When the Dead Rise Series 1
The Beginning

By C.M. Fick

Contact: cmfick@yahoo.ca
Website: www.cmfick.com
ISBN: 978-0-9880802-5-6

Volume 1: Patient Zero

Before Contamination...
Cliff Holbrook was the lead scientist in the R&D department of Synergy Pharmaceuticals, located in San Antonio, Texas. His current project was a top-secret military study of the application of the synthesized drug, Obsepire. It was derived from a theoretical study of Congenital Insensitivity to Pain, otherwise known as CIP. The goal of the project was to block the pain receptors in a soldier's brain so they had the ability to complete a mission despite the condition of their bodies.

Unfortunately, the scientists working on the project had several setbacks. After they'd administered the drug to the subjects, they discovered the human body wouldn't metabolize it. In one hundred percent of the subjects, it passed harmlessly through the body leaving behind no trace of the inhibitor - that was until the powers-that-be brought Cliff onto the project. After much research, he decided that using a virus as the delivery vehicle would be the most effective way of getting the body to accept the inhibitor.

Cliff's theory started with the Varicella Zoster virus, known to cause shingles and chickenpox in humans. When this combination alone didn't produce the long-term, full body results the military was looking for, Cliff went back to the drawing board, adding a second strain that would allow the altered Varicella Zoster virus to travel to the brain: Meningitis. The theory behind adding the second strain was that the first strain of Varicella would hold the synthesized drug and the second strain of viral Meningitis would transport the pain inhibitor to the brainstem where it could take hold and deliver the payload.

The subject would then be kept in quarantine for two weeks while their system fought off the viral infection created by the Meningitis, and for the drug Obsepire to alter the brains receptors permanently. Cliff knew the dangers of their experiments, but with a new mortgage and a child on the way, he was more concerned with the bonus he'd receive once Obsepire completed the first wave of successful human trials. And so, Cliff ignorantly continued his work. If he'd known what he was creating, he may have been more careful - or perhaps tried to convince Synergy of the dangers of manipulating nature. But of course, Cliff didn't know until it was too late to stop the spread of the disease, which reanimated the dead and brought on the end of civilization as we know it.

The night the end of the world began, was much like any other night for Cliff. He'd finished the last of his notes on the successful delivery and effects of Obsepire on the primate test subjects and was putting away the samples when someone burst into his lab behind him.

"Cliff!" the man barked making Cliff jump.

Startled by the intrusion, the test tube Cliff had been holding slipped from his fingers, shattering on the floor at his feet. He sighed as he thought about the work that went into creating that small sample and turned to face his boss. "Yes sir?"

Hugo Farner stood in the lab's doorway with bright red coloring his puffy cheeks. He was a round man with round glasses and a mostly bald head, making him look, to Cliff, a little like the dough boy in a suit. "I was expecting your report on my desk before three," Hugo barked, his face growing redder with each passing moment.

Cliff's shoulders slumped as the countless late nights weighed down on him. He didn't need a lecture from Hugo; he'd been working as quickly as the process allowed and still it wasn't fast enough for the department head. "The report is printing." Cliff waved his hand towards the whirring machine where the printed pages already created a small pile. "I needed to verify some of the results before giving you my final report." Cliff rubbed his hands over his sore eyes before finally admitting. "I believe we're ready for human trials."

Hugo seemed to deflate all at once, his anger replaced by surprise, quickly followed by the gleam of greed in his eyes. "So it's done?" he asked, finally moving from the doorway, into Cliff's small lab. He pulled the printed pages from the paper tray and began to scan the report on Obsepire's progress.

"Yes," Cliff sighed again, this time in relief. "The subjects are fully recovered and the drug has the desired effect of blocking any pain." Cliff waved to the room off his lab where his three primate test-subjects lived.

"I'm happy to hear of your progress and look forward to reading your report in full tomorrow morning." Hugo clapped Cliff on the back, all traces of his anger gone. By completing Obsepire, Cliff had ensured the military contract with Synergy would be ongoing and very profitable for both parties. Hugo hummed happily to himself as he waddled from the room, leaving Cliff to clean up the mess on the floor.

Cliff's mind wandered as he plucked the largest pieces of the broke test tube from the floor. He thought about how his bonus would pay off their new mortgage and allow a small nest egg for Cliff and his pregnant wife, Helena. He thought about Helena's fast approaching due date, and how excited he was to see the birth of his little girl. He thought about the promotion that he'd receive once Obsepire was in full production, about the pay raise that would accompany his new position.

Cliff's mind was on everything but the mess he was cleaning up, so when a sliver of glass pierced his skin and a small drop of blood welled on his fingertip, he pulled it out without a second thought. Cliff disposed of the trash in the incinerator and left for home.

Falling Ill...

Cliff had a hard time pulling himself from his bed the following morning. He had an odd neck ache and felt as if he were coming down with the flu. Not wanting to pass his illness onto Helena, he skipped breakfast and headed straight to work. He stopped by Hugo's office on the way to his lab and the men shared a congratulatory drink - it didn't matter that it was only nine in the morning; they were both about to become insanely wealthy men.

After his congratulatory drink with Hugo, Cliff made his way back to his office to begin the tedious process of creating several new cultures of virus-altered Obsepire. He needed to replace the specimens lost the night before in order to move forward with human trials, but the ache in his neck persisted, distracting him from his work. Finally deciding he'd worked hard enough, Cliff went back to Hugo's office to inform his boss he'd be taking the remainder of the day off.

"What can I help you with Cliff?" Hugo spoke without looking up from the papers on his desk.

"I just wanted to let you know I wasn't feeling well and am going to head home before it gets worse." Cliff mumbled, feeling a sudden chill. His whole body ached and he'd begun having terrible dizzy spells that the walk from his office exacerbated. The only thing keeping Cliff upright was the thought of his nice warm bed waiting for him at home.

"Of course," Hugo waved his hand without glancing up from his paperwork. "I wouldn't want something to happen to the man who saved the company." Hugo finally looked up at Cliff with a wide grin, which faltered as he finally took in Cliff's state. "Are you okay to get home on your own?" Hugo asked with sudden concern. He got up from his desk, helping Cliff into a nearby chair.

"I don't know what's come over me." Cliff scrubbed his face with his hands, trying to wake up his senses.

"When did this start?" Hugo asked as he poured Cliff a glass of water.

"Just this morning." Cliff nodded his thanks when Hugo extended the glass to him. He tried to raise the water to his lips with shaking hands, but the glass slipped from his weak fingers, crashing to the floor and spilling the water all over Hugo's expensive rug. The room tilted and spun around Cliff as he fought to remain conscious.

"Cliff, are you okay?" Hugo sounded panicked, but Cliff couldn't determine where the large man stood, the room was spinning too rapidly.

"Hugo, I..." Cliff was about to explain about last night's accident and the possibility of infection, but a wave of nausea washed over him. His body shook with the chills as bile rose in his throat. The room continued to spin.

"Cliff?" He heard the anxiety in Hugo's voice as he shook Cliff's shoulder; the motion intensified the spins. Hugo's voice shook with panic, "Cliff answer me."

Cliff felt his body pitch forward followed by the feel of cool wet carpet beneath his burning face. The last thing he heard was Hugo calling for the paramedics.

Quarantine...

Cliff awoke in a white sterile room, confused by his surroundings. After several moments of studying the room around

4

him, he realized he was in Synergy's basement quarantine unit. Cliff remembered seeing a room, similar to the one he was in, in the basement of the pharmaceutical company on his initial tour of the facilities. Then he'd been on the outside looking in. Panic blossomed within Cliff's chest. How long had he been unconscious for? To block the rising panic, Cliff turned his attention to his body. In a clinical manner, he noted that the extreme fatigue was still present along with the stiffness in his neck; his whole body ached and his head throbbed. The dizziness was absent, but Cliff suspected that if he stood, the world would begin spinning again. He was also having a hard time breathing and was thankful for the oxygen tube he felt pressed against his upper lip.

The sound of shuffling fabric drew Cliff's eyes to the side of the room where he saw two technicians in biohazard suits, standing at a table filled with lab paraphernalia. They had their backs turned to Cliff.

"What am I doing here?" Cliff rasped, only now realizing how dry his throat was.

Both technicians started and turned simultaneously, staring at Cliff in disbelief.

"You've been infected with a form of meningitis we've never seen before," the first technician spoke in an educated tone. "The director of your department requested that you be quarantined until we can determine whether or not the virus is communicable, and if it is, how it's transmitted."

Every employee who worked at Synergy knew of the quarantine protocols. Hell, they'd all had to sign a release form stating that, should a contagion infect an employee, Synergy had the right and duty to the public to ensure the contagion was contained within their facilities. *What's going to happen to me?* Cliff shuddered knowing there was nothing he could do but allow the technicians to perform their tests. Once he'd been cleared to go home, there would be yet another confidentiality form to sign, but at least Cliff would be able to get on with his life - he just had to wait out the viral infection.

"What did they tell my wife?" Cliff asked, silently calculating how many weeks he'd be stuck in quarantine compared to Helena's due date. She still had a month and a half before the baby was due, but everyone knew babies came out when they were ready - not necessarily when their parents were.

5

"We are unsure," the second technician answered, coming over to Cliff's side. He unzipped the hood of his suit and removed his respirator to monitor the machines beeping along with Cliff's body. "Just before you awoke, we determined the contagion is not air-born." Cliff sighed, but realized his relief was premature when the tech continued, "We still have yet to determine its communicability. We do not know how long you will be ill or if your body will be able to fight off the virus and until then, we cannot tell your wife anything specific."

Cliff froze at the technicians words. If his body would be able to fight off the virus? What would happen to him if it didn't? Was he going to die? Was he going to end up a lab rat, stuck in Synergy's basement? Could they even do that?

Cliff's heart thundered in his ears at the prospect of dying from something he'd engineered. Couldn't they give him anything to counteract the virus? Cliff shook his head - the very reason why he'd used the viral form of meningitis was that the body had to fight off the virus, making it stronger while allowing the Obsepire time to do what it was designed for. Antibiotics, if he'd used the bacterial form, could have corrupted the Obsepire making the viral form so much more efficient - even with the two week recovery time from the meningitis.

"I need to speak to Hugo," Cliff finally said. If anyone had answers for him it would be his superior. He needed to know what restrictions he was contractually under and what those limitations would allow him to divulge to those working his case. He wanted to explain what he'd created and its effects, assuring the techs that he would recover.

"Mr. Farner is unavailable," the technician said coldly, turning back to his microscope.

Cliff pushed himself into an upright position, swinging his feet to the cool tiled floor beneath his bed. "That is unacceptable. I deserve answers. I need to make sure my wife's okay and that she knows I'm safe. She's having a baby..." Cliff's head spun as he stepped towards the technicians, but he couldn't give up - he needed to know his wife hadn't picked up the virus from him. The first technician moved to the inner door of the room and without concern, pressed a small round button beside it.

The door swung open and two large men in white scrubs and latex gloves marched in, picked Cliff up under his arms, and dragged him back to the bed; the techs went back to their microscopes. One man secured Cliff's arms and legs with restraints while the other held him down. He bucked, he kicked, he screamed obscenities but nothing fazed the men - until the one holding him down let his arm get a little too close. Cliff lashed out with his teeth, as they were his only remaining defence, sinking them into the man's tender skin.

The man howled, but held Cliff firm. "You crazy son of a bitch," he growled before looking over his shoulder to speak to his partner. "Are you almost done? I have to go get this sterilized before my immune systems' compromised."

The last buckle slid into place and the man stepped back. He held out the arm Cliff had bitten for his partner to inspect; the bite mark was an angry red and blood trickled down the man's arm.

It must hurt like a mother... Cliff thought smugly to himself.

"Dude," the other man said after inspecting the crescent shaped marks, "That's totally nasty. Make sure you report the incident." Cliff heard the uninjured man say before the door closed silently behind them.

Cliff tested his restraints but all he accomplished was further exhausting his already tired and sore body. His mind reeled from the shock of the situation he found himself in. He was an American citizen... He had rights... He paid his taxes and was considered a pillar within his community... He shouldn't be treated this way. "I need to speak to Hugo!" Cliff screamed as he twisted, uselessly, in his restraints. Hugo would know what to do.

One of the techs pulled out a small syringe and filled it from a vile before walking briskly to Cliff's bedside. "You need your rest and this," he held up the syringe, squeezing the plunger until a small stream of liquid spurted from the tip, "will help you do so." Cliff didn't feel the prick of the needle but he did feel the drug's effects as it pulled him into darkness.

Final Breaths...

Over the next two weeks, Cliff's immune system raged an intense war against the virus within him. Hugo never came to Cliff's bedside as he tossed in fevered delirium. None of the techs would give him any information on his wife, despite his desperate pleas. There'd only been one other occasion where restraints were necessary and to Cliff's surprise, a different man appeared with the one who'd strapped him in bed during his first days in quarantine. When asked where the man he'd bitten was, the response was simple: called in sick the day after the bite and never returned to work. This news worried Cliff, but no one would listen when he voiced his concerns.

Cliff grew more ill as the time passed, and the amount of time he spent awake and lucid decreased until all he did was sleep between tests. He was unable to keep food down - not that he had an appetite - dizziness plagued him constantly and his cough worsened until he was coughing up clots of blood; then the shakes began. Cliff recognized the signs of his body shutting down and resigned himself to the fact that he'd never get to see his child or his beautiful wife again. And then, just as his two week quarantine was coming to an end something strange happened - the techs didn't come to his room for his morning check-up. The day wore on and no one came to check on Cliff's condition. He was too weak to get out of his bed but shouted until his voice grew horse. Still, no one responded. It was sometime that night that Cliff took his final, laboured breath.

Dead Rising...

He awoke from the nightmare with a start; the dream of his own death etched into his memory. Cliff remembered watching his eerily still body, lying on the bed beneath him. At that point, he'd been sure he'd died. Now he was clearly back in his body, but it felt somehow alien to him. Unwilling to open his eyes, Cliff reached out with his other senses to anchor his mind back to reality. He could tell it was dark because the normally bright lights of the lab weren't glaring through his eyelids. He heard the faint sound of an alarm, far down the hall but nothing else moved in his immediate area. The air, which normally circulated through the room, was stale but to Cliff's relief, the pain he'd endured was gone without a trace.

Cliff finally opened his eyes and sat up, staring at his surroundings as if seeing them for the first time. The world was bathed in milky wash making the objects around him indistinct and difficult to see. Cliff raised his arm to scrub the film from his eyes and was alarmed when it only jerked outward, clumsily and uncoordinated. He shifted, allowing his legs to fall over the side of the bed but when he tried to stand, he found himself pitching forward. His arms flailed uselessly as his feet tangled together and he tried to break his fall with his unresponsive arms.

Cliff hit the floor and expected pain to explode through his body on impact, but it never came. He lay on the floor for a moment studying his body - shockingly, he felt nothing. Fear filled him as he realized something in his experiment had gone terribly wrong. He hadn't felt the explosion of air from his lungs when he'd fallen. He couldn't feel his heart beating nor did he feel the coolness of the floor beneath him. *I need to get out... I need to go home.*

Awkwardly, Cliff struggled to his feet, irritated by his lack of coordination. He shuffled to the closed door of the quarantine unit and was about to open the door when he heard voices in the hall, making him hesitate.

"Dude," a muffled male voice said, "the information on the virus has to be here somewhere. Make sure to check those rooms as well." Cliff could hear the people opening and closing the lab doors in the hall; he shuffled behind his room's door just before it swung open, hiding him from the intruders.

A flashlight shone into the room as a female voice spoke excitedly, "Hey! I found something," she called down the hall to her companions, "This is a quarantine unit that was in use until recently." The sound of running feet echoed in the hall and slid to a stop outside Cliff's room. "See?" Two more flashlight beams joined the first, sweeping every inch of the room. Cliff remained unmoving; he was terrified of being discovered but wasn't sure why.

The people moved into the room cautiously, checking behind the equipment and under the bed. "Whatever was in here is long gone," one of the guys, now searching the cupboards, said to his companions. He moved closer to Cliff's hiding place, almost within reach.

A sudden, gnawing hunger consumed Cliff and he leapt from his concealment, onto the unsuspecting man who shrieked in panic. Cliff's arms tightened around the man with unnatural strength, and before he knew what he was doing, he bit into the man's shoulder. His teeth broke the skin and blood filled Cliff's mouth. The skin tore with a satisfying snap. The warmth of the flesh surprised Cliff as he began to chew. The woman screamed.

"Get out Trina," the second man ordered.

9

Trina's voice was panicked, "But Andy, we can't just leave Paul here."

Cliff couldn't pull his attention away from the warm flesh in his arms and bit down again. The one they'd called Paul stopped screaming and now only twitched in Cliff's arms.

"He's gone Trina. Go!" Andy ordered again.

"Come with me Andy. Paul is that thing's first kill. He won't leave it until the body's cold or Paul's risen." Trina and Andy ran down the hallway, the sound of their pounding feet fading until all Cliff heard was the whine of the alarm.

Cliff didn't understand what she'd meant. *First kill? Cold body?* It didn't matter - nothing mattered other than getting more of the warmth inside him. His iron grip on the warm flesh loosened, allowing it to slip to the floor. Cliff fell on the exposed belly and continued to gorge: more warmth - he needed more... somehow, it made him feel alive.

Soon, Cliff felt he'd gotten enough of the warmth inside of him and starred down at his meal. With a sudden jolt, Cliff realized what he'd done... what he was covered with... what was causing the satisfying heat in his belly. He wanted to retch, but couldn't. To his horror, Cliff watched as Paul's body twitched just before the now empty eyes popped open.

Cliff tried to speak to Paul; to apologize for killing and consuming the young man, but all that came out was a pitiful moan. Paul got to his feet and returned Cliff's moan before shuffling from the room. Cliff followed, trying to figure out how a man with a gaping wound in his neck and torso could be up and moving around. It didn't make sense to him, but the irresistible urge to eat human flesh hadn't been sensible either.

Needing to understand what was happening, Cliff made his way to the emergency exit where the door was propped open. Overhead the alarm sounded and behind him, he sensed the presence of the man he'd killed and eaten. Laboriously, Cliff began the three-story ascent with the shambling Paul close behind him. *I need to get away from that thing,* he thought with every step.

Upon reaching the main level, Cliff stopped, not believing the destruction in the building's lobby. The large picture windows running the lobby's length were shattered. Bodies lay strewn haphazardly about; many with gaping holes in their heads. Papers fluttered in the breeze. Beside Cliff, Paul moaned a long mournful sound that triggered a moan from Cliff. He hadn't meant to respond to the call, surprised when another muffled moan sounded outside. Paul shuffled through the lobby just as another person appeared on the street in front of Synergy's main entrance.

Cliff was about to warn the person away, when he saw the missing arm and bite marks trailing up the leg. The person in the street wasn't a person, Cliff realized, he was a zombie - just like Paul... just like Cliff. The realization hit him like a ton of bricks, grief overwhelming him, driving him to his hands and knees. The once warm flesh in his gut felt heavy and no longer gave him that 'alive' feeling he craved.

A Familiar Face...

Cliff's mind returned to awareness and he was surprised to find that, not only was it now the middle of the night, but that he was in a suburb far from Synergy's laboratory. He wasn't sure how he'd gotten there or where his consciousness had gone during the lapse. There were car accidents blocking the street, some of them with wisps of smoke still rising from blackened cars. The chatter of automatic gunfire sounded the next block over, almost swallowed by a chorus of moans. Cliff heard shattering glass, screaming, several blasts from a rifle and then silence - he instinctually knew whomever had been defending their position, had lost the battle against the horde.

An instinct Cliff hadn't realized he possessed, told him there were living humans close by and the hunger flared with a vengeance in his gut. He craved the warmth the flesh had given him even as his mind revolted at the thought of killing and consuming another living person. A dog barked, pulling Cliff's attention away from the hungry moans the next block over and the desperate cravings he didn't understand. He turned and studied the mangy black and white dog, snarling at him from the sidewalk, surprised to realize he recognized it as his neighbours.

Cliff ignored the dog and stumbled down the street searching for his home. How could he have forgotten about his wife and their baby? Silently, he prayed they were both alive and safe. When he found his house, Cliff was relieved to see the house's main floor windows had been boarded up and all looked secured. He wandered

11

closer, hoping to catch just a glimpse of his wife and was making his way around the side of the house, when he heard a man's voice at the front door.

"I'm going to make sure everything's clear out here; then we can head out. Make sure we have everything packed Helena."

At the sound of his wife's name, Cliff turned back to the corner of the house, pausing there until he heard the shuffle of feet in front of the houses two-car garage. The barrel of a shotgun appeared from around the corner first, and then a hand followed by an arm. Cliff couldn't hold himself back as he lunged, sinking his teeth into the exposed flesh. The man howled in pain, swinging the barrel of the gun towards Cliff's head; he flung up an arm, awkwardly blocking the blow.

The man tore his arm away, leaving behind a warm chunk of bloody flesh in Cliff's mouth. The man stumbled back, trying to aim with his shotgun but Cliff was faster. Grabbing the man by the shoulders, Cliff pulled him close, eagerly waiting for the moment he could eat more flesh to warm his insides - the first bite had only intensified the need. He bit down hard on the man's neck, cutting off the scream of pain and Cliff followed the man to the ground as he tumbled backwards, viciously tearing at the exposed flesh.

He felt the warmth inside him growing with each bite. He didn't want to stop or maybe it was that he couldn't stop, until a muffled gasp drew Cliff's attention up from his feast. Standing on their small front porch was Helena with a shaking hand clasped over her mouth; her eyes wide in horror.

She was safe and healthy, as was her swollen belly. Relieved, Cliff staggered to his feet and stumbled towards her wanting to gather her in his arms and comfort her.

"Stay back Cliff." Helena, eyes filled with tears, began backing towards the open door. "Oh God; stay back!"

He tried to reassure her he wasn't going to do anything to hurt her, but it only came out as a hideous moan. He reached for her, wanting her to see he was still inside himself, trapped in his mind, but with a sob, she turned to flee into the house.

Cliff's hand snaked out, faster than he realized he could move, encircling Helena's wrist before she made it up the two steps and into the safety of their home. She cried out in pain as he pulled her back towards him and cringed away from him, trying to free her arm with little success. Cliff stared down at her pale skin and thought about how wonderful she'd taste and how warm she'd make him feel. Shocked by his thoughts, Cliff relaxed his grip just long enough for Helena to pull free. As she fled into the house, relief and horror washed through him. The door slammed and to his relief, Cliff heard the snick of a lock. Grief filled him as he stood, staring at the closed door. He'd been ready to kill his wife and his unborn child. What was happening to him?

Movement beside Cliff drew his attention away from the door of the house. The man he'd just attacked struggled to his feet and once gaining his footing, shuffled to the door. He moaned and began beating on the boards of the home he'd used as a refuge only minutes before.

"Go away Cliff," Helena cried from inside the house. He tried to warn her, to tell her to flee, but once again, the only sound that came out was the eerie moan.

Cliff shuffled to the man pounding on the door and tried to push him away, distract him from Helena. It was Cliff's fault that she was now on her own, pregnant and scared. Moans rose in chorus behind Cliff and he turned, horrified to realize that the moans from him and the new zombie attracted more of the dead to his wife's position.

The whirr of the garage door opener sounded, drawing both Cliff's and the man's attention back to the driveway. The man shuffled quickly to the rising door and raised his arms, clawing at the barrier between him and living flesh. Cliff understood the need and felt it himself but he wouldn't - no - couldn't hurt his beautiful Helena.

Before the door was fully raised, Helena's burgundy SUV shot out of the garage, cracking the bottom of the door and ploughing into the man who'd been her companion through this nightmare only a short time ago. There was a sickening crunch as the SUV's back tire bounced over the man's skull, effectively ending his suffering. Helena swung the vehicle onto the street, fish-tailing for a moment before speeding away from the house they'd shared together. He'd never see his wife again, Cliff knew. He could only pray that she'd find safety.

Last Meal...

Cliff's consciousness once again returned to his body, just as the sun was beginning to rise over cookie cutter homes. He found himself in a group of zombies, making their way down an abandoned

13

street Cliff didn't recognize. Several zombies on the outskirts of the group wandered in front of the houses lining the streets, pausing momentarily to sense for any movement within. As the horde made their way down the street, Cliff grew more concerned about the lapses in time and wondered what would happen to him once his consciousness was completely suppressed by the instincts growing stronger within him.

He studied the others around him, wondering if they too were trapped within their dead bodies as he was, but all he saw were pale, empty eyes. Cliff grunted in an effort to get a response from one of his horde, but knew after studying those around him that he was alone. He didn't understand what set him apart from the others - perhaps it was because he'd been patient zero. He pondered this for a time and decided he was correct in his assumption; the zombies around him had all been bitten and turned after succumbing to the wounds - he'd suffered through two weeks while the virus ravaged his body, turning him slowly. Being trapped in his rotting body was his punishment for creating such an aberration that would turn humanity into mindless, ravenous monsters. He couldn't blame whatever higher power cursed him to this fate.

A vibration hummed through the horde when they came to a T-intersection, startling Cliff from his musings. To Cliff, it seemed as if they were communicating with each other, determining which way they'd go. The vibration stopped and the group split down the center; the left side moving down the street to the left and the right going in the opposite direction. They'd split up to better search for living flesh, Cliff realized and wondered at the hive mentality of the horde he travelled with.

After several minutes, the lead zombie in Cliff's group let out a low moan, which rippled through the horde alerting all in the area of living flesh close by. The throng around Cliff became frenzied, pushing forward, not caring that some of their group fell and were trampled beneath dead feet. A scream tore through the air and panicked cries echoed throughout the neighbourhood. Cliff struggled through the drove, pushing his way out to the fringes, searching for a glimpse of their prey. He saw a group of the living, shouting as they scrambled for cars and SUV's while others stood on top of the vehicles shooting into the horde.

Cliff watched as one of his fellow zombies took a bullet in the chest, stagger one step back from the force of the gunshot, before regaining his balance and pressing forward once again. A second shot rang out and the zombie who'd taken the chest shot crumpled to the ground. Cliff couldn't help but stare at the gaping hole where his eye should have been. He shuddered. Would his life end in a similar fashion? He prayed that if it did, he wouldn't see the bullet coming.

By the time Cliff reached the small grouping of vehicles, those who'd lived only minutes before had already joined the undead. Hunger gnawed in his gut and the craving for the warmth of living flesh overwhelmed Cliff as he stumbled forward. He thought back to the man in the lab - the first person he'd killed. He remembered the numbness he'd felt when first waking, the feeling of the flesh as he chewed it between his teeth, and the satisfying warmth as it filled his belly.

A small whisper of sound reached Cliff's ears and he spun, trying to find the source of it. The horde continued to move forward, bumping and jostling Cliff as he searched, unwilling to alert the others of the living flesh nearby. He caught sight of movement between the homes, the milkyness of his vision blotting out all color. Excitement filled him and he couldn't control his shuffling feet as he moved silently between the buildings.

Cliff stood scanning the yards, patiently waiting for whatever he'd seen to move again but saw nothing. He was about to return to the zombie parade when the shifting of gravel caught his attention. The building beside him had a large wooden structure protruding from its rear - Cliff couldn't remember what he would have called it when he'd still been alive; he thought hard for a moment but the word escaped him. The noise came again; just a small shift in the stones from beneath the wooden thing. Cliff made his way around, clumsily avoiding the corner, until he spotted a portion of the crisscrossing cover moved aside.

He dropped to his knees, trying to see into the darkness with little luck. He slithered into the dark space knowing he'd eventually find what he was seeking. Then he heard it, the muffled panting of one of the living. He struggled over the hard little things beneath him, no longer concerned with the loss of the word he'd understood moments before - he wanted flesh, he needed flesh; warm flesh that would give him life.

He scrabbled forward, searching for his prey in the darkness until his hand closed around a foot and the person shrieked, kicking him squarely in his face. He heard a crunch of ... but he couldn't remember what the solid structure beneath the skin on his face was called - he didn't care because he finally had his hand around the warmth he'd become desperate for. The foot he held tried to shake free, but he wasn't going to let go so easily. This is what he'd been searching for; this is what he'd needed. There was a crack of the barrier behind the living, followed by a flood of light and the living scrambled out of the new hole, dragging him behind, still attached to the thing that kicked him.

This was his! Excitement grew into frenzy as he clawed at the living, pulling it closer.

It almost shook him free as it struggled to stand upright, but he wasn't going to let it go so quickly. He grabbed the other thing as it tried to kick out, once again towards his head - where he lived. It stumbled and fell. Already, that feeling of being alive began to fill him as he dragged the squirming thing towards him. He bit into the warm flesh just above where he gripped it. A leg maybe? But he no longer cared what the name for the flesh was - it was warm and that's what mattered. There was a howl of pain; a concept he no longer cared about -something which had been from another life he no longer remembered. He bit in again savouring the snap as the flesh was consumed.

He continued to eat, filling himself with warmth, savouring every bite. The last remnants of the man who'd once had a wife, a home, a job, a life; slipped away leaving only the primal behind. When the zombie rose from his meal his only thoughts were on where he'd find the next living flesh and the hunger which would never be satisfied.

Volume 2: And it All Began with a Bite

A day like any other...

Maggie, her arms full of groceries, tossed the keys on the small table in the entryway and kicked the door closed behind her. She hurried into the kitchen to put the perishables into the fridge and begin preparation of dinner for herself and her boyfriend Tyrone.

Maggie was a nurse at the Methodist Children's Hospital in San Antonio, Texas while Tyrone, also trained as a nurse, worked for Synergy Pharmaceuticals. It irritated her to no end that he wasn't allowed to discuss the details of his position with her, but his weekly paycheck more than made up for the lack of communication in that area. In addition, he never brought home baggage from work, unlike herself. Maggie worked in the terminal care wing of the hospital and what she witnessed on a daily basis left her emotionally drained by the end of her shifts. Today had been an especially hard day for Maggie; she'd lost a seven-year-old boy to leukemia and was looking forward to spending a mind numbing night in front of the television.

As she began to prepare a simple dinner of steamed vegetables and barbecued chicken, Maggie turned on the radio to keep her mind distracted from wandering to thoughts of the boy. Just as she brought the chicken into the house, she heard Tyrone's car pull into the driveway.

After washing off her hands, she stuck her head out the side window and called to Tyrone. "Make sure to leave me enough room to leave in the morning - I need to be in for six-thirty." Without waiting for a reply, Maggie pulled her head back inside and closed the window before returning to dinner preparations. When the front door slammed, she turned to greet Tyrone with a smile, but it quickly faded when she took in his paler than usual complexion and the gauze bandage wrapped around his forearm. "What happened?" She hurried over to him as he sunk into the nearest chair.

"It's nothing," Tyrone growled in a tone that warned Maggie not to push him too far.

Her immediate instinct was to check his temperature; his skin was burning beneath her touch. When she reached down to check the wound's wrapping, he pulled it from her reach.

"Don't touch it Maggie," he growled again.

With such a high fever, she wasn't going to put up with his attitude for a minute longer. Putting her hands on her hips, Maggie glared down at the big man. "Tyrone Martell Evans," she smirked when he flinched at her use of his full name, "you will allow me to look at that wound and you will not argue with me about it. I've had a hard enough day without you fighting me over simple first-aid."

Tyrone looked up at Maggie with his large brown, blood-shot eyes. "Peter?" Maggie nodded, struggling to hold back the tears that suddenly sprung up. "I'm sorry darling," he said gently, as he squeezed her hand in a sympathetic gesture and nodded towards the sink. "Do what you need to do."

Maggie hurried over to the sink, glad for a moment to collect herself, and dug out the extensive first-aid kit she kept for occasions such as these. While a bowl filled with water, she grabbed several clean dishtowels from the drawer. Placing the bowl of warm, clean water on the table, Maggie sat in a chair opposite him and began to unwrap his arm. She gasped when the wound was finally visible. "Is this a human bite mark?"

"Yeah, I was restraining a guy at work today..." Maggie looked up, shocked at Tyrone's sudden willingness to share about his day. She began to ask why he needed to restrain a man at a pharmaceutical company, but Tyrone held up a hand. "I am unable to discuss the man or why he needed to be restrained." Maggie dabbed a little harder than necessary as she cleaned the odd wound. "Ow, you did that on purpose," Tyrone grunted, but after a moment he went on with his story. "I was restraining him and he began flipping out. My arm got too close to his chompers and he decided to take his frustration over his situation out on my arm."

Maggie pressed her lips together, trying to suppress her smile. "He bit you hard enough to break skin?" Now that the wound was cleaned Maggie could see faint lines spreading out in a radial pattern from the teeth marks. "How long ago did this happen?"

"Just before shift end. I sterilized it and had Mark wrap it before leaving for the day."

"Well it doesn't need stitches but you are going to have to go on a strict anti-bacterial regiment," Maggie spoke in a mock-serious voice before sobering. Her eyes returned to the veiny lines; their appearance unsettled her. "Human mouths are filled with nasty shit and we can't take any chances you will come down with an infection." She distracted herself by liberally applying topical cream to the rough edges of the bite, before rewrapping Tyrone's arm with clean gauze. "I think you should survive big man." Maggie bent, kissed him on the forehead, and then began to pack up her kit. Scooping up the bloody towels, she threw them into the laundry room and poured the dirty water down the drain. "Ready for dinner?" she asked, as she washed out the bowl.

Tyrone stood and fetched the plates and silverware, setting the table without being prodded; Maggie's unease grew. It wasn't normal for her boyfriend to be so accommodating. As they ate, Maggie told Tyrone about Peter's final hours, the relief she felt that the boy was no longer in pain and the guilt that she felt relieved.

Finally, Tyrone pushed back from the table and stood. "I'm going to bed. I'm exhausted and not feeling well. It seems to be getting worse and I can't afford to take any sick days right now."

Maggie glanced down to his plate - he'd barely touched his food. It looked like he'd taken a few bites, but hadn't done much more than push his food around on his plate. "But you barely ate," she said, following him into the bedroom where he flopped down on the bed. "Maybe we should take you to the hospital. Get you checked out to make sure you didn't catch anything from the guy who bit you."

"No hospital Maggie," Tyrone warned in his 'I'm serious' tone.

"But Tyrone..." she whined, hating herself a little for the petulant tone, "what if it's serious?"

Tyrone's eyes snapped open and he grabbed her arm tightly. "No doctors. Promise me you won't take me to the hospital."

His fingers bit into her wrist painfully, scaring her. "I promise," she said quickly, pulling from his grasp. *There will be bruises on my wrist in the morning.* She stood and watched him a moment longer, before hurrying from the room to clean up dinner.

19

More than just the flu...

Nine o'clock that night, Maggie stuck her head into the bedroom to check on Tyrone. She'd made some noodle soup and poured him a glass of orange juice, just in case he was hungry when she checked in on him. She set the soup on the nightstand and turned on the bedside light. She gasped when she saw his scrubs had been soaked through with perspiration, as were the sheets beneath him.

"Tyrone?" Maggie nudged him gently. She needed him to wake up so she could check his symptoms, which were obviously getting worse. "Tyrone, I need you to wake up babe." He groaned and rolled over, turning his back to her. "If you don't let me check your vitals, I'm going to call an ambulance."

That woke him up. He rolled back to his former position, squinting up at Maggie. "No hospitals," he croaked. "Can we turn off the light?"

Maggie pulled out a thermometer from her pocket, turning it on before putting it beneath Tyrone's tongue. "Not until I check your temperature." She waited in silence while the thermometer measured his temperature. It beeped, indicating the reading was done, and the knot of unease grew when she saw the readout: 103.5 degrees Fahrenheit. She knew if his temperature rose another two and a half degrees, his brain cells would start dying. She had to get his temperature down.

"I'm going to get some ibuprofen and cold compresses." Maggie stood with a sudden urgency. If Tyrone wasn't going to allow her to call the hospital, then she'd have to get his fever down on her own.

"Can I get a blanket?" Tyrone shivered, despite the beads of sweat on his clammy skin.

Maggie draped a thin sheet over him, not wanting to increase his temperature with a heavier blanket. "I'll be right back; then we can go over your symptoms. This is serious Tyrone and proper medical attention may be necessary." She hurried out of the room, ignoring his protests.

She returned several minutes later with a glass of water, two ibuprofen, and five makeshift compresses. She only had two icepacks in the freezer and had to put ice cubes in zip lock baggies for the other three. Tyrone complained about the cold as she placed the ice beneath his knees, in his armpits and beneath his neck. She lifted his head, allowing him to drink and swallow the pills easier before gently placing his head back on the soaked pillow.

"Now, tell me where it hurts," she said in her professional nurse's tone.

"Everywhere," Tyrone groaned.

"I need you to be more specific than that," Maggie chided.

"My neck is sore and stiff; my whole body aches; I'm cold then hot and where my clothes stick to my skin it hurts." He struggled to speak as Maggie's dread grew. She wasn't prepared to care for Tyrone at home, not with his symptoms. She also knew that he'd do more harm to himself if she tried to force him to go to the hospital.

"If you get worse or your fever doesn't come down, I'll have to take you to the hospital Tyrone." Maggie hoped, no prayed, he'd see reason and allow her to get proper care for him.

His eyes shot open, startling Maggie with the intense anger burning in his bloodshot eyes. "I told you no hospital."

"You might die if I can't get the fever down Tyrone... please!" Maggie pleaded, but could see she wasn't going to get the answer she wanted. He was being a stubborn man.

"Promise me Maggie," Tyrone's anger faded and she could now see what it had been hiding - his fear. "You can't take me to the hospital. They'll run tests and see that what I have isn't normal. They'll start asking questions that I can't answer - my contract clearly states I cannot discuss my work with outsiders. Especially this." He weakly squeezed Maggie's hand. "My system will fight it off babe; it'll just take some time." Resigned, Maggie promised not to call an ambulance - for now...

A long night followed by a long day...

Maggie stayed up through the night to keep watch over her boyfriend. At midnight, things took a turn for the worse. While Tyrone's fever maintained at 103.5 degrees, his other symptoms progressed. When he started violently coughing and vomited what little dinner he'd eaten earlier, she was sure he'd contracted some viral form of meningitis. He began to have difficulty breathing just after midnight, and once again, Maggie tried to convince him to let her take him to the hospital. Again, he refused; what if he was contagious? That thought scared Maggie. She didn't want to catch whatever was inflicting Tyrone. At the same time, she also knew that they couldn't risk spreading whatever he had through a hospital, should it be communicable.

Around two in the morning, she removed the bandage on his arm to clean the wound again. The fetid odour that emanated from the bite marks made her stomach revolt. After spending a few minutes in the bathroom disgorging her own dinner, Maggie hurried back to Tyrone's side, determined to clean the obviously infected area. The radial lines she'd noticed earlier were now dark brown, extending further up his arm than she remembered. Another bad sign was the pus building just beneath the wounds scab. She feared it was already septic and causing septicemia, which would spread, requiring immediate medical attention in the near future. Immediately she set about cleansing the wound with warm salt water and gently pressed on top of the pus-filled area to squeeze out the accumulated fluid. She followed up with a liberal dose of antiseptic cream and a loose wrapping to keep any further pathogens from getting into the infected area. Once she'd ensured Tyrone drank what she deemed to be an acceptable amount of fluids, and she was sure he'd fallen back into a fitful sleep, Maggie finally allowed herself to break down and cry.

For the remainder of the night, Maggie sat in a chair dozing beside Tyrone. Every time he coughed, she woke and held out the pail for him in case he needed to throw up again. She checked his temperature, which never fell below 103.5 degrees, every half hour, and woke him to coax more fluid into him. Keeping him hydrated and his temperature from spiking further was all she could do; he was either going to take a turn for the better or she'd have to take him to the hospital in the morning - regardless of his protests.

When Maggie's alarm went off at five, she went to the kitchen and called into work, apologizing for not being able to make it in for her shift. When she explained that her boyfriend came down with something nasty, and that she didn't want to pass it to the children, they were happy she'd chosen to stay home. The last thing you wanted was to bring a bug into the ward while working with children with less than stellar immune systems. If she went in for her shift, she'd be putting all the children at risk.

Maggie made a similar call to Tyrone's immediate superior at Synergy, but changed the symptoms and downplayed the severity. If this was something he'd caught at work, the last thing he needed was to be put in quarantine by his employer. She recalled a phone conversation she'd overheard. One where Tyrone told his co-worker that he would rather die than go through Synergy's quarantine protocol. She shuddered at the thought of someone barging into her house in white biohazard suits and taking them to some secret facility for study.

"Maggie?" Tyrone's raspy voice had her running back to the bedroom. Did he sound stronger than he had last night? Maggie wasn't sure until she stepped into the bedroom and saw his wide fevered eyes.

"What can I get you?" she asked softly, walking to the bedside to check his temperature.

"Nothing." His eyes closed. "I had a dream you'd been hurt. When I woke up, you weren't here, so I got worried that something happened to you."

"Nothing's happened. I'm fine." The thermometer beeped and her heart sank when she read the readout; 104.0 degrees. Not even the cold compresses were working to lower his temperature now.

"I'm cold Maggie," Tyrone complained.

"Well we can get you into a cool bath, I'll change the sheets and start a load of laundry and afterwards we can get you into fresh scrubs. You should feel a little more comfortable after that." She wasn't quite sure how she'd get the big man into the tub, or out if he lost consciousness, but it was a risk she'd have to take. A cool bath should help lower his fever and it was her last resort before calling for medical help.

"Okay," Tyrone groaned as Maggie helped him into a sitting position.

"Now, just stay here while I run the bath for you and try not to lie back down." She pressed her lips to Tyrone's burning forehead before hurrying from the room to get the bath underway.

With Tyrone settled into the bath, Maggie set about stripping the old sheets from the bed and placing a new set on. She wasn't sure if she wanted to bother washing the bed sheets or if she'd be better off throwing them out and buying a new set to replace them.

"I'm too tired to decide right now," Maggie sighed and dumped the heap of blankets onto the back stoop. She sat for a few minutes on the steps, soaking in the sun's warmth; it felt good to be out of the stuffy sick house.

Her peace lasted less than ten minutes. When Tyrone started screaming, Maggie was back on her feet ready to face the next challenge - she'd decided that Tyrone was going to pull through and she needed to be the one to help him through it.

She ran to the bathroom where Tyrone was sloshing about in the water screaming: "Get them off... Get them away from me."

"What is it?" she asked, frantically searching for the cause of his agitation.

"The snakes," he shouted shrilly as he thrashed. "They're all over me."

Maggie knew this wasn't a good sign. If he was delirious, the fever wasn't getting better in the cold water. "There are no snakes Tyrone," Maggie said as she calmly pulled the plug of the tub and helped him out. As the water receded, Tyrone slowly calmed.

"Get me out of here," he barked, when the last of the water drained. "They're gone for now but they'll be able to find their way back up the drain. I want you to close the bathroom door and shove a towel in the crack."

"There were no snakes Tyrone," she said again, as she toweled him off. "It's just the fever playing tricks with your mind. Let's get you into clean scrubs and get you back to bed."

Maggie redressed the wound on Tyrone's arm without looking at it too closely this time; it smelled worse and the lines were darker and longer. It wasn't a good sign and her hopes of Tyrone's recovery ebbed into fear. *At this point, I'm not sure that he's going to survive, even if I can get him to the hospital.* She choked back a sob. *I've left it for far too long.*

Even in his delirium, Tyrone refused her offers to get medical help. She'd even gone as far as to suggest they call Synergy to ask for the equipment she needed to deal with the blood poisoning. When that sent him into a fit, she knew she couldn't propose that option again; all she'd accomplished was to get him worked up and expend energy he didn't have.

The morning wore on and Tyrone's delirium grew worse. He had an episode where he thought maggots covered his entire body and another where he was sure the meat in the soup were chunks of human flesh. The worst was when he'd woken up screaming that the house was on fire. He'd made it all the way out to the front porch before Maggie had been able to convince him that there was no fire and get him back to bed.

Around one that afternoon, Tyrone began to shake uncontrollably. At first Maggie thought he was seizing, but quickly realized none of the standard seizure symptoms were showing. There was no fluid coming from his mouth and he wasn't shaking violently, with whole body spasms; it was almost as if he had a really bad case of the chills. Tyrone became increasingly hard to waken for the fluids Maggie insisted on giving him every fifteen minutes. Then came the blackish vomit. Every time she tried to give him water, he'd swallow and almost immediately, his stomach would reject it and vomit it back up.

With the bedding covered with black smears, Maggie was on the verge of panic. Ridiculously, all she could think was that she shouldn't have changed the sheets earlier.

Immediate medical attention no longer required...

Maggie sat with the phone clutched in her hand for what seemed like an eternity. She'd been arguing with herself about whether to call 911 or if she should respect Tyrone's wishes, and let him continue fighting whatever he'd contracted, on his own. With her knuckles turning white around the phone, she listened to his laboured breathing and, for a frightening moment, thought she'd waited too long when she didn't hear the next inhalation. With the next wheezing breath, Maggie decided she'd waited far too long already and punched in the numbers. She no longer cared what promises she made about keeping the doctors away.

The operator answered in a calm tone, "Nine-one-one, what's your emergency?"

Maggie wasn't sure what to tell the operator: if she told the truth, they might revoke her nursing licence for not bringing Tyrone in sooner, but if she lied, Tyrone wouldn't get the treatment he desperately needed.

"Hello?" the operator spoke again, filling the silence. "What is your emergency?"

Maggie choked back a sob, "I need an ambulance for my boyfriend. He came home last night and didn't feel well and he's gotten much worse throughout the night."

"What is his condition ma'am?" the operator asked in that calm tone.

"He's barely breathing. He's started vomiting blackish fluid about twenty minutes ago." This time Maggie couldn't hold back the sob and burst into tears.

"I am dispatching an ambulance to your location. Why didn't you call earlier ma'am?"

"Because he made me promise not to." Maggie wailed, unable to control her emotions. "I'm a nurse and I knew better, but he made me promise. I did what I could with my limited resources at home... I did the best I could. It just wasn't good enough."

"Help is on the way ma'am; I'll stay on the line with you until..." Maggie hung up; the house, she noticed, had fallen silent. She rushed into the bedroom and stared in shock at Tyrone. He wasn't breathing. He wasn't moving.

Maggie crumpled to the floor in the doorway, shock paralyzing her - Tyrone was dead. *I waited too long.*

The dead didn't look the same as the living, Maggie knew from experience; they looked deflated, as if the part of them that made them human was gone. What they left behind was only a shell. She broke into fresh tears as she stared, unable to pull her eyes away from the lifeless corpse that lay in hers and Tyrone's bed.

Maggie wasn't sure how long she sat on the floor with tears streaming down her face. It wasn't until Tyrone's hand twitched, that she returned to her senses. Had she imagined the movement or was it just the last electrical impulses firing off in his brain? She wiped the tears from her eyes and sniffled to clear the snot running from her nose. In her attempt to clear her sinuses, she was assaulted by the scent of ammonia; his bladder had released its contents meaning he was truly dead.

"Post-mortem spasms," Maggie whispered to herself, wishing for the moment that she didn't understand so much about death.

Tyrone's hand twitched again, as did his foot. Maggie got to her feet and slowly walked to the bed, intending on pulling the sheet up over Tyrone's head - she didn't want to witness more. Just as she pulled on the sheet, Tyrone's eyes flew open. Maggie staggered back with a squeak, bumping into the nightstand, which upset the light causing it to crash to the floor. She'd never heard of post-mortem spasms causing the eyes to open like that. In the dim light peeking through the curtains, Maggie watched in horror as Tyrone struggled to sit up.

"Baby?" she asked almost in a whisper - she'd been sure he was dead.

At the sound of her voice, Tyrone's head whipped to face her and Maggie saw the milky white of his eyes. This wasn't her boyfriend any longer - she didn't know what this thing in her boyfriend's skin was. The thing tracked Maggie as she scuttled for the door, not daring to turn her back on the creature. She watched in horror as it swung its legs over the side of the bed and attempted to stand. Its belly filled with air, puffing out like an emaciated child's, and a long low moan escaped its lips.

Maggie's fear paralyzed her. She'd never seen anything like this creature before - other than in zombie movies... She went cold; this was exactly like a zombie movie and the stupid idiot who discovered the zombie always got eaten first. Maggie didn't want to get eaten by this monster. She watched as the thing shuffled forward, closing the gap between them. Its legs tangled in the sheet and it pitched forward, falling onto Maggie. It gnashed its teeth and clawed at her shirt, trying to gain purchase, but Maggie was able to wiggle free from its grasp. It collapsed in a heap to the floor. For being a zombie, it was incredibly uncoordinated. Maggie laughed at the absurd thought - how did she know what a zombie was supposed to be capable of? Her experience with zombies went as far as what Hollywood portrayed on screen and how could they know what a zombie was truly like?

Standing there watching as the zombie struggled to its feet was wasting precious time - she needed to get somewhere safe, even if it was only temporarily. She ran down the hall, dashing into the spare room, and slammed the door closed behind her. Her heart was beating wildly as her mind raced to catch up with the reality of her situation. She leaned against the closed door and began to laugh; she sounded manic even to herself. Her fit of laughter quickly subsided when something heavy hit the door from the other side, making the room shudder. The monster trying to get into the room and eat her flesh moaned again and crashed into the door for a second time. Maggie realized she had to act quickly if she hoped to get out of the house before the thing got in.

She cast a quick glance around, settling on a heavy waist-high dresser against the wall beside her; Maggie prayed the door would hold until she could maneuver piece of furniture into place. It took several heart-pounding minutes to push the dresser, all the while, the thing kept banging away. Once she heard a splintering sound, she knew the room wouldn't be safe for long. With the dresser barring the door from being opened - not that the thing knew how to open it anyways - Maggie rifled through the room searching for the gun Tyrone kept hidden there. She found it in the last place she looked - the bottom dresser drawer locked in a small metal box; there was no key.

"You're an ass hole," Maggie shouted through the door. "What use is a gun, locked in a metal case without a key?" There was no response, but she hadn't expected the zombie to respond. The monster just kept up its incessant banging on the door.

The door splintered off its hinges, the loud crack making Maggie jump. She was thankful she took the time to move the dresser; otherwise, it would already be in the room with her. She quickly changed into an old pair of scrubs she'd found in the closet, thankful she'd kept the oversized clothes after losing thirty pounds last year. She cursed when she realized her cell phone and keys were in her purse, hanging from a hook in the kitchen. She'd just have to try and sneak in the back door before that thing heard her.

The door shuddered in its frame again, making loud cracking noises as the pounding increased in speed and strength. With one final crash, the door snapped in half, falling to the floor at Maggie's feet. The zombie stared at Maggie with its milky eyes and stumbled forward, falling over the dresser and landing in a heap inside the room.

"You fucker!" Maggie shouted, as she pulled up the window, knocking out the screen. She struggled to get one leg out, and then ducked her head in an attempt to squeeze through the small opening. She could hear a siren close by and realized the paramedics are on their way to get Tyrone.

"Too late now," she muttered, looking back to the zombie shuffling across the floor. Straddling the window ledge, she looked down to the ground beneath the window, relieved that she lived in a single story home. If she were on a second story, the fall would be a lot further and hurt a hell of a lot more. Realizing that she'd be unable to get her other leg through the opening without falling to her ass, Maggie took a deep breath, preparing herself for the fall. It was too late. Cold hands clasped her leg and she screamed as teeth sunk into her calf.

Shocked, Maggie lost her balance and toppled out of the window, feeling her flesh tear free from the zombie's teeth as gravity forced her to the ground. She stared up as Tyrone's head popped through of the window, blood dripping from his maw and his mouth working in a chewing motion. In life, Tyrone was a large man, and now he was unable to force his body through the small opening of the window.

"Small miracles," Maggie muttered.

Food for the hungry...

There was loud banging on the front door and the zombie's head disappeared from Maggie's view. She gingerly pulled up her pant leg to inspect the damage to her calf and had to swallow back bile as she inspected the bite - he'd taken a chunk of skin from her leg. Was that what he'd been chewing on? The banging on the front door continued, pulling Maggie back from the brink of hysteria. She knew she had to warn the paramedics not to open the door.

"Hello? Did someone call nine-one-one?" a male voice called loudly, followed by three more heavy bangs on the front door.

Maggie stumbled to her feet, trying not to put too much pressure on her wounded leg, and stumbled towards the front of the house.

"We're responding to a call made to nine-one-one. We are entering the house in case you are unable to answer the door yourself," the voice shouted again.

Maggie rounded the corner, a warning on her lips, just in time to watch the paramedics push the front door open. The Tyrone-shaped zombie fell through the door, latching its teeth into the closest paramedic and bit deeply into his neck.

There was a grotesque gurgling sound followed by the second paramedic shouting, "Get off of him." He pulled at Tyrone's arm, as his partner struggled beneath the big man's weight. When that didn't distract the zombie from his gorging, he pounded on its back and head. Maggie watched in stunned horror as Tyrone ripped chunks of flesh from the man's neck and shoulder, oblivious to the man standing above him. When the man beneath Tyrone stopped fighting and stilled, his attention turned to the living man standing over him. The paramedic gasped and stumbled back as the zombie reached for him. Opening its gore-filled mouth open, the zombie let out a low, inhuman moan that started from deep within him. The sound made Maggie shudder.

She watched, unwilling to draw attention to herself by calling out a warning as the paramedic turned and dashed into the house. He swung the door closed behind him, but wasn't quite fast enough. Tyrone stumbled to his feet and reached through the doorway, stopping the swinging door before it was able to fully close.

"It may have saved him if he'd gotten inside sooner," Maggie snorted as she watched the zombie push open the door and disappear inside. Within the minute, she heard the screams of the second paramedic before those too were silenced.

Hobbling across the yard as quickly as her leg would allow, Maggie prayed that Tyrone hadn't taken her spare set of keys from the glove compartment of her car. He'd always hated knowing they were so easily accessible to someone who might want to steal her beat-up-hunk-of-junk. She flung open the door and fell onto the seat, slamming the door closed behind her. Ignoring the searing pain in her leg and the lightness of her head, she ransacked the glove compartment; there was momentary panic when Maggie couldn't find the spare keys amidst the clutter. When her fingers touched the cold metal of the keying, she breathed a sigh of relief and turned her attention to her leg. Blood pooled on the floor of the car. She knew that if she was going to make it to her sisters while she was still conscious, she needed to wrap the wound and stop the bleeding.

In the back seat, Maggie found a cotton t-shirt she'd left in the car after one of her more grueling shifts and quickly tore two strips from the bottom of the shirt. She wadded up the remainder to use as an absorbent pad. With practiced skill, Maggie staunched the flow of blood in under a minute and cracked open a bottle of water. *Fluids after blood-loss is a must!*

Just as she was putting the key into the ignition, movement in her peripheral vision made Maggie turn her head. It was the first paramedic; he stumbled into her car door. She cranked the key and the car roared to life. Throwing the car into reverse, she stomped on the gas. It flew down the drive. The tires squealed when Maggie spun the steering wheel as far right as it would go. The car swung onto the street then stopped, swaying from the violent turn. Maggie fumbled with the shifter as she watched the paramedic stumble towards her. With the car finally in drive Maggie sped past the house just in time to see Tyrone and the second paramedic stumble off of her porch.

Poor choices...

Maggie didn't remember the eight-minute drive to her sisters or her frantic banging on the door; she only remembered seeing her sister's panicked face when the door finally opened.

"Oh God Maggie, what happened to you?" Anne exclaimed after taking in her sister's state.

Maggie collapsed, bawling, into her sister's open arms. "Tyrone..." she gasped, unable to catch her breath, knowing she was going into shock.

"Tyrone did this to you?" Anne asked incredulously.

"Yes... No.. He's dead Anne." Maggie managed to get out between sobs.

"Dead?" Now it was Anne's turn to be shocked. "How?"

"He was dead but now he's not. He's walking around biting people Anne and they die and get back up to bite more people." Maggie looked up into her sister's frightened face. "I'm going to die and come back like them. I'm going to eat people too."

"No baby," Anne stroked Maggie's hair gently as she spoke in a calming tone, but felt none of the calm she was trying to impart to her sister, "you aren't going to die or eat people. I don't know what you've been through, but you're a mess; you're in shock. Let's get you inside so I can take a look at you."

Maggie went wild, thrashing against her sister's embrace. "No, not inside. I'm not going to put you at risk. If I die I'll come back and eat you."

Anne looked down and noticed the wrapping on Maggie's calf; Anne's blood ran cold. Something very bad had happened to her baby sister. She was going to find out who'd done this to her and make them pay. "What happened to your leg sweetie?" Anne asked, unsure if she truly wanted an answer.

Maggie's hand went down to the makeshift bandage, loosening the ties. Anne gasped when the cloth fell away revealing a nasty bite and a missing chunk of skin. "Who bit you?" she asked, unable to mask the horror in her voice.

"Tyrone," Maggie wailed.

"Well we're going to take you to the hospital..."

"No!" Maggie screamed. "No hospital!"

"Well baby, if I can't take you inside and I can't take you to the hospital, what do you expect me to do with you?" Anne wasn't sure what to do; she'd never seen anything like this before.

Maggie looked up to Anne with glassy eyes. "Do you have any orange juice or lemonade? I need to keep my fluids and sugar up because of the blood loss."

Anne sighed; for someone in shock she'd at least retained her medical training. "Sure thing baby. You wait right here and I'll be back in a few minutes with some juice for you." As Anne hurried back into the house to pour a glass of juice she remembered the sleeping pills she'd been prescribed a year earlier. If Maggie wasn't going to be reasonable, then she'd just have to make sure she was calm until Anne could get her to the hospital. It didn't take Anne long to crush the tiny blue pill, mixing some of the powder in with the juice. Before long, she was handing the spiked drink back to her sister, who chugged the whole thing in one breath.

Anne sat rocking Maggie on the porch of her home, trying to decide what she'd do after dropping Maggie off at the hospital. She could go confront Tyrone, but the big man frightened Anne. She could go to the police and report the incident - but what would they do... Maggie had been bitten. *Is biting considered abuse? Assault?* "It sure as hell is," Anne said indignantly.

Maggie gave a soft groan from Anne's lap; she was asleep at last.

Volume 3: Wildfire

Shifts end...

Officer Rick Powell and his partner Officer Brett Lewis pulled into the stations parking lot, glad the day was finally over. Their final call of the evening had been a domestic dispute where the woman refused to press charges against her dead-beat husband; those type of calls always infuriated Powell. He'd been a cop for twenty-one years and knew he'd never understand why a battered woman would always stand by her man once the cops showed up. *At least the day's over.* He was looking forward to going home, taking a long, hot shower, and spending an evening with his wife and children.

"What are you up to tonight Lewis?" Powell asked his partner as they exited the patrol car.

"I was going to grab a drink with Tanya from booking when her shift ends." Lewis gave his partner a lewd look and Powell rolled his eyes. Lewis was twenty-six and fresh out of the academy. He hadn't yet learned that dating the women he worked with was a bad idea. That knowledge would come with time and experience.

"Are you still..." Powell began but was cut off by a screech of tires. Both officers looked to the end of the parking lot as a car swerved around the bank of parked vehicles. "What's this now?" he sighed, lifting his arm to flag the car down.

"Watch out Rick!" Lewis grabbed Powell, yanking him back, just as the car swerved in their direction and smashed into the cruiser next to them. Both officers ran to the driver's side door. It opened and a short woman with bleached hair struggled to free herself from the wreckage.

Powell immediately took in the woman's condition; her wild eyes were glazed, she had a cut just above her left eye and he noticed her side was drenched with blood.

"Get on the ground," Lewis shouted as he drew his weapon.

"Easy." Powell placed a hand on his partner's arm, forcing the rookie to lower his weapon. "She's been hurt - let's get her out of the car and see what's going on." It took some manoeuvring but soon the woman stood on shaking legs, glancing wildly around the parking lot.

Powell took the woman by her shoulders and gazed into her glassy eyes. "Where are you hurt? What is your name?" but his questions weren't to be answered; the woman collapsed in his arms. Lewis stood gaping, his mouth moved but no words came out. "Help me get her inside Lewis," Powell barked.

They carried the bloody woman into the waiting area, laying her across several of the plastic seats. He gingerly lifted the side of the woman's shirt and both cops gasped when the shirt peeled away from two bloody holes in her side. Powell turned to his partner, who looked at the woman in shock. "Go get a first aid kit and tell whoever's working the desk to get another officer down here to take this woman's statement."

Lewis didn't move. "Why didn't she go to the hospital?"

"Does it look like I can ask her?" Powell snapped, motioning to the unconscious woman. "Just go do what I asked - and have whoever's there call an ambulance."

Lewis had just disappeared from sight when the woman moaned and her eyes fluttered open. Powell squatted beside her, taking her hand in his large one. "Ma'am?" She moaned again and mumbled something he couldn't make out. "What is your name ma'am?" Powell spoke loudly, trying to draw the woman back to consciousness. The woman screamed, sitting bolt upright, and then grimaced as she grabbed her side. Her eyes met Powell's and the terror he saw there frightened the veteran cop. "What's your name ma'am?"

Her whole body shook as she spoke in a trembling voice. "Roslyn. Roslyn Macpherson. Where am I? "

"You're in the police station. You crashed into one of the cars in our parking lot." Powell paused for a moment, giving Roslyn time to acclimate herself with her surroundings; she still looked like she was in shock. He spoke in a low calming tone, "What happened to you Roslyn? Why did you come to the police station and not go to the hospital?"

"They're eating my neighbours. They tried to eat me. My neighbours have gone crazy. They've started attacking and eating people. I couldn't go to the hospital because someone needs to go there and stop them from eating people," Roslyn rambled.

Powell sat in disbelieving silence; this woman was further gone than he'd thought. *She must have lost a little too much blood.*

"My daughter... my daughter will be home soon and she doesn't know that he's going to try to eat her too." Roslyn shifted into a sitting position, grimacing with each movement. "You have to go warn my little girl and arrest my neighbours. They're killing people."

"Can I look at your side Roslyn?" Powell said calmly, although he didn't feel calm. His guts twisted a little more with each word Roslyn spoke. She'd obviously been through something traumatic, but he couldn't bring himself to believe that there were people in his city eating one another.

"You'll go right?" She reached out with a bloody hand and clasped Powell's arm tightly. "You're going to go..."

"I promise to send someone. My partner is getting help right now." That seemed to appease her and she lifted her shirt, baring her bloody side for Powell.

The bleeding appeared to have slowed but Powell couldn't make out much beneath all the blood; he'd have to wait for Lewis to come back with supplies. To the veteran cop, it looked almost as if she'd been bitten by another human. Cold chills ran down his spine. "Is this the only place you're hurt?" he asked cautiously, unsure if he wanted to know the full extent of the woman's wounds.

"My back." Roslyn tried to pull her shirt up further, but it was too painful for her and Powell sat beside her, lifting it for her. He was glad she couldn't see the horror on his face as he inspected the long scratch marks on her lower back. He bent closer; there was something imbedded in her skin, at the bottom of the longest scratch, just above her pant line. Without thinking Powell pulled it out, making Roslyn cry out in pain. He studied the crescent shaped object, wiping away the blood from its jagged surface. He felt bile rise in his throat as he realized what had been imbedded in Roslyn's back: he'd just pulled a human fingernail from the poor woman's flesh.

"Tell me what happened Roslyn," Powell said in a tone he hoped didn't alert her to how shaken he was.

"I don't know anymore. It just doesn't seem real." She looked at Powell; fear, confusion, pain, and uncertainty radiated from her eyes.

"Just tell me what you remember, no matter how unbelievable it may seem." He was surprised when Roslyn took his hand in hers, squeezing it tightly.

She inhaled deeply, letting the exhalation out in a slow, controlled breath before beginning. "I'd just gotten home from the grocery store. I'd been kept late at work and picked up tacos for dinner because it was quick. The kids love it when I make tacos for dinner." Tears splashed down onto Powell's hand, but Roslyn went on without noticing. "I called to Peter, my son, to come help me unload the groceries. I was angry that he'd left the garage door open and his skateboard in the driveway again, so I'd shouted loudly for him. I began pulling bags out of the backseat when I saw his shadow. I started to say that if he didn't get his stuff put away properly that I'd take it away for a month and it would teach him to take better care of his things." Roslyn looked up at Powell with more tears shimmering in her eyes and a small sad smile on her lips. "Do you have children Officer?"

Powell nodded, remembering the many time's he'd done the same thing to his twelve year old son Stevie. "I have a son and a daughter," he said around the lump growing in his throat. He wasn't sure if he wanted Roslyn to continue with her story; he had a very bad feeling about the direction it was headed.

"Then you know how they are." Roslyn's tears spilled over, leaving streaks on her cheeks. "He was always such a good boy; strong like his father and smart like me. He just had a problem putting things away."

She broke down into sobs for what seemed, to Powell, like forever. He was used to dealing with hysterical women - it was part of his daily job - but this was different and his gut knotted with anxiety. As a cop, he always trusted his gut instinct and now it was telling him to grab his family and head for the hills. No matter how badly he wanted to trust his instinct and go, he knew he couldn't do that. "Go on Roslyn," he gently prodded.

"Well I'd started to scold him when I felt cold hands on my back. I yelped because the cold was unexpected and I started to back up so I didn't hit my head on the car roof. Then pain shot up from my side and I began to scream; he'd bitten me hard enough that he'd broken skin. My first thought was that it wasn't him, that some sicko had hold of me. I scrambled over the groceries in the back seat and had just gotten the passenger side door opened when he pulled me back through the car and bit me a second time. I managed to get out from under him - get through the car again - when I felt his fingers dragging down my back, trying to find another hold. There was another stab of pain in my lower back but I kept going. I knew that if I didn't get out, I'd be eaten alive right there in my car. My groceries would get all bloody and dinner would be ruined." She let out a small mirthless laugh, "Silly isn't it?"

More tears splashed on Powell's hand and he squeezed reassuringly; he wasn't sure if he completely believed Roslyn's story... no, he believed her - he just didn't want to.

"I fell out the other side of the car and kicked the door closed behind me. I think I was already going into shock at that point. I got to my feet and starred into the car - into my son's face; but it wasn't my son... not really. It was his body clawing at the window sure, but my sweet little boy was gone. His eyes were cloudy and white. He had part of his neck torn out and his mouth was filled with blood and skin - my blood... my skin..." another sob burst out, and Roslyn's small body shook. Powell wanted to tell her to stop. Tell her he didn't want to hear more but knew she wasn't done.

Roslyn took another shuddering breath and continued with her story. "I noticed movement behind me in the window's reflection. I turned and saw old Mrs. Demarsh stumbling around the corner of my house. I think I gasped when I saw her blood covered nightgown and that her arm was missing below her elbow. She stopped when she saw me, and her belly puffed up. It was so strange. Then she moaned." Roslyn shuddered as if recalling the sound. "It was the most horrible, unnatural moan I've ever heard. I heard Peter moan in the car and then there were more moans coming from the surrounding houses. It was like Mrs. Demarsh rang the dinner bell and everyone was coming for the feast. I knew I couldn't stay there but I didn't know where to go. Thankfully I noticed a car idling in the street. The door was open and so I ran to it and jumped in. I didn't look back as I turned around and drove away." Roslyn ran a hand over her face, leaving a bloody streak on her cheek. "I wasn't sure where I was going to go until I saw the station. You know the rest."

Powell wasn't sure what to say once Roslyn finished her story. Only then did he notice Lewis standing down the hall; eyes wide and his dark skin unnaturally pale. "I'll be right back Roslyn." Powell squeezed her hand once, before pulling it from her iron grip.

"Don't leave me," Roslyn half shrieked. She clutched at Powell's uniform, looking up at him with fear.

"I'm just going to go talk to my partner." He spoke slowly as he motioned towards Lewis, "I'll be right back with some first aid supplies to clean your side and back. Will you be okay for two minutes? You'll be able to see me the whole time. I promise." Roslyn nodded, slowly releasing her grip on his uniform. Once free from her clutches, he hurried over to Lewis who handed him the first aid kit. "How much of her story did you hear?" He asked in a low voice, not wanting Roslyn to overhear him.

"Enough," Lewis croaked.

"Did you call an ambulance?"

Lewis nodded, casting wary glances over Powell's shoulder to where Roslyn sat. "No one's coming though."

Powell frowned. "What do you mean no one's coming?" he hissed.

Lewis looked as if he were about to hurl. "There was a disturbance at the hospital. They called in and requested several officers to be sent over. A woman apparently came in, went into cardiac arrest and then started biting people." Lewis lowered his voice to a whisper as he leaned towards Powell, "They told dispatch that there were a lot more patients biting people now and they needed help controlling them. They sent over three units and when they stopped responding to dispatch, they sent another four units in riot gear to see what was going on. They've lost contact with those units as well."

"What the hell is going on?" Powell growled. "What are we supposed to do with her?" he jerked his head back towards Roslyn who sat crying silently.

Lewis shrugged. "Clean her up, bandage her wounds as best we can and put her in a conference room until they figure out what's happening." Powell sighed; his hot shower would have to wait. "There's one other thing... and you aren't going to like it."

Powell scrubbed his hands over his face. He was supposed to be off duty and they were sending him back out. He wasn't happy with the turn in events, but overtime was often part of the job. "Give it to me." He motioned in a 'bring it on' gesture with his hand.

"There are two paramedics who responded to a call early this afternoon in Pecan Valley. They haven't returned. With all the confusion at the hospital, no one's reported them missing until just now. They've asked us to head over there and see what's going on."

"Did you just say Pecan Valley?" Roslyn called from her seat behind Powell; Lewis nodded. "That's where I live... Swan Forest, just off of Southeast Drive. That's where everyone's gone crazy. Will you go and find my daughter? Will you keep her safe and bring her to me?" Roslyn's eyes were pleading with Powell; how could he say no to a woman who's been through so much already.

He sighed; his shift was over but he knew he couldn't turn his back on this situation - someone needed to go look into what was happening in Pecan Valley. "I will, but first we have to clean your side and back. There is something going on at the Baptist hospital and it may be a while before someone can get here to take you in for proper treatment."

Roslyn's eyes went wide. "What's happening at the hospital?"

"Nothing you need to worry yourself about." Lewis smiled weakly at Roslyn, but Powell knew it didn't ease her fears. She saw the truth in his eyes.

"What's your daughter's name?" Powell asked, as he took the first aid supplies from his partner. He was glad Lewis had enough presence of mind to grab a bottle of water and a towel on his way back. A quick splash of water had most of the blood running down Roslyn's side.

She grimaced when he dabbed the edges of the wound. "Marcy." Her voice quivered when she spoke.

"Sorry," he muttered, concentrating on the task, "I'm going to have to disinfect it and it's going to hurt. How about you tell me about Marcy and try not to think about what I'm doing here."

Roslyn gave Powell a weak smile before turning back to face Lewis who reached out and held the woman's hand tightly. "Marcy's a firecracker. She just turned sixteen and runs like the wind..." She screamed in pain as Powell dabbed at the largest bite with an antiseptic towelette.

When she took in several gasping breaths, Powell feared she'd hyperventilate and pass out; at least then, she wouldn't feel the

39

pain. "Go on." Powell urged when she'd calmed enough to speak. Now that he was seeing beneath all the blood, he realized the bites were much worse than he'd first assumed. Two large chunks of skin were gone, revealing the muscle beneath. *She's going to need a lot of stitching up and some heavy-duty antibiotics.*

"Marcy's the top long distance runner on her high school track team and is always changing the color of her hair - this week she has bright pink streaks." Roslyn laughed but Powell could hear the tears in her voice. "Next week they'll be green." She screamed again as Powell dabbed at the second, smaller bite. Mercifully, this time she did pass out.

Powell finished cleaning the wounds on Roslyn's side and back in silence. He wrapped them in gauze as best as he could. He had Lewis carry the woman to one of the conference rooms while he ran the address for Roslyn. If he were going to keep his promise, he'd need to check her house for signs of Marcy. He wasn't looking forward to missing the hot dinner waiting for him at home but knew his wife would understand.

Carnage in Pecan Valley...

Lewis made the turn onto Swan Forest and slammed on the breaks. Powell's heart thundered in his chest as he looked out the car window; there'd been an accident at the corner leaving the road impassible for the cruiser.

Powell cursed under his breath. "Well I suppose we get out and walk from here."

Lewis turned to him with wide eyes. "You want us to walk the three blocks to the Macpherson's home?" Powell nodded to his partner, unable to speak. The street beyond the accident was littered with garbage and dark splotches. In the dim light, he could see two more accidents and several other cars abandoned in the street. "What if we come across any of those... those things Roslyn was talking about?"

"Zombies..." Powell said wearily; Lewis spluttered incoherently. "What else do you call something that's walking around eating other people?" he snapped, "I know it sounds unbelievable, but you saw those bite marks."

"Does that mean Roslyn's going to turn into a zombie?" Lewis shrank back in his seat.

I hadn't thought of that. If we are dealing with zombies, then it's likely. Did we close the door to the room that she's in? What he said to his partner was, "We don't know what's going on here Lewis; do you really think the dead can get up and walk?" Powell shoved open his door. "I was just making a comparison to movies - for all we know these people are infected with a type of rabies." As an afterthought, he told Lewis to leave the keys in the ignition. If they needed to get out of the area quickly, he didn't need to be searching for the cruiser's keys.

Lewis got out, glaring at his partner over the cruiser's roof. "You know, rabies doesn't sound any better." He slammed the door then flinched as the bang echoed down the street.

"Just shut up and let's get moving," Powell snapped. He shouldn't have said anything. Now Lewis would be afraid of his own shadow, but a nagging feeling that he was right with his first description, crept over him as they walked down the empty street. There was movement to Powell's right, and on instinct, he pushed Lewis behind the cover of one of the abandoned cars.

"What the hell?" Lewis hissed as Powell peeked over the car's trunk; what he saw made his blood run cold.

A woman, dressed in a business suit, staggered across a lawn in front of them. She had an odd gait and Powell quickly realized it was because she was missing one of her high-heeled shoes. Her face and neck were covered in blood while a gory trail of what Powell guessed were intestines, hung from beneath the suit's jacket; two of her fingers were missing. He heard Lewis retch behind him and was glad he hadn't eaten anything in the past several hours. The woman paused, slowly turning towards the sounds Lewis was making. Powell clamped a hand over his partner's mouth and pressed a finger to his own lips, indicating Lewis needed to be very quiet. After several tense minutes of absolute silence, the woman began her uneven shuffle down the street once again.

"We need to get moving," Powell finally said in a low voice, once the woman had moved three houses down. "Try to stay as close to the cars as possible. I don't want to be caught in the street without cover."

They made it down to the next cul-de-sac, silently creeping from car to car, before Lewis stopped Powell. "This is the street where the ambulance was called to." He pulled his flashlight from his gun belt and shone the powerful beam down the street. Three houses up the ambulance sat in silence. "Should we go check it out?" Lewis looked to Powell and missed the shambling figure that stumbled out from behind the ambulance. He had a paramedic's uniform on but Powell could see the missing flesh from his neck.

A scream, followed by gunshots further down the street, had both officers turning to see where it had originated. All the surrounding houses were dark, which was unusual for being so early in the evening. Lewis turned his flashlight, shining it further down the street they were on and they could see figures moving in the dark, beyond the light.

"I think we should get to Roslyn's house and check for her daughter. Then I think we need to get back to the station." A low, unnatural moan came from the other side of the car they were hiding behind. "Fuck!" Powell cursed as goose bumps prickled down his arms; he'd been distracted by the scream and had forgotten about the paramedic.

"What? What?" Lewis spun back to Powell.

Powell withdrew his weapon and peered over the hood, knowing what he'd see. The zombie - he was now sure that's what these dead things were - stood no more than ten feet away. His eyes were milky and his once crisp uniform was wrinkled and covered with large splotches of blood; gore hung from his mouth. Lewis gasped beside Powell, as he realized what his partner was looking at. The zombie's belly puffed out and another low guttural moan came from the creature; a responding moan came from behind the pair of men, further down the street.

Lewis jumped up from behind the car as soon as the zombie started shuffling forward. "Freeze," he said with too much volume. Powell cringed; these things seemed to be attracted to sound and Lewis with his loud mouth was going to get them both killed. "I said stay back," he commanded, as the zombie continued his shuffle towards them. "If you don't stop, I will shoot." Powell could see the gun shaking in Lewis' hands and felt sorry for his partner. He knew the rookie had never shot a person before.

The gun fired. Powell scanned the street for movement; he could see the woman in the business suit shambling towards them with a few friends. The gun fired a second time. "What are you doing Lewis? You're making too much noise," he hissed.

"He-h-he took two shots in the chest." Lewis whimpered.

Powell looked back over the car and was shocked to see the paramedic was still approaching them. He raised his own gun, took aim, and pulled the trigger. The bullet entered the man's forehead, right between the eyes, and the zombie slumped to the ground.

"Head shots Lewis. We have to move," Powell growled, pulling his partner further down the street in search of somewhere he could easily fortify while he radioed for backup. The gunshots had brought out more shambling figures into the streets. Where it used to be still and silent, the street was now filled with movement and those awful moans. Powell saw at least twenty figures ahead of them but was sure they'd be able to navigate around the slow figures, shooting any that came too close.

"Look there." Lewis pointed to the end of the street, at the house on the corner. From the second story back window, Powell could see someone signalling with a flashlight.

"It's Morse code; SOS I think. There have to be people alive and holed up in that house." He shot a closing zombie in the head, feeling satisfaction as he watched it topple to the ground and skid across the asphalt.

"How are we going to get in?" Lewis said as they rounded the corner and onto the cul-de-sac where the Macpherson's lived. Powell knew he'd never be able to make it past the five houses on the street to the end where Roslyn lived. There were just too many zombies in the streets right now; their gunfire had drawn out hundreds from the surrounding houses and they were closing in. "Has everyone in the neighbourhood been turned into one of those monsters?" Lewis asked after seeing the sheer number lumbering towards them.

"Over here," a man's voice called from the corner house.

"There's a ladder." Powell pointed before sprinting across the lawn, glad they wouldn't have to try and close a door behind them. He wasn't sure how smart these things were but didn't want to risk them getting in, and trapping him in the breached house.

His foot had just hit the first rung when Lewis shrieked, "Get it off of me!"

Powell spun around and was horrified to see a small little girl, no older than five, clinging to Lewis' leg. A dark spot blossomed from where the little girl had sunk her teeth into the flesh of his thigh. "Brett, watch your hands," Powell shouted as he lifted his gun and without hesitation, shot the little zombie in the side of the head. When she fell away, Lewis clamped his hands over the bit and started blubbering; he couldn't understand what his partner was gibbering about.

Powell was about to go after his partner and help him to the ladder when the man on the roof spoke again. "You can't do anything for him now; a bite means he's as good as dead. Either you come now or I'm raising the ladder and you can find somewhere to hide with your partner until he turns into one of those things and eats you."

"Help me." Lewis reached towards him, his eyes pleading for help.

Powell turned to the man on the roof. "Please just let me bring him up and once he goes, I'll take care of him myself. I can't leave him out here to be eaten. He's still alive and I can get the bleeding stopped. I just need enough time to radio into the station and figure out how we're going to get out of here."

The man shook his head slowly, placing a hand on the ladder. "I'm sorry. I have others here I need to look out for."

A burst of gunfire made Powell spin back to Lewis. His partner dropped three of the closest zombies, but too many were closing in. Lewis was slowly backing up towards the house when the ladder began to rattle back up to the roof. "Wait." Powell raised his hand, palm out in the universal signal for stop.

Lewis screamed, making Powell turn back around. He watched in horror as a massive man in scrubs held Lewis in a bear hug. He pulled something away from the side of Lewis' face and his partner screamed again. "He can't be helped," the man shouted over the screams and the moans. "Are you coming or not?"

Powell waved for the man to lower the ladder. "I'm coming." As he climbed, he felt his eyes begin to burn with tears he refused to shed. Lewis had been a foolish rookie and possibly made their situation worse, but he hadn't deserved to die at twenty-six for those mistakes. Abruptly, Lewis' screams became choked gurgles and Powell turned at the top of the ladder to look down at his partner, lying on the ground with the big man - *No, he isn't a man,* Powell reminded himself, *he's a zombie* - bent over the twitching body of Officer Brett Lewis.

The man from the roof pulled on Powell's arm. "Come on man, we have to get the ladder up." He helped Powell navigate around the top of the ladder and sat him down on the extended portion of the porch roof. He hauled the ladder onto the roof and sat down beside Powell. "I'm Ron." He held out a hand and Powell took it in a daze.

"I'm Rick," he mumbled, watching as his partner stopped twitching. The big zombie struggled to his feet and Powell pulled his gun, aiming for the zombies head. It killed his partner and now he was going to kill it.

"Don't," Ron whispered, placing his hand on the gun's barrel. "The report will alert them to our location. They don't seem to understand how the ladder works. Once they can no longer see the living person or where they went, they will wander away and spread out again. I don't know how, but if a living person goes through a door, they'll follow, but the ladder seems to have confused them so far. We haven't had any breaches yet."

Powell watched, half in fascination, half in horror, as Lewis' corpse began to move. The entire right side of his face, along with his ear, was gone and he was missing one of his eyes but still, he sat up and struggled to his feet. The squawk of Powell's radio made him jump.

"Turn that bloody thing off," Ron hissed. The zombie, who was once his partner, turned and stared up at Powell with grey, flat eyes that were already beginning to turn milky; he lifted his arms and moaned. Powell spun the volume dial on his walkie as Ron got to his feet. "That moan seems to bring more zombies in. We'd better get inside before they find us and figure out a way to get into the house."

Powell didn't remember climbing through the window or lying down on the bed - he knew he was going into shock but couldn't do anything about it. He didn't remember the call on his radio or even his promise to Roslyn as the world faded into black and he found a reprieve from the waking nightmare.

In the light of day...

Powell woke to sunlight pouring through the open window. At first he was afraid he'd slept in and missed the beginning of his shift, but soon the memories of the night before came flooding back. Roslyn coming to the station with bite marks... the zombies in the streets of Pecan Valley... the little girl clinging to Lewis' leg... Lewis staring up at him with one dull eye and half of a face...

"You're finally awake," a woman's voice interrupted his thoughts. "Sit up and have something to drink; you must be thirsty." Powell turned his head and saw a plump woman who appeared to be in her forties, not that he'd ever been good at guessing a women's age. He blinked, slowly rolling to his side in an attempt to delay becoming vertical once again. Once he was up, he'd have to figure out what his next plan of action would be and where he was going to go from here. "I've made you some toast as well, but that can wait until after you've gotten some fluid into you." She held the glass to his lips and he took a sip of the offered water.

He hadn't realized how dry his mouth and throat were until those first few drops hit his tongue. He sat up, taking the offered glass, and drained it in one long gulp. "Thank you," he croaked, wiping the back of his hand across his mouth.

The woman set a plate with a piece of toast on it in Powell's lap and plucked the empty glass from his hands. "I'll give you a few minutes. Eat the toast and I'll be back with a bigger glass of water." She smiled gently and left the room.

The clock on the nightstand informed Powell it was just after two in the afternoon, reminding him he hadn't called his wife last night to let her know what was happening. He dug into his pocket, pulled out the cell phone she insisted he carry, and grimaced when the screen read there were four missed calls and two voicemail. He didn't bother listening to the voicemails; rather, he hit the key to call home and took a bite of the toast.

"That won't work." The woman stood at the door holding a large glass of water. She was right; the phone beeped a fast busy in his ear. "I'm Ruth. Whenever you're ready, we're down in the basement. We don't want anyone on the main floor for too long as it might attract unwanted attention," she said, as she handed him the glass of water and retreated, leaving him alone once again.

Powell took another long swig of the water and stood, going to the window and looking down onto the street. He could see Roslyn's house from here, but the garage door was still open along with the inner door and his hopes in finding her daughter inside faded. Turning on his radio, he called into the station but there was no response. He watched a zombie wander aimlessly along the street as he shoved the rest of the toast in his mouth. He needed to relieve himself, he realized, and wandered into the hallway of the small home.

Just as he was washing his hands, his radio squawked. "Who was that trying to call in?" the strange female voice, he didn't recognize, asked in a whisper.

"Officer Richard Powell," he responded. "Why wasn't there an answer when I first called in and who is this?"

"Oh thank God! This is Tracy from booking Officer Powell. Is Brett with you?" Tracy was still whispering, making Powell's stomach drop. The bread he'd just eaten felt like a stone in his gut; something wasn't right.

"Negative," he responded, unsure how to answer the next question he knew was coming.

"Wh-what happened?" Tracy's whisper quivered as if she'd started crying.

"You don't want to know Tracy. Where is everyone? What happened at the station?" The response that came back was drowned out by banging in the background. "I didn't get that Tracy, please repeat."

Now it was obvious that Tracy was crying. "The woman you brought in died in the night. Someone covered her up and closed the conference room door. We noticed banging on the door a short time later and someone went in to check, thinking that she hadn't really died. She bit them and then went around the station biting other people. I managed to lock myself in the dispatch room but they're outside the door now. They're trying to get in Officer Powell."

"The same thing that happened here..." Powell was about to go into more detail but was cut off.

Over the splintering noise in the background, Tracy shouted, "They're breaking down the door." Loud moans were the last thing Powell heard before his radio fell silent.

Shaken, he made his way down to the basement and was surprised to find twelve people; some standing, talking in hushed tones while other sat huddled on the cement floor. On the floor, he noticed several children, two teens and a handful of adults comforting the youngest of the bunch. He couldn't imagine what they'd gone through, but every set of eyes that met his were haunted - they'd never be the same again.

Powell cleared his throat and the four people standing turned in unison; he immediately recognized Ruth and Ron. He gave Ruth a weak smile and lifted the glass, nodding his head in silent thanks while Ron made his way over to him.

"We were just discussing what our options are," Ron said, clapping Powell on the back in a friendly gesture. "Everyone's eager to meet you." He held out his arm, indicating Powell should join the group.

"You've already met my wife Ruth. This is Thomas," Ron indicated an older man with grey hair, whom he guessed was close to seventy although he appeared to be fit for someone his age, "and this is Peter." Ron indicated a man who was in his mid-thirties and wore thick glasses. "We were discussing gathering supplies from the surrounding houses, but no one's willing to risk going out and possibly getting eaten in the process."

Thomas spoke up, "I was a marine in Nam, and after fighting those gooks, I think I can handle a few walking corpses. I just have to get back to my house and load up on more ammo for my glock." He patted the bulge at his waistline. "I have enough to arm everyone here and then we can go out and take back our neighbourhood from those flesh-eaters."

Ruth smiled indulgently, patting Thomas' arm. "I know you have an arsenal, but we can't risk losing more people." Thomas glowered at the woman and Ruth shrank back; Powell was glad he wasn't on the other end of Thomas' stare.

"Now, now..." Ron held up his hands, "We need to come up with something because we can't just hide in here, but we can't go charging out with guns blazing either." He looked to Powell for support.

Powell held up his hands, "I'm not sticking around. I need to get back to my car and home to my wife and kids. I'm going to blow town and hide up at my cabin until this situation is resolved. My station's been overrun and I know a hospital has been as well. I'm sure the army's been called in and they'll close down all roads in and out of the city until it's been declared safe; I need to get gone before that happens."

"Then why did you come if it wasn't to help?" Ruth glared at Powell accusatorily.

"I made a promise to a woman named Roslyn that I'd come look for her daughter..."

A quiet voice behind Powell spoke, "You saw my mom?"

Powell turned and his heart leapt at the sight of the girl with pink streaks in her hair, sitting on the floor. "You must be Marcy." He blew out breath, feeling a weight he hadn't known he was carrying lift.

"Is she okay?" Marcy asked, getting to her feet, hope shining in her eyes. He swallowed a lump in his throat and slowly shook his head. Marcy's shoulders slumped momentarily and he expected tears, but when she lifted her head and straightened her shoulders, he only saw determination in her eyes. "I'm going with you." She ducked her head and shrugged, "that is if you're okay with me tagging along."

Powell smiled back, "I told your mom I'd look out for you and I wouldn't feel right leaving you here."

"Now wait one minute," Ron said, stepping forward. "You can't just leave with Marcy. We don't know you from Adam and I will not allow a sixteen year old girl to take off with a stranger."

"I'm going too," Thomas said, as he put a protective arm around Marcy. "I knew Roslyn better than all of you and if she asked this officer to look after her little girl, then I say she comes with us." Ron and Ruth spluttered in comical unison but Thomas wasn't having any of it. "She's lost her whole family and has the right to decide how she's going to survive this. I think she stands a better chance with Officer Powell, than holed up in this house with the lot of you."

Escape from Pecan Valley...

It took some convincing, but after assuring Thomas that he had enough at home for them both, the old man finally agreed to leave without first stopping at his house to get more guns and ammunition. They'd found a talking dolly and a remote controlled car to use as a distraction while the three escaped the house. The distraction also gave Ron and two others Powell hadn't been introduced to, to get to the surrounding homes to search for supplies. They taped the doll, already turned on, to the remote controlled car and opened the garage door just enough to allow it to roll into the driveway. It zoomed down to the end of the street, coming to a stop in

49

the Macpherson's open garage; zombies shuffled towards the home to investigate the possibility of fresh meat. The distraction worked perfectly, allowing Powell and his two new companions the opportunity to escape. They made it back to the cruiser with little incident, only having to dispatch with two zombies on the way. Soon they were driving north; the city around them oddly quiet.

A sinking feeling came over Powell when they finally pulled into his townhouse complex. He immediately noticed the dark splotches in the driveway and how quiet it was - he couldn't even hear birds chirping. He didn't see any of the undead wandering about, but wasn't going to take a chance. As soon as he'd stopped in front of his unit, Powell popped the trunk of his car, handing Thomas a shotgun and fresh clip for his glock. He put an extra clip of ammo for himself into his pocket and started towards the house, gun drawn but at the low-ready.

"What about me?" Marcy asked in a petulant tone.

"You're too young to handle a weapon, Marcy," Thomas replied, as he loaded rounds into the shotgun's barrel.

"I know how to use a gun." She crossed her arms over her chest, stomping after Powell.

"Keep it down," Powell snapped as he inserted the key and turned; the thump of the lock sliding back sounded too loud to his ears. He turned the knob and opened the door, before stepping into the entryway of his home. Thomas and Marcy followed him inside, closing the door quietly behind them.

Powell suppressed the urge to call out for his wife and children as he poked his head into the living room; it was dark and empty. He went into the kitchen; it was clean and looked as if dinner hadn't been made the night before. He saw movement in his backyard and stepped up to the patio door, peering into the sunlit yard; whatever had been there already moved past his fence.

"Can you close the living room curtains?" he asked Marcy, as he pulled the blinds over the patio door. She nodded and hurried back to the living room.

"Powell," Thomas' voice sounded grim, "you'd better come see this."

Not wanting to go, but unable to stop himself, Powell holstered his gun, made his way down the hall, past the laundry and stopped cold. Thomas stood in front of the door to the garage where the portable phone was lying in a dry puddle of blood at his feet. Bloody handprints marked the inside of the door.

"I'm sorry," Marcy said behind him. All three stood there staring at the blood until a loud thump came from upstairs, startling them all into action.

"Marcy, you gather all the non-perishable food from the cupboards. Make sure to fill anything you can with water - we'll need lots of water." He turned to Thomas who stood with the shotgun in the crook of his arm. "My gun safe is in the closet of the laundry room." He pointed to the only door off the hallway. "The combination is twenty-four, eighty-three, o-one. Put everything in the duffle beside the safe and grab all the ammunition from the top shelf. Everything will need to go into the SUV in the garage." Thomas nodded, mumbling the combo to himself as he went. Marcy bit her lip and Powell patted her shoulder, trying to reassure the young girl although he didn't feel the same reassurance. "Go on, I'll go upstairs and see what's making that noise."

At the bottom of the stairs, Powell stopped and listened. The bumping noise came again, but he couldn't tell where the sound was coming from. He pulled his gun and held it pointed at the ground as he walked up the steps, glad they didn't creak beneath his feet. Once he reached the top, Powell paused, took a deep breath and stepped into the hall. His wife stood in front of the closed bathroom door, dragging her fingers down its surface. She lurched forward and bumped into the door, stumbling back two steps before reaching out and dragging her fingers down the door again.

When he cocked the gun, she turned and his heart stopped. Her long hair was bloody and matted. A chunk of it torn away from her temple. Her sleeveless, flowery dress revealed a nasty bite mark on her bicep and her eyes were that strange milky colour. A sob broke from Powell as his wife lurched towards him; he raised his gun and pulled the trigger.

"Daddy?" Stevie's scared voice came from beyond the bathroom door and Powell's heart restarted.

"Stevie? Are you okay? Is your sister with you?" Powell turned the knob but the door was locked. "Open the door son," he said in a calm tone; what he really wanted to do was break the door down.

"Is mommy still out there?" he asked, almost too quietly for Powell to hear.

"She is, but she can't hurt you or Gillian anymore. Open the door Stevie." The lock clicked, and the door swung wide, revealing his frightened children. He stepped into the bathroom wrapping them in his arms, not caring that they saw the tears streaming down his face. When he saw the nest they'd made in the bathtub with towels, he realized they'd spent the night trapped in the bathroom by their dead mother.

"I'm so sorry I couldn't come home sooner." He placed one hand on Stevie's face and the other on Gillian's, looking at one then the other as if they were miracles. Gillian, who was eight and had grown out of the thumb sucking two years ago, now had her thumb placed securely in her mouth. Stevie's eyes looked like he'd grown into an old man over night; the boy was only twelve. "Can you tell me what happened?"

"Gilly hasn't said a word since we locked ourselves in here," Stevie started.

Powell looked at his daughter and asked, "Why don't you want to talk baby?" She only shook her head and buried her face into his shoulder, thumb still in her mouth. He turned back to his son. "What happened Stevie?"

"We came home and mommy pulled into the garage as always. She closed the door but didn't see that someone came in before she closed it. We got out and went inside while mommy was getting the groceries from the trunk. She screamed..." Stevie got a distant look in his eyes as he trailed off and Gillian trembled in Powell's arms.

"Go on," he urged gently. Not wanting to, but still needing to hear the story.

Stevie swallowed, and glanced over Powell's shoulder to where their mother lay on the floor. Powell kicked himself for not having the presence of mind to cover her before opening the door. "She came running into the house; the side of her head was bleeding and her arm was too. She slammed the door and told me and Gilly to go upstairs and lock ourselves in the bathroom. That she was going to call you and not to open the door unless she told us to come out or you did. A little while later, it was after dark by then, something started banging on the door and I said 'mommy is that you?' but she didn't respond, so I made a bed for Gilly and me and we stayed in here until you came home."

Powell swallowed another lump in his throat and pulled Stevie into a tight squeeze. "I'm just glad you two are safe." His voice was tight with a flood of emotions.

There was a shout from downstairs and after a moment the shotgun went off, making them all jump. "You two stay here." He looked back at the body of his wife and changed his mind. He scooped up his children and hurried to the stairs, setting them down halfway down the stairs. "Stay here," he said again. "If I tell you to run, go back up and lock yourselves in the bathroom again." Stevie wrapped his arm around Gillian trying to look brave, although Powell could see the fear beneath the façade. In that moment he was so proud of his son.

There was a second blast from the shotgun and Powell jumped down the remaining stairs, running to the back hallway. "What the..." he slid to a halt when he saw Marcy standing over two bodies - one was his neighbour and the other was Thomas' - Marcy held the shotgun in trembling hands.

"He attacked Thomas when he opened the door to the garage. By the time I got here it was too late for Thomas." Powell could see the old man's neck was torn open. "He'd set the gun by the laundry so I shot the zombie and then I had to shoot Thomas in the head when he bled out." Her voice trembled as she spoke.

"You did the right thing." Powell gently peeled the gun from Marcy's fingers. "My kids are on the stairs. Do you think that if I get these bodies moved to the side of the garage, you can get them and load up the food and water? I need to get the guns loaded and I want to sweep the garage." Marcy nodded and went back towards the kitchen as Powell dragged the bodies back through the garage door, depositing them unceremoniously on the cement floor. He cleared the garage and grabbed the duffle, listening to Stevie chatter away to Marcy as he carried the heavy bag to the back of the SUV.

The kids screamed and Powell rushed back into the kitchen noticing the banging on the patio door. "What's wrong?" he barked; his gun already drawn. Marcy stood with the kids protectively behind her, facing the back patio door as it shook from the force of each blow. He didn't need to look to see what was in his backyard - he knew that another zombie had been attracted by the gunshots. "Okay, Stevie, I need you to go upstairs with Marcy, pack a bag of clothes for you and your sister and get my shave kit and all of our toothbrushes from the bathroom. Do you think you can do that quickly?"

Stevie looked frightened, but nodded. Marcy grabbed his hand and turned towards the stairs. "Marcy, you can grab some of my wife's clothes, they will be a little big, but they should work until we can get more. Do you think you can pack a bag of my clothes as well?"

"Sure thing," Marcy called over her shoulder.

Powell scooped up Gillian, who stood stalk still, staring at the door. "I won't let anything happen to you," he told her, grabbing several of the grocery bags Marcy pulled together. After securing Gillian in the SUV, Powell went back to the kitchen for the remaining bags and containers of water. The glass of the patio door gave a loud crack and he knew he didn't have much time left. He ran to the bottom of the stairs. He was about to shout up, when Marcy and Stevie barreled down the stairs, loaded with bags.

"Let's go!" He grabbed the bag Stevie was struggling with, pushing the boy past the door and down the hall to the garage. Just as he swung the door closed behind them, Powell heard the glass in the kitchen shatter. While Marcy helped Stevie into the back, he shoved the remaining bags into the back and closed the hatch. Jumping in the SUV, he hit the door opener and started the engine. As soon as the door was clear, he backed out onto the road that looped around the complex.

"Where are we going?" Marcy asked from the seat beside him.

He put the SUV in gear, suppressing the urge to tell her to be quiet, but also knew that by talking he'd calm his children. "Our cabin in the mountains. It's not far from Cripple Creek. We have a seventeen hour drive ahead of us but we'll be safe there." Or so he hoped.

Volume 4: Confessions, Quarantines and Cover-ups

Investigative Journalism...

By the age of forty-two Allegra Lozano of Austin, Texas had won a Selden Ring Award, a Worth Bingham Prize, a Pulitzer Prize, and two IRE Awards for her Investigative Journalism works. She'd recently wrapped up two years of research on the true cost of the Iraq War and its effects on the US economy; she hoped to earn at least one more award for the piece. Initially, she'd wanted to research pharmaceutical companies, specifically a large company named Synergy and their processes for testing and pushing drugs through the FDA, but was immediately blacklisted by Synergy's legal, public relations, and communications departments.

Allegra's most promising insider had been a young woman named Sabrina Manahan who was the administrative assistant of Synergy's R&D department head. Sabrina had initially been eager to work with Allegra but after the legal department issued a warning to their employees about the ramifications of giving her information, Sabrina stopped responding to all correspondence. When Allegra hadn't been able to find another reliable source within the company, she'd moved onto the Iraq War while keeping tabs on the pharmaceutical giant. So when an email from Sabrina appeared in her inbox with the subject 'URGENT', Allegra opened it with both apprehension and excitement, knowing this could be her opportunity to root out and expose the unethical practices of Synergy Pharmaceuticals.

The email was short and included three video files; Allegra read with growing unease.

Dear Allegra,

I'm sorry, but this email isn't what you're expecting. I don't think anyone expected what's currently happing in San Antonio and I don't believe it can be stopped. I'm sending you this, in hopes that you will be able to spread the word to the American people so they can prepare themselves for what is coming.

Enclosed you will find three videos; the first is titled 'Confession' - Hugo Farner's confession. The second is a recording taken in our primary quarantine lab two days ago, titled 'QUAR-04-23'. The third, titled 'Sab', is a video from me attempting to explain the events that led up to the first two videos. I fear that by the time you read this, I will no longer be alive and so I leave it to you to warn people of what's coming.

Sincerely,
Sabrina Manahan
Administrative Assistant to Hugo Farner, Director
Research & Development Department
Synergy Pharmaceuticals
San Antonio, TX.
Encl: Confession.avi, QUAR-04-23.avi, Sab.avi

After reading the email several times over, Allegra prepared herself to witness whatever story the videos were going to tell. She clicked on the file titled 'Confession' and sat back to watch with her trusty notepad and chewed-on pencil at the ready.

Confession...

Hugo Farner sat at his desk with a look of utter defeat; his complexion, which normally held an unhealthy red hue from high blood pressure, was pale and drawn. He looked into the camera with empty, bloodshot eyes.

"This is my final confession because I fear that my actions have doomed humanity." Perspiration stood out on his balding head and he wasn't wearing his usual round glasses, possibly because he kept rubbing at the bridge of his nose as he spoke.

"First off, I want to apologize to Clifford Holborn and his wife. I can only hope and pray that you are safe Helena, and that somehow, you will escape the city unharmed and find a safe place for you and your child. I am sorry the baby will never know its father, and for Cliff who will never see the birth of his child if you are fortunate enough to survive." Hugo chuckled mirthlessly and a distant look unfocused his eyes. "Perhaps he or she will be smarter than Cliff, and one day, be able to figure out what we've been unable to. I suppose that will depend on if people can succeed in halting the spread of the virus. If life, as we know it, goes on."

Hugo's eyes refocused on the camera, not caring or unconscious of the tears streaming down his face. "I also want to apologize to Tyrone and Maggie - if they can hear me from whatever afterlife they are in." Hugo lifted his hands to cover his face and choked back a sob. "Oh God! I hope they aren't trapped in this hell we've created." He sniffled, wiping the back of his hand under his nose. "I should have never let you leave Tyrone. I should have never let you out of that quarantine unit; I knew better but didn't want to deal with the additional paperwork and for that I'm sorry.

"If I'd only taken the time, Maggie wouldn't have gotten sick. She wouldn't have been taken to the hospital, where my wife sat on the board of directors, and they'd both still be alive." Hugo's head dropped to his chest and his shoulders heaved in silent sobs.

After a minute, Hugo straightened, with sad determination in his eyes. "I'm sorry for what we've unleashed. I'm sorry we haven't been able to find a cure. We didn't know what we were doing... We didn't know how virulent the virus would be... I'm sorry Arlene; I'm sorry our children are gone, but I thank God they will never know what I've done."

Hugo reached his hand out, grasping something on his desk. He lifted the gun and put it in his mouth. He closed his eyes and pulled the trigger.

The sound of the gunshot made Allegra jump and she watched in horror as the window behind Hugo's head was splattered with gore.

"Is everything alright Mr. Farner?" a female voice came from the speaker of the phone on his desk. "I thought I heard something that sounded like a gunshot." There was a long pause. "Mr. Farner?" the female voice sounded worried and a little frightened. "Mr. Farner!" the voice barked his name but of course he couldn't answer. "This isn't funny Mr. Farner. I've just received word that the second and third floors have been breached from lobby level - I need to know what you wish for me to tell the employees." There was another long pause before the phone clattered and fell silent.

The door opened and a gasp came from behind the camera then footsteps could be heard clicking across the floor. Soon a young woman with dark skin, wearing a brightly colored dress came into view. With trembling hands she pressed her fingers to Hugo's neck.

"God damn you Hugo. I hope you rot in hell," she spat venomously. Something on the computer screen caught her attention and with a look of disgust, she rolled Hugo's slumped body away from the desk. Turning back to the computer, she leaned down and clicked the mouse; the video ended.

Allegra sat in shock in front of her own computer, staring at the black screen as the image of Hugo blowing out his brains replayed over and over in her head. She didn't realize that she was breathing heavily or that a light sheen of sweat now coated her skin. She wasn't sure if she wanted to watch the next video.

"Allegra," she told herself, "You are an investigative journalist. You deal with shocking shit all the time. Just open the file." She inhaled deeply, slowly blew out the breath and clicked on the second video.

QUAR-04-23...

The handheld video camera focused on a woman strapped to a gurney as she was being wheeled down a long stark hallway; her eyes rolled with fear as she struggled against her bonds.

58

"Hugo? Hugo!" she cried, trying to catch a glimpse of something just above her line of vision. "Why are you doing this? Where are you taking me?" she screamed, as she pulled against her restraints.

The camera swung up when a man shouted, "You have to let me talk to her. At least let me hold her hand until we get her into quarantine." One orderly pushed the gurney, while walking behind him were two others who held Hugo Farner's arms ten paces behind, red-faced and kicking. "I am the head of the R&D department. I sign your paychecks and you need to listen to me."

"Mr. Farner," a calm voice interjected, "your judgement in this crisis has now been compromised. You can no longer make unbiased decisions and therefore do not need to be included in this study." The camera panned to a short waif of a man wearing a lab coat and a stethoscope. He trotted along beside the gurney making notes on a clipboard. There was a shiny bald spot on the top of his head and his skin was deeply tanned. "I do not wish to remove you but that can be arranged if you do not allow me to do my job." The man smiled at the camera, pleased when Hugo's protests became muttered curses.

"Dr. Alvarez?" A female voice spoke from behind the camera.

"Yes, Dr. Nguyen?" The short man with the clipboard responded without bothering to look up.

"Besides running the blood work on Mrs. Farner, is there anything else you'd like me to do?" The camera zoomed in on Dr. Alvarez's clipboard, but the notes were scribbled in too small and tightly spaced words to read.

"We will need to hook her up to an EEG, a monitor for her vitals, and get a saline drip started. It's unfortunate that there is no medication to treat viral meningitis, not that we can treat the effects produced by Obsepire either." He made a few more notes on his clipboard before hanging it on the rail of the gurney. He looked up, staring at the camera in grim resignation. "All we will be able to do is monitor the levels of the virus in her system until she succumbs and then when she reanimates, she will need to be observed before being put down."

Mrs. Farner began to scream incoherently and thrash about while Hugo shouted in the background. "You will do no such thing! You will find and synthesize a cure before that happens," Hugo raved.

The procession abruptly stopped in front of a set of double doors. Dr. Alvarez, ignoring Hugo, pulled a key card from his pocket and swiped it at the key card lock to the right of the doors. The doors slowly swung open, revealing a large room filled with medical equipment, an observation window, and a sterile white room beyond the glass. The orderly wheeled a still screaming Mrs. Farner through the doors, but Dr. Alvarez stopped the orderlies holding Hugo.

"I will give you a choice Mr. Farner. You can either come in and observe quietly, or I can seal the door with you out here where you can scream and shout until you give yourself a heart attack." The doctor's eyes were suddenly filled with a dark fury. "Need I remind you that this virus is of your making? That if you hadn't pushed Cliff so hard to complete Obsepire, that perhaps he would have realized what he'd created before it got out into the general population?" Hugo's jaw dropped open and his red face blanched at the doctor's words.

"Or perhaps I should remind you that without Cliff we have no hopes of developing a cure. The best we can do at this point is pray that Cliff pulls through and with enough antibodies for us to synthesize a vaccine - so others do not succumb when bitten. Mind you, by the time that happens it will be too late for most people. The spread of this virus has already gotten out of hand and all of our lives will never be the same."

Hugo spluttered but Dr. Alvarez went on. "I could tell you the chances of Cliff recovering; I have seen his charts. I could also tell you the rate at which this will spread throughout the world, killing billions of innocent people all because of your greed. I could give you statistics that would leave you with nightmares until the day you die by the teeth of one of those abominations your drug created." The doctor's tone changed and his voice became light; the venom gone. "But I suppose you'll behave yourself and allow me to do my work, won't you Mr. Farner?"

Hugo visibly swallowed and nodded his head slowly. Dr. Alvarez waved his hand in the air, giving Hugo a cold smile. "Good!" He said in a cheery voice as he entered the room followed by Hugo, his two large escorts and finally Dr. Nguyen, who turned and swiped a key card over the inside lock. "Dr. Nguyen, I need your assistance please," Dr. Alvarez called from deep within the room.

"Coming doctor," Dr. Nguyen replied before turning off the camera.

Allegra had chills. *What's happening? What does the virus do to people?* Was whatever was going on in San Antonio really as far out of control as the doctor suspected? Was this the end of modern civilization? *Is that even possible?* Other questions began to surface in her mind, but her computer screen flickered and a new image flooded the screen, chasing all thoughts from Allegra's mind.

Dr. Alvarez sat, slumped on a loveseat in what appeared to be a small break room. He looked exhausted and stressed, with dark bags under his eyes and what little hair he had, in a disheveled mess atop his head. His once-pristine lab coat was now wrinkled and spattered with sickly green spots.

"We'll start with the outbreak at the hospital," Dr. Nguyen spoke from her place behind the camera. "Tell me what you know doctor."

Dr. Alvarez pressed his fingers against the bridge of his nose, squeezing his eyes tight before sighing. "What we know is that a woman was brought in by her sister with a bite on her leg. While her identity has not been confirmed, we believe that she was the girlfriend of an orderly employed by Synergy; the one who received a bite from Clifford Holbrook while trying to restrain him. Cliff is currently alive and in the secondary biohazard quarantine unit below us. While he is exhibiting some of the symptoms, the rate at which they are manifesting is far slower than any of those bitten. We are unsure if this is because he was infected with the undiluted drug or just that his immune system is responding better than most have to the virus."

"The hospital, doctor?" Dr. Nguyen pressed gently.

With a shake of his head Dr. Alvarez continued, "Right, right. We are unsure why the woman, brought into the hospital, went into cardiac arrest - it could have been any number of reasons - but what we do know is that she could not be resuscitated. After the doctor declared time of death and left the nurse to take care of the machines, the woman would have reanimated and killed the nurse who was in the room with her. We do not know the exact timeline of the events at the hospital but within an hour of her recorded time of death, the hospital was overrun with the undead.

"I use the term undead only because this is what they appear to be. I have reviewed what little footage we were able to obtain from the hospital and some of the wounds we noted on those infected would have been fatal." Dr. Alvarez scratched at the stubble now

61

shadowing his chin. "Fatal wounds and yet they were still walking, or rather stumbling around, biting and infecting those who were still alive. Again, I digress," the doctor smiled tiredly into the camera. "The objective after we lost the hospital was to simply contain the walking corpses within the facility."

Dr. Alvarez sighed again, shaking his head slowly; he looked as if he'd aged ten years in a matter of hours. "Then Hugo received a phone call from his wife, who'd become trapped in a small conference room on the first floor with another woman. She said the woman she was with had sustained a nasty bite but that she'd been able to staunch the flow of blood. Hugo arranged for two transport vehicles to go bring his wife back to the lab from the hospital. Three brave police officers went in to get Mrs. Farner, escorting her and her companion to safety. I do not know when or how Mrs. Farner received the bite, but it was only a small one on the knuckle of her index finger. It broke the skin, however, effectively sentencing her to death and reanimation.

"When her transport arrived back at the building, we were already waiting in the lobby with a gurney for the wounded woman. Her transport never made it back to the office; we were told by the driver of Mrs. Farner's transport that it swerved and crashed ten minutes before reaching us. Again, we are only assuming, but I believe that the woman died and attacked her driver before we could get her into containment. When I noticed the blood on Mrs. Farner's finger, I asked her how it had happened. She explained that someone tried to bite her and caught her finger in their teeth - that is when I decided she was possibly infected. You see, all the other victims we knew of, had bites which broke the skin and all eventually died before getting back up and biting others. I asked that she immediately be restrained and taken to my quarantine lab where I could run tests in a safe environment, despite Hugo's protests."

"But now she's experiencing advanced symptoms," Dr. Nguyen said and Dr. Alvarez nodded.

"Within three hours of her arrival her fever spiked, and from there the symptoms progressed like a textbook case of viral meningitis. The only difference is that her body cannot fight it, as it's progressing too quickly. Fifteen hours later, and she's in the final stages."

"How much longer do you think she has?" Dr. Nguyen asked.

"At this rate," Dr. Alvarez ran his hand over his eyes, "I would guess, three maybe four hours. Whatever the disease is doing to her body could take up to twenty four hours given the final stage should be a coma, but I doubt her body will sustain a coma state for long. I've never been in this position before where I don't know how to fix it." He looked past the camera to Dr. Nguyen; exhaustion, frustration and grief etched into the lines of his face. "I'd like to rest for an hour; we can continue with the summary once I've had a short nap."

"Certainly doctor." The camera angle dropped to the floor. "I'll wake you if her condition changes." Dr. Nguyen stood, still holding the camera pointed down and walked to the door, dimmed the lights, and swung the door closed behind her. She sighed, leaning against the closed door before turning the camera on herself.

Allegra was finally able put a face to the voice behind the camera. Dr. Nguyen was of Asian descent; her dark hair cut in a sensible bob with a heavy fringe of bangs. Her hooded, almond shaped eyes had dark smears beneath them but the woman couldn't have been much older than thirty.

Dr. Nguyen pushed her bangs from her eyes with the back of her free hand. "I never thought I'd see the day when the dead rose up and killed the living. Hugo locked down the building just after ten this morning. Only half of our employees came into work today and now they are trapped here with us. They are unable to leave - unable to return to their loved ones.

"An hour ago I went up to the lobby to take some time for myself and there was a group of people at the security desk shouting. The guard was doing his best to calm them but all they wanted was to get out. Of course he couldn't accommodate them, igniting their fear and irritation over the situation further. One of them noticed someone stumbling through the parking lot and cried out, diverting the group's attention from the guard and out the large windows. It was a man in a business suit. He staggered closer, everyone falling silent when they saw the blood dripping from his chin and the tear in his neck. Upon reaching the window, the man didn't stop. He walked straight into it and stumbled backwards, before regaining his balance and coming towards the window again. He clawed at the smooth surface with his face pressed against the glass. His bloody mouth worked up and down, as if he could chew his way through the glass, and his tongue smeared the blood transferred from his face across the surface."

Dr. Nguyen put a hand over her mouth, swallowing hard. "It wasn't like anything I've ever seen before. His eyes were cloudy and some of his nails were missing; while we watched, he actually bit off a portion of his tongue and didn't seem to notice. One man, who'd been standing at the desk, walked towards the window. I can only guess that the macabre sight piqued his curiosity. The reanimated man puffed up and let out a moan that the glass walls only muffled. It gave me chills." Dr. Nguyen shuddered at the memory.

"Soon more appeared in the parking lot and the group, now terrified, quickly retreated back upstairs to their offices; I returned to my lab. I don't think I'll go back upstairs for a while." The doctor glanced around the room before speaking in a low voice, so only the camera would pick up her words. "I don't know how we'll get out of the building once Dr. Alvarez realizes there's nothing we can do. I'm afraid they're going to keep coming and block the exits. I don't know what's worse, being stuck in here with the possibility of starving once the food runs out or taking my chances on the outside." The camera dropped to Dr. Nguyen's side and shook, along with her body, in silent sobs. After a moment, the camera clicked off.

Allegra pressed pause on the video, which was three quarters of the way completed. She needed a drink. Pushing back her chair, she got unsteadily to her feet and half stumbled to her fridge. She pulled out a bottle of tequila and a shot glass from the cupboard. With shaking hands, she poured the tequila, filling the shot glass until the gold liquid spilled over the rim. Allegra slammed back the shot, cringing as the fire burned down her throat and erupted in her belly. She took another shot before digging through her junk drawer and pulling out a stale pack of smokes she kept for emergencies; this classified as an emergency.

The smoke shook in her fingers as she placed the filter between her lips. She fumbled with the lighter, cursing when it didn't light on the first few flicks. Allegra shook the lighter and tried again, ready to throw it across the room if the flame didn't appear. Thankfully it did and Allegra inhaled deeply, feeling her nerves loosen ever so slightly. She poured herself another shot and leaned back against the counter, the smoke in one hand, the shot glass in the other.

"This can't be real," she spoke to the empty kitchen. A manic laugh escaped her lips as she spoke again, "the dead don't walk. This has to be a hoax." But why someone would plan such an elaborate hoax was beyond her. Hugo's brain matter splattering on the window replayed in her mind and she knew that whatever was going on in San Antonio was real. She slammed back the shot she held and ashed the cigarette in the sink before digging out an ashtray from a bottom cupboard. Allegra grabbed the bottle and the pack of smokes on her way back to her desk. For the first time in her life, she didn't want to finish what she'd started.

When the video resumed Mrs. Farner was laying, strapped to a bed in the white room; she was still and pale. There was a network of wires taped to different areas on her head and a needle was stuck in the back of her hand. It connected to a clear bag hanging from the pole beside her. The blips on the machines surrounding her, tracking her vitals, slowed and within moments flat lined.

"Nooo!" Hugo wailed and a scuffle could be heard in the background. "Let me go," he shouted. The camera stayed trained on the body of the late Mrs. Farner.

"Mr. Farner," Dr. Alvarez's voice boomed with authority. "These nice gentlemen are keeping you from being eaten by your wife when she reanimates."

"We need to go see Cliff. He can tell us what to do to stop this." Hugo sounded frantic but seemed to have stopped struggling. "He's not far and I'm... I'm sure he'd be happy to help us figure out how to get her back. You just need to restart her heart and keep her alive a little longer while I go talk to Cliff. At least try to revive her; don't just leave her like that."

There was a long pause and when Dr. Alvarez spoke again, he sounded weary. "Cliff has been in quarantine for close to four days with the best virologists Synergy could find. They've been diligently working around the clock, trying to find the key to a vaccine. From their reports, they've had no success in locating a single antibody in Cliff's endless blood work. Even if they had, it wouldn't work on someone already infected. Regardless, from the progress reports I've received, Cliff is in no condition to answer questions at this time."

The camera, which hadn't been turned away from Mrs. Farner, shook slightly when the fingers of the corpse twitched. "Um, Dr. Alvarez..." Dr. Nguyen spoke in a shaky voice, "I think she's reanimating."

"Come Dr. Nguyen, we should review the EEG results before the next stage progresses much further."

The camera swung to a large bay of computers, where Dr. Alvarez sat clicking on a keyboard; the screen before him was filled with a series of wavy horizontal lines. "These are the results we received two hours ago. What do you see Dr. Nguyen?"

"Normal brain activity; this is when she was still responsive but unconscious," Dr. Nguyen responded easily.

The results scrolled quickly across the screen until a point where the peaks and valleys of the lines changed, becoming less prominent. "And here?" Dr. Alvarez asked.

"This is when she fell into a coma and became unresponsive." The change in the horizontal lines was obvious even for someone untrained.

"Now we'll forward to time of death." The screen scrolled quickly until a sudden change in the results appeared. The steady horizontal lines with minor peaks and valleys became drastic vertical lines for a span of several inches on the screen before straightening out into a solid horizontal line.

"The last spikes before brain death," Dr. Nguyen explained without being prompted. "But here," she pointed to the far right of the screen where only a few of the lines resumed minor activity, "what's this?"

Dr. Alvarez moved forward. "Very interesting," he mused. "It appears that some brain activity has restarted."

"Does that mean she didn't really die?" Hugo asked from behind the doctors.

"No you idiot," Dr. Alvarez snapped. "Her vitals have dropped off all together and didn't restart when the minor brain activity resumed. She's dead," he said irritably. "This is showing us what parts of the brain are reactivated by the virus."

"It appears that the hypothalamus is responding highly in certain areas, while the primary motor cortex and parietal lobe are functioning in a limited capacity. The cerebellum has almost no activity at all." Dr. Nguyen seemed to be puzzled.

Dr. Alvarez hummed as if it made perfect sense to him. "Hypothalamus drives hunger and primary motor cortex and parietal lobe allows the virus to control the body. As these creatures seem quite uncoordinated, I'm not surprised to see little activity in the cerebellum; perhaps it is too complex for the virus to control so many systems at once. There's also faint activity in other parts of the brain but a majority of the brain remains dead. The amygdala, hippocampus, temporal lobe and a majority of the frontal lobe show no activity at all."

"Enough of the doctor speak," Hugo snapped. "Look, she's sitting up - how can she be dead?"

The camera spun back to the window where, sure enough, Mrs. Farner was sitting up, face turned towards the window. "Incredible." Dr. Alvarez got up from the computer and shuffled over to the window; Dr. Nguyen followed slowly.

When the doctors moved to the glass the corpse of Mrs. Farner struggled to raise her arms but couldn't because of the bands of fabric around her wrists. She pulled her feet over the side of the bed and awkwardly stood, straining against the straps holding her back.

"We need to secure her properly." Dr. Alvarez suddenly seemed concerned. "Stu, can you please go in and gag her before strapping her to the bed? We cannot allow her to free herself from the restraints." The doctor turned to the orderly standing beside him.

"M-m-me?"

The camera didn't move from Mrs. Farner and the woman's hauntingly milky eyes, but Allegra imagined how scared the man must have looked.

"Yes you," The doctor snapped, handing something to the man. "We need to run a series of tests and she must be gagged for it to be safe for us to enter the room. How stupid I was not to think of it sooner," he shrugged, "but there's nothing to be done for it now except go in and ensure she cannot bite anyone going forward." There was a moment's hesitation from Stu and Dr. Alvarez spoke calmly to the man. "She cannot grab you. All you will need to do is go in, and when she opens her mouth to try and bite, just slip this in her mouth and tie it behind her head."

"You can't do that!" Hugo sounded like he was crying when he spoke. "That's my wife."

"Your wife is gone Mr. Farner," Dr. Nguyen said softly. "That is only her corpse." There was a thump on the floor and everyone turned; Hugo had passed out.

A door opened and the camera turned back to the room as the orderly crept towards the corpse, who was now leaning forward, thrashing against her bonds and clacking her teeth together. A loud pop echoed in the room and the corpse jerked forward, halting Stu in his tracks. He looked warily through the glass, his eyes pleading for Dr. Alvarez to call him back.

"She just dislocated her shoulder," Dr. Alvarez spoke through the intercom. "Go on Stu; the faster you get the gag in her mouth the sooner you can come back out."

Stu's jaw clenched, but he turned back to the corpse who was leaning awkwardly away from the bed as she gnashed her teeth at him. He'd only taken three more steps and was reaching forward with the gag between his hands, when the sound of shattering bones filled the room. Suddenly the corpses left arm was free. . Her mangled hand appeared to have several broken the bones, allowing it to slip free from the bonds. Even with a dislocated shoulder and a broken hand, the forward momentum and additional freedom allowed Mrs. Farner to swing her body into Stu's. The shock and surprise, along with her dead weight, toppled the man to the floor. Mrs. Farner flopped on top of him, searching for purchase with her teeth.

Both doctors gasped and the other orderlies rushed forward. "Don't," Dr. Nguyen ordered and they came to a faltering halt. Stu screamed when the corpse bit into the flesh of his left side. "It's too late for him now," she said resignedly.

Stu thrashed, trying to push the dead woman off of him but only succeeded in pushing her further down his body. She bit down again, this time on his inner thigh and dark blood gushed from his leg.

"The femoral artery," Dr. Alvarez said with a sigh. "We won't be able to study Stu's change now and soon we won't even be able to get into the room. We can monitor how long between attack and reanimation at least."

"Are you serious?" one of the orderlies shouted just before Dr. Alvarez's small frame was lifted into the air and slammed against the glass. "You were the one who sent Stu in there, you cold-hearted bastard."

Pulled from the hand holding it, the camera was set none too gently down on the table. A white lab coat fluttered into view and Dr. Nguyen shouted, "Put him down Jacob. Let him go." There was a grunt and Dr. Nguyen fell to the floor, leaving only Dr. Alvarez's thrashing legs in the view; gasps could be heard from the floor where she lay.

"Shut that thing off," Jacob snapped, and after a few brisk steps heard coming towards the camera, the screen went dark.

Sab...

Allegra's head was light and a calming warmth spread out from her belly; the tequila bottle sat empty beside her and she needed more smokes. She'd just watched the scoop of the century if it was true, but she couldn't bring herself to believe what she'd witnessed. The dead didn't walk - couldn't walk - and yet somewhere deep inside, she couldn't fully disbelieve either. What was this drug the doctor mentioned, "Obsepire," she said after referencing her notes. There were too many questions to be asked but no one to ask them to, especially if Hugo and Sabrina were dead. *Is Sabrina really dead?*

Opening her email client, Allegra hit reply to Sabrina's email and furiously typed. "I have questions," she said aloud as her fingers flew across the keyboard, "questions that I need answers to, if I'm going to release this to the public. Call me or email me back if you can." She signed her name and hit send, praying Sabrina would receive it.

With a sigh, Allegra opened the final video titled 'Sab' and sat back to watch, hoping the woman would provide at least some answers to her many questions.

The woman from the first video, the one who discovered Hugo's cowardly way out, sat at Hugo's desk still wearing the brightly coloured dress. The lights were on in the office but the sun had already set in the world beyond. Her once neatly tied back hair hung limply around her face and her dark eyes kept darting from the camera to the door. She began to speak in hushed tones.

"Hello Allegra. I'm Sabrina Manahan. I'm sorry we didn't have the opportunity to meet in person. I now wish I'd had the courage to tell you what was going on at Synergy Pharmaceuticals when you approached me two years ago." Sabrina's shoulders slumped. "Perhaps this could have been avoided back then, but it's too late now. The genie's out of the bottle and no one can seem to stop it; the spread is too quick. I hope that with this video, I'll be able to answer some of the questions I'm sure you have since I won't be here to answer them myself.

"Hugo had a top secret project he was working on and since I was his admin, I saw a lot more than I'm sure he intended. There were confidential emails and letters sent from an unknown branch of the military on a drug called Obsepire. Apparently, it was supposed to create a type of super solider, one who could withstand or perhaps not feel any pain. I don't know much more than that on who commissioned and paid for the project. Hugo was very careful to destroy any evidence linking back to the people he reported to.

"Clifford Holbrook was the lead scientist on the project and he somehow combined the drug with two viral strains. I don't know the details, but I think it was a form of chicken pox along with meningitis. Hugo kept praising Cliff on his ingenious use of the viral strains because they couldn't be cured or tainted by antibiotics." Sabrina ducked her head. "All of it is way above my pay grade so I don't understand enough of it to explain it to you properly.

"Cliff somehow became infected with the virus and is currently sealed in the secondary biohazard quarantine unit in Synergy's basement, and while he's still alive, I don't think his prognosis is good. The unit he's in is now in lockdown as there was a breach in the lobby early this morning. We've been stuck in the building for the past two days but at least we were safe until some idiot smashed open a lobby window." Sabrina blinked back tears and took a deep breath to calm herself.

"It could have been contained with Cliff, but an orderly was bitten before going home for his shift. I don't think anyone could have foreseen what happened, but the orderly died the following day. He began biting people who in turn bit others and now these monsters have overrun the city. I know the army was here, but I think they've fallen back now - I haven't seen any of their vehicles in the past twenty four hours.

"I've been trapped in Hugo's office for the past twelve hours now and had to listen to the screams as other people, barricaded in offices, are found and killed by..." Sabrina shuddered, "them." Banging started on the door to Hugo's office and Sabrina's eyes went wide, as she stared beyond the webcam; she began to speak rapidly as she searched for something amongst the papers on Hugo's desk.

"The doctors from the second video are dead. Hugo told me that the orderlies locked them in the white room, before taking off. He was pretty shaken up when he brought the camera back to his office."

The banging continued more frantically in the background and Sabrina fell to her knees, searching the floor.

"The only way to kill them is to destroy the brain. This can be accomplished with severe blunt force trauma to the head but..." she visibly sighed in relief when she found what she'd been looking for. Sabrina struggled back up into the chair and held up a gun in shaking hands as the banging on the door intensified, "but a bullet to the head works best."

She placed the gun beside her on the desk and began typing at the keyboard while she went on. "The phones and internet have been shut down city wide - I'm not sure how the government managed that, but they did. I think they are hoping to contain it in San Antonio. I don't believe that they can stop it here, however; it spreads too quickly. The only way I'm able to send this information to you now is because Hugo had an independent link to a Synergy Global satellite that I was able to find the access codes to."

Sabrina's eyes filled with tears when a splintering sound came from the door; she took in a shuddering breath before continuing. "You have to spread the word Allegra; to warn people and tell them to gather what supplies they can and get away from the city centers. I believe the cities will be the first to fall because of the condensed populations and how quickly the virus is spread. All it takes is a single bite. I don't have much time left and need to get this sent before they get into the office. Goodbye and God's speed." With those final words the video ended, leaving Allegra in silence.

Searching for the truth...

After checking her email, disappointed she hadn't yet received a response from Sabrina, Allegra began to search the internet about disturbances in the San Antonio area; not surprised when she found nothing. She pulled up the San Antonio local newspaper, the San Antonio Express-News, but they hadn't updated their site in over three days. The lack of new news confirmed what Allegra had begun to fear - this wasn't a hoax, this was real, it was happening. She was possibly the only person outside of San Antonio and the government who knew what was coming.

After twenty minutes of scouring the Express-News website, Allegra finally found a link to an article that held promise. It was titled

'Bizarre outbreak at local hospital', but when Allegra clicked on the link it came up with a page cannot be displayed error. Allegra frowned, clicking back on her browser, but when the page loaded, the link was gone.

"What the hell?" Allegra refreshed the page, knowing she hadn't been seeing things. "Gone," she whispered, as she closed the browser confused by the article's disappearance. Opening a new page, Allegra Googled the paper a second time and clicked on the first link to the paper's main page. This time, it didn't load the news, even the four-day-old news, now it redirected to a page that claimed the site was undergoing maintenance.

Allegra's honed journalistic sense told her that someone, most likely the government, was covering up what was happening. Her determination to blow the whole thing open, grew with each unsuccessful click. They - whoever they were - were going to be blindsided when Allegra spread the word of the virus and intentional cover-up. She knew the American people didn't take kindly to being kept in the dark, especially if it meant the difference between their survival and possible death.

Opening her email client again, Allegra forwarded Sabrina's email to her most trusted colleague; another investigative journalist named Paul Davis. She began to type.

Paul,

Watch the videos but don't do anything with them until you hear back from me. I need someone I trust to know the truth - I can't be the only one who knows. I'm going to San Antonio to try and get into Synergy and find some more answers. I also want firsthand accounts and pictures for when we share this with the public. If you don't hear from me within ten days, assume I didn't get back out of the city and blow this thing wide open. Do NOT come after me. I don't know what it's like in there or what, if anything, I'll find.

They're trying to cover it up, so be careful with whom you trust this information to. Make sure you have several secure backups just in case your computer and servers are somehow compromised. I'm pretty sure they have someone searching for and destroying all evidence of the information I'm sending to you - just look online and you'll realize the same truth I've found.

Allegra

After hitting send, Allegra began to pack for the trip, unsure what she'd find in San Antonio. She was sure that it wouldn't be good.

Volume 5: Class Dismembered

Floresville, TX - population 6,574...

Marcus Tanners taught Physical Education. He was a big city boy living in a small town; relocating from Philadelphia to Floresville after accepting a teaching position at the local high school. He'd taught at the school for five years now and found he enjoyed small town life. He loved how he could walk down the street and say hello to his neighbours or run into friends and acquaintances each time he went out to the diner. He enjoyed his early morning two-mile runs into the countryside - something he'd never been able to do in Philly - but also sympathised with the teens when they complained about the lack of entertainment in the small town.

The day everything changed, began like any other for Marcus. He woke up at 5:15 AM, ran his usual mile route out to the San Antonio River and back, jumped in the shower, had breakfast, and was in his office off the gymnasium by 6:45 AM. The cross-country training began promptly at 7 AM followed by regular classes straight through until lunch. Fifth period, however, didn't go as planned, turning everyone's life upside down forever.

The end of the fifth period...

Marcus stood at the gymnasium doors as winded students filed back inside after their track and field lessons. While he hadn't noticed on the field, Marcus now realized that three of the classes known slackers, were missing. "Where are Mark, Eddie and Trina?" Marcus asked the last student through the doors.

Diego shrugged. "I think they went to the fence for a smoke."

Rolling his eyes, Marcus thought, *Of course, they stopped for a cigarette.* Irritated, he turned to the gym full of students. "Stretch and hit the locker rooms; good job today everyone." As Marcus made his way along the back of the school, heading towards the fence, he heard the groans of his students and couldn't help but smile. Despite all of their complaining, they were hard working kids.

Marcus rounded the corner of the school and stopped dead. Twenty or so paces from the fence he saw Trina sprawled face down on the grass while a group huddled over two more prone figures next to the fence line. Fearing the worst Marcus sprinted towards the figures. "What happened?" he called, as he approached Trina. The figures didn't respond.

He knelt beside the unmoving girl, noticing the spray of blood tinting the grass and the patch of skin torn away from her neck. His fingers trembled as he pressed them to the unmarked side of her neck... there was no pulse. Marcus' heart broke; she was only fifteen.

"Hey!" Marcus shouted to the figures, as he stood unsteadily to his feet looking at the group of five adults hunched over the sprawled bodies of Mark and Eddie. Shocked when he recognized the long dark ponytail and blue custodial uniform, Marcus started towards the group. "Lonzo what happened?" When Lonzo didn't acknowledge Marcus, he called out to the boys. "Eddie? Mark? Are you guys okay?" Still no response.

Now that he was closer, Marcus could see that the people huddled around the boys were reaching down and bringing something red up to their mouths. "What's going on?" he asked, as one of the people turned towards the sound of his approach. The woman's eyes were milky and she clutched a piece of long glistening rope in her hands. Red liquid dripped from her chin and Marcus could see her chewing. It took a moment for his brain to register what he was witnessing, and when it finally did, he bent and retched.

The woman dropped the meat she held in her hands, staggering to her feet with arms outstretched. Marcus took a stumbling step backwards. The group of adults were eating his students, he realized with dawning horror. The thought punched Marcus in the gut and he felt bile rise in his throat. "What have you done?" his voice cracked when he spoke.

The woman's belly puffed out and a long, low moan emanated from her lips. Four more sets of eyes turned towards Marcus and the chorus of moans gave the stunned teacher chills. They dropped their meal and lumbered to their feet as Marcus backed further away. He could see a chunk of skin missing from the janitor's cheek and his bloody shirt, torn to shreds, revealed more missing flesh. His skin was sallow and his vacant eyes remained unblinking, as he stumbled forward. An innate sense warned Marcus that these people weren't right, that something vital within them had been destroyed, leaving behind a monster.

Turning to run, Marcus tripped over something, which sent him sprawling face first onto the ground. Cold hands clutch at his exposed ankles and he quickly scrambled to his feet. Spinning around to see what he'd tripped over, Marcus watched in horror, as Trina struggled to her feet. Her eyes were the same milky color as the others and he could see the skin on her neck had been torn away, revealing the muscles beneath. She reached out, as if she were going to embrace Marcus, her teeth clacking together. She took a stumbling step forward, not in full control of her limbs.

"But you're dead." He'd meant to shout, but the words came out as a whisper. Behind Trina and the five stumbling adults, he noticed that Eddie and Mark begin to move as well. Marcus turned, his flight response taking over his body, and sprinted towards the school swallowing the urge to vomit a second time.

When he rounded the corner, Marcus saw one of his students standing in the open door of the gymnasium. "Close that door," he shouted.

The student started, giving him a bewildered look. "I just needed to speak to you about..."

Marcus cut her off, "Close the God damn door," he stopped beside another rear entrance, waving for the girl to go, "and don't open it for anyone. Keep the rest of the student in the gym. I have to go to the office and I'll be there shortly." The girl stood for a moment with her mouth hanging open. Turning, Marcus saw Trina and Lonzo stumble around the corner of the school. "Go!" he screamed. Relief washed over him as he watched the girl hurry back inside and close the door behind her.

Bolting up the three steps to the door, Marcus flung the first set of fire doors open and pulled it closed behind him just as Lonzo appeared at the bottom of the steps. Awkwardly, the janitor managed to reach the top step, stumbling only once, and collided with the door;

Trina was close behind. Lonzo pressed his face against the glass, clacking his teeth together, as his hands left bloody streaks down the window. Obviously, the janitor no longer understood that he only needed to reach down and pull on the handle to open the door. It was clear that he wanted to make Marcus his next meal.

Going through the second set of fire doors, Marcus finally took a moment to process what he'd just witnessed. *This is a dream; I'm asleep and this is all a horrible, horrible nightmare.* Putting his hands to his knees, Marcus dropped his head allowed himself a short moment to breathe. For someone who ran every day, he was winded from the short sprint from the fence. He had a stitch in his side and his heart felt like it was about to explode out of his chest or just stop all together.

I'm going to die from a heart attack! The thought sprung, unbidden, to his mind. "It's just the adrenaline," Marcus reminded himself aloud. His body's reaction was simply from fear and given the circumstances, a completely normal response.

Loud banging on the outer door made Marcus look up. All the flesh-eating monsters were pressing together, slamming their hands and heads against the glass.

"Okay, they can't get through the fire glass." Marcus tried to reassure himself. A loud crack echoed down the hallway and Marcus saw the glass spider web into a million tiny fractures. "Or maybe they can..."

There was another bang and the glass bulged inward, crackling further beneath the blow. After a third blow, the wire mesh holding the glass in place gave an audible pop and an arm broke through. Marcus could see long, deep gouges in the skin from the mesh, but no blood flowed from the wounds. When the owner of the arm attempted to pull it back the door opened slightly and grasping fingers reached through the crack. To his relief, it shut with a bang from the weight of the others pressing against the door. The reaching fingers broke with a muffled snap and dropped to the floor; the expected cry of agony didn't come. The things might not have enough sense to pull open the door but they'd eventually get in with sheer luck and persistence.

Marcus closed his eyes and swallowed hard. If he vomited now, he'd have to clean up the mess since the janitor was one of the bodies pressing against the door. "Now that's a pleasant thought," he mumbled.

Quickly slamming the top and bottom locks of the inner doors home, Marcus knew he needed to get to the office and warn the students.

"What's going on Mr. Tanners?" a female voice from behind him asked.

Marcus turned and saw one of his first period students standing in an open class door. "Keep everyone back from the windows," he said just before he heard Mrs. Silva from within the classroom say:

"Jacob, come back inside and close the window."

"But there's a bunch of people banging at the back door," Jacob responded. "Hey Luke, isn't that your mom?"

Desk chairs squealed across the floor and Marcus heard a rush of feet heading towards the classroom windows. *Of course the idiots run towards the danger.* He pushed past the girl and into the room. "Get back. All of you get away from the windows," he shouted over the excited chatter of the students but it was too late.

One of the boys hanging out was suddenly pulled through the window and bloodless hands clasped another student's arm. The boy who'd been pulled from the class began to scream and blood spurted from the girl whose arm had been grabbed. The classroom erupted into panicked chaos. Several of the boys rushed towards the girl, pulling her free from the monster's grip. At the sight of the blood, Mrs. Silva's hand fluttered to her chest and her eyes rolled back, as she crumpled to a heap on the floor.

Marcus turned back to the girl who'd come to ask him what was happening. "You need to get the students back from the window. Close them. Get everyone to head down to the gym quietly and in an orderly fashion." The girl's eyes were wide with fright and when he spoke, she only nodded vaguely. He took her by the shoulders and shook none too gently. Snapping out of her shock, the girl tore her eyes from the hands reaching into the classroom. "Do you understand?"

The girl blinked several times before nodding slowly. "Get them back. Get them to the gym." Her eyes flicked back to the windows and Marcus was relieved to see the glaze over her eyes clear. She was still obviously terrified, but Marcus felt reassured that the girl would now follow his instructions.

"Have someone close all the fire doors on your way through the halls but don't lock any of them," he instructed; the girl nodded again. Another student screamed as a window shattered and they were pulled through, flailing helplessly against the groping arms.

The girl turned and with a look of determination, ran to her fellow students. "Get back!" she shouted, pushing those closest to her away from the nightmare outside.

When the bell rings...

Marcus jogged towards the stairwell, which would take him to the office. When he came across curious students poking their heads from the classrooms, he instructed them to get back into their classes, close the door and not to open it for anyone; above all - stay away from the windows. He felt bad he'd left a young girl in charge of rounding up her fellow classmates, but what other choice did he have? Disgust for Mrs. Silva rose in Marcus. It was her responsibility to ensure her student's safety in a crisis and if she hadn't been so weak, the responsibility wouldn't have fallen on a child. He'd been responsible for Trina, Mark and Eddie and now they were dead. Their deaths were on him, and he'd eventually have to face that fact - but not now, not until everyone had been warned and was safe.

Marcus stopped briefly at the bottom of the stairs to release the fire doors, and again at the top, when he reached the main level hallway. The closed doors might be hindrances for the students, who'd have to pull them open to gain access to the stairwell, but at least those things couldn't pull them open for themselves.

"I need to use the PA system Maria," Marcus said when he entered the main office. "We have a situation and I need to tell the students to remain in their classes after the bell."

Maria frowned. She was a sour woman who should have never been given a job working with students; she just didn't have the patience needed to deal with the issues of so many teens on a daily basis. "You will do no such thing without permission from Mr. Hansfield," she said indignantly, rising from her chair behind the long administrative counter in the office.

He glanced at the clock, realizing the bell that would end fifth period, would ring in the next two minutes. "This is an emergency Maria." Marcus balled his hands at his sides, as Maria shook her head and picked up the phone to call the principal. Knowing he didn't have the time to explain, Marcus made his way around the counter and over to the PA system.

"Wait, Mr. Tanners, you can't do that without authorization." The phone clattered in its receiver. Maria snatched the PA mic from Marcus' hands, glaring at him. "I cannot allow you to..." the bell rang, dismissing fifth period.

Doors banged open, echoing down the hallway. The usual bustle of student chatter and lockers opening and closing filtered into the office. A long shrill scream sounded from outside and the noise in the hallway fell silent.

Maria started looking to Marcus with wide eyes. "Wh-what's happening?" she stuttered.

"That's what I was trying to tell you," Marcus snapped, peeling the mic from Maria's hands. He depressed the button, which would activate the system and spoke quickly. "Attention students. There is an emergency outside and we need everyone assemble quickly, but safely, in the gymnasium. We will explain once we have the school secured. If you see anyone acting strangely or attacking someone, please do not approach them. Do not go near the windows. Do not go outside. If you find yourself unable to get to the gym, please take cover in the nearest classroom and someone will be by to collect you as soon as the situation is under control."

Another scream from outside broke the silence in the still hallway. Chaos erupted as students began to push past one another beyond the office doors. "Mr. Tanners?" Maria's voice quavered.

He glared at her. If she'd just allowed him to make his announcement a few moments earlier, perhaps this could have been avoided. "What?" he snapped.

"What do you need me to do?"

"I heard screams. What is going on?" Mr. Hansfield burst from his office.

"I don't have time to explain," Marcus said over his shoulder, turning back to Maria. "I need you to gather any medical supplies you have and head to the gym; contact the school nurse and tell her to do the same. I'm going to run up to the third floor and close all the fire doors I can on my way down. They don't seem to know how doors work, so I'm hoping we can keep them from completely overrunning the school."

"What are you talking about? Who are 'they'?" Mr. Hansfield asked angrily. Marcus turned, ready to explain as best as he could, but his expression must have said enough. Mr. Hansfield's face paled and he waved Marcus away. "Go do what you must, but there'd better be a damn good reason for this Marcus. My school is in chaos because of you."

"Oh there's a good reason," Marcus said, as he hurried back around the counter and out into the chaotic hallway. Some students still stood searching through their lockers while others tried to run through the crowd. "Get to the gym now!" he shouted over the din, as he pushed his way towards the end of the hall.

"Mr. Tanners," someone called from behind him; he spun, searching the pressing crowd for the voice. "Can I do anything to help?"

Marcus spotted Tyler, the basketball team's center, waving over the sea of students. "Close all the fire doors on this level and then get to the gym." Tyler saluted and turned into the crowd around him.

Releasing the doors at the end of the hallway, he pushed through the flood of students coming down the stairs from the third floor. Again, he closed the fire doors at the top of the stairs before heading into the now silent third floor hall. Some of the classroom doors were closed and he could hear hushed voices talking inside. For a moment, he thought about telling the hiding students to go to the gym, but quickly decided that if they felt safer in a classroom, rather than being crowded into the gym, he was okay with that.

After closing the three other fire doors on the third floor, Marcus ran down the steps, which would let him out of the stairwell on the bottom floor's common area outside of the cafeteria. He was unprepared for the situation he found himself walking into. The large room was bathed in blood; arms severed at the elbow, disembodied fingers, discarded shoes and chunks of gore lay strewn across the linoleum floor. There were pockets of students hunched over prone figures, while others rushed through the open expanse, trying not to look too closely at the grisly scenes around them.

Cameron, Zach and Noah, three football players, stood at the end of the common area, guarding the hallway to the gym; each of them holding one of the school's baseball bats. When one of those things, which had once been a student but no longer was, came too close, they'd swing their makeshift weapons. The football players already had a small pile of twitching bodies lying around them. *Ex-students,* Marcus thought as his guts churned sickly. One of the ex-students struggled to pull itself from beneath the pile and Cameron brought the bat down on its head with a sickening crunch.

"How many are in the gym?" Marcus called to the boys who moved aside for two girls. One limped from a wound in her thigh while the other had an arm around the wounded girl's waist, helping her along.

"Maybe two hundred," Noah called back. "There are a lot of people hurt in there Mr. T."

"Are Maria and the school nurse helping the injured students?" A bloody ex-student stumbled towards Marcus. He sidestepped her reaching grasp, and she tumbled over a dismembered body lying at her feet.

"They're in the gym," one of the boys replied.

Marcus glanced around the common area one last time, not understanding how it had spread so quickly. There'd been eight outside and none inside but now, there had to be at least thirty in the common area alone and he could see more carnage through the open doors of the cafeteria. Someone beyond the caf doors screamed and the three boys started forwards, but Marcus waved them back. "They can't be helped; you'll only get yourself killed." He turned to the boys and saw fear in their eyes. They'd seen terrible things happen to their friends but had been brave enough to keep the entrance to the gym secure, giving others a chance to make it to safety.

Moans echoed down the hall and the heads of the ex-students looked up, answering the moan with a chorus of their own. Chills ran down Marcus' spine at the unnatural sound. "I think we'd better get into the gym and secure the doors," he said to the boys in an unsteady voice.

"Wait," Zach said; the sound of running footsteps from the hall beyond the common area grew louder. "Come on!" he shouted to the runner in encouragement.

A petite girl in a cheerleading uniform ran into the room. "Vickie!" Zach cried as he broke from the line, rushing towards the girl who slipped on the slick floor.

"Zach," she squeaked, flinging her arms out towards the football player just as she lost her balance and went sprawling. Her momentum and the blood-slicked floor propelled Vickie right into the leg of an ex-student who was chewing on a severed arm. The ex-student looked down, puffed up and moaned. The dismembered arm fell from its hands, thudding to the floor. It reached out and tangled its fingers into the cheerleader's long ponytail. It jerked her towards its dripping teeth. Vickie cried out in pain and struggled to her knees, trying to back away from the thing, but the blood-drenched floor beneath her made retreat impossible.

Zach darted around a cluster, swatting away the arms that reached for him. He was almost to Vickie when the thing holding her bent down and bit into her shoulder. Vickie screamed. When Zach reached her, he grabbed a fistful of the ex-students hair and pulled it to its feet. Vickie screamed again as a chunk of flesh was torn from her shoulder and her hair, which was still entwined in the things fingers, yanked her backwards. Marcus stood with his mouth hanging open. With a roar of anger, Zach punched the thing in the face before tossing it to the floor. He swung the bat in an arc over his head and brought it down on the skull of the ex-student. Its fingers went limp, allowing Zach to free Vickie's hair. The commotion drew a lot of attention from those feasting around them. The football player quickly scooped up the cheerleader and barreled towards the hall, shouting for his friends to clear the way.

Marcus finally came back to his senses and rushed after Zach while the ex-students stumbled to their feet around them. "Here." Marcus held out his hand when he reached Zach's side. "Give me the bat." With a weapon in hand, Marcus cleared the way through the stumbling ex-students. Bones crunched under the force of each blow but those not hit in the head, didn't stop their progress towards the retreating trio - they didn't even cry out in pain when the bat broke rib cages or arms. Noah and Cameron still stood guarding the hallway but were being driven further back into the hall under a fresh assault from the ex-students.

"Take Vickie Mr. T, I can clear through this group," Zach said, holding out the sobbing girl. He settled Vickie into Marcus' arms just as another group stumbled into the room from the opposite hall with a loud chorus of moans. "Let's go," Zach said and charged into the group, clearing a path for Marcus to follow.

Just as he cleared the last of the ex-students, something pulled Vickie's leg and Marcus almost lost his hold on the girl. Thankfully, Cameron was nearby and brought the bat down on the clutching arm. The bone splintered and the grip slackened just enough for Marcus to pull Vickie free. Ahead of them, Noah reached the fire doors at the top of the gymnasium steps. He pulled the door open and held it as Zach, Marcus and Vickie dashed through.

"Come on Cameron!" Noah shouted to his teammate who still stood in the hall, swinging the bat at the advancing ex-students. Cameron turned and ran. Noah waited, holding the door for his friend.

Marcus handed Vickie back to Zach, opening the lower set of doors for the boy. "Take her into the gym and have the nurse look at her."

Zach nodded, "Thanks Mr. T."

Marcus spun back to the short set of stairs when Noah and Cameron tumbled through the door. They turned in unison, pulling on the handlebars so the door closed before grasping hands could reach them.

Marcus blew out a breath as he stared at the thick, solid steel doors at the top of the steps. "Good job boys," he said, making his way back up the stairs to secure the top and bottom locks of each door.

Noah, who'd sunk to the top step and covered his face with his hands, looked up at Marcus' approach. "What's going on Mr. Tanners?" he asked, his eyes brimming with tears.

"I don't know," Marcus replied, patting the boy on his shoulder. When the snick of the bolts sliding into place echoed in the small space, relief washed over him. Finally, they were safe.

"Didn't you see Noah?" Cameron asked wide-eyed. "They were dead. They were walking. They were eating other people..." He trailed off and sighed. It seemed to Marcus that he didn't want to say what they were all thinking.

"They were zombies," Noah finally whispered.

A loud bang shook the doors, making them all jump. Marcus glanced warily over his shoulder. "We'd better get into the gym."

Hopefully, with two sets of steel doors between the living and the dead, the ex-students... *call them what they really are Marcus,* he chided himself even as his mind reeled in disbelief. *I hope that the zombies lose interest and wander back to the common area, giving us time to deal with wounded and come up with a plan.*

Horrifying questions...

It would be a gross understatement to say the gym was chaotic. Students, who'd been injured in the rush to get to the gym, sat on the bleachers to the left of the entrance while able bodied students pulled mats out of the storage room for the seriously injured to lie down on. The school nurse worked her way through the crowd, tending to those wounded in order of severity. Some students sat in groups attempting to comfort one another; their reactions ranged from shell-shocked to hysterical. Marcus could barely hear himself think over the din. With a student population of over one thousand, Marcus felt dismayed when he realized there couldn't be more than two hundred students and teachers who'd made it to the gym.

"We need to regain some semblance of order," Mr. Hansfield spoke from beside him.

Marcus turned to face the principal. "Is that," he pointed to the sealed doors of the gym, "a good enough reason for what I did?"

Mr. Hansfield's face turned scarlet; he cleared his throat and loosened the tie around his neck. "You acted quickly and appropriately, Mr. Tanners. I appreciate your quick thinking in the situation. We do need to calm the students and regain control of the remaining student population before determining our next course of action."

Marcus gritted his teeth; hadn't he done enough? Wasn't it now the principal's responsibility to address and deal with the situation? He studied Mr. Hansfield and knew the tall, bird-like man would be of no help to him. "Gather the teachers in my office and get me a clipboard with some paper on it. We need to get a proper headcount. We also need to know who's been wounded and the cause of their wounds." Mr. Hansfield gave Marcus a curious look, "I'm afraid this isn't over yet." With a wary look and a curt nod the principal turned, hurrying across the gym to Marcus' office.

Scanning the bleachers, Marcus soon found Anita, the school nurse, wrapping Zach's hand with gauze. He made his way over to them and asked, "What happened?" as he approached. Zach met Marcus' gaze only briefly before dropping it to Vickie who lay on a nearby mat.

"Oh it's nothing serious," Anita replied, not looking up as she taped the gauze. "He's just cut his knuckles on something. What did you say it was dear?"

Zach flinched as the nurse pressed down to secure the tape. "I think it was the teeth of that student I punched."

The sick feeling he'd had since discovering the bodies of Trina, Eddie and Mark, grew. If this situation was like the movies, which seemed likely given the rapid infestation of the school, anyone bitten could be infected. The transfer of the saliva into the bloodstream through any open wound could also mean infection. *I suppose the answer would depend on the communicability of whatever this thing is.* Marcus shivered and Zach met his eyes, giving him a sickly, knowing smile. *He's asking himself the same thing and believes he knows the answer.* He swallowed hard, turning to Anita. "And Vickie?"

Anita's eyes flicked from Zach to Vickie before finally meeting Marcus' gaze. She gave him a worried look, her eyes suddenly brimming with unshed tears. "She's badly injured and needs immediate medical attention." She inched closer and lowered her voice. "The wound is deep and there's been damage to the subclavian artery. It's likely she'll bleed out." Anita waved to her meager pile of supplies sitting in a carrier. "With my limited resources, I'm afraid a lot of the injured students will simply die from blood-loss. Some of the students are so badly injured that I don't think even a hospital with a fully prepped medical team could help them now."

Marcus lowered his eyes to the young girl, lying pale and still on the gym mat. Her breathing was shallow and blood leaked from beneath the saturated gauze covering her wound. How many others were not going to make it? What were they going to do with the bodies? Were the students who died from being bitten going to come back like the others had? What about the students who hadn't been fatally bitten - what would happen to them? Unable to take his eyes off the cheerleader, Marcus' mind spun with questions.

Anita's light touch on his arm startled him from his thoughts. "I really must tend to the others. There are thirty or so students with grievous wounds and another twenty-five that need patching up," she said, her voice sounding weary.

Marcus looked into her tired face for a moment before glancing into the crowd. Relief filled him when he saw Mr. Hansfield hurrying back across the room with a clipboard in hand. "It's okay." Marcus patted the hand on his arm without looking back to the nurse. "I have things I must attend to as well. Come get me if anyone's condition worsens," he said before hurrying towards the principal.

"The remaining teachers are in your office Mr. Tanners," Mr. Hansfield said, handing Marcus the clipboard with lined paper and a pen.

"Good, tell them I'll be in momentarily," Marcus replied, turning away and walking to the front of the gym where several chairs lined the wall. Stepping up on a chair, Marcus faced the students and blew his whistle in one long shrill blow. The room quieted and everyone turned to face him. "I know you're all scared and want to know what's going on... but unfortunately we don't know."

"Zombies attacked the school," a male voice said, but Marcus couldn't determine who'd spoken in the sea of pallid faces. Whispers buzzed through the crowd and several students broke into sobs.

"We don't know that," Marcus shouted to be heard over the chatter. "For now we're safe in here. I'm going to meet with the teachers and figure out what we're going to do next. What I need is for everyone to write your name on this," he held up the clipboard, "so we have a list of all the students present and accounted for. If you have an injured friend, please write their name down on the second list along with the injury they've sustained. Once I've spoken to the teachers, we'll announce our next plan of action."

"Can we call home? Most of us don't have our cell phones because there wasn't time to stop at our lockers," someone shouted.

"I'll bring my phone out of my office and put it there." Marcus pointed to the small table outside his office. "You may line up and call home in an orderly fashion after your name's been added to the list. Because I know not all of you follow the rules..." snickers rippled through the crowd, "those of you with cells, please share it with those around you once you've made your own calls. Tell your parents that there's been an emergency, but stress to them that you're safe and under no circumstances should they come to the school to get you."

"You can't keep us here," a student shouted from the back of the crowd.

"Do you want to go outside and not only risk your lives but the lives of those in here as well? It's not safe out there since we don't know if this thing has spread throughout the town. This thing, whatever it is, wasn't brought onto school property by a student."

"You don't know that!" another voice shouted.

"I say you should let those of us who want to leave, go," a different student said and the gym erupted with mingled shouts of agreement and argument.

Marcus blew his whistle again, this time blowing until the room was once again quiet. "While you are here, you are our responsibility. We can discuss letting those who want to leave do so after I've spoken to the remaining teachers and we decide our next course of action. For now, sign the list and call your parents." The crowd began to break up and cluster into small groups. A sudden thought crossed Marcus' mind and he shouted over the growing din, "I'd also like to speak with those on the football and basketball teams for a minute by the side doors." Marcus jumped down from the chair, walking past the students who still stood along the length of the room. He ignored their questions.

Mr. Weber, who taught English, stood by the small table outside his office, holding the phone from Marcus' desk. "I overheard and brought this out for you."

"Thanks Pete," he tried to smile, but was afraid it looked more like a grimace. "Can you please tell the other's I'll only be another minute?" Pete nodded, taking the clipboard from Marcus. He patted Pete on the back in thanks, and turned to where the team players congregated by the outside doors. He saw Zach, Cameron and Noah standing with three other football players and Tyler with two other basketball players. Was this all that was left of his two teams - nine players?

"What's up Mr. T?" Noah asked as Marcus approached.

"Is this everyone?" he responded with a question of his own, glancing through the crowd of students.

"No," Tyler replied. "There are three other b-ball players but one of them has his cell and they were more concerned with calling home."

"There are two injured from the football team," Zach said solemnly. "I didn't think they should get up so I told them to stay put."

Nodding, Marcus brought his attention back to the players before him. "That's fine. I think the nine of you will be able to handle what I'm about to ask."

"Anything for you," Noah gave Marcus a ghost of a smile.

"Thanks!" Marcus tried to smile in return. "I need you guys to watch the doors. I don't want any of the students trying to get out while we're in my office."

"I don't think anyone is going to try to get out," Tyler said.

"I don't necessarily agree with you. If they can't get a hold of their parents, then they might try. Those things are out in the yard and I don't want more casualties than we already have." Marcus met the eyes of each of his players "Think you can keep these doors sealed?" They all nodded. "Good! I'll be back shortly."

The teachers crowded around Marcus, asking questions the moment he'd closed his door.

"Give the man space and let him explain," Mr. Hansfield boomed from Marcus' desk chair.

As soon as he had breathing room, Marcus told the story of the afternoon's grisly discovery without interruption; the teachers only stared in wrapt horror. With his tale complete, Marcus let out a long breath.

"There are also students who didn't make it to the gym. Some of them stayed in classrooms and we'll need to get to them somehow. We also need to call the police and hope they can come help us deal with this."

Ms. Sanchez, the economics teacher, was the first to speak. "I was already in here when Mr. Hansfield brought the others in. I was trying to contact the police but all of their lines were busy. I tried the county sheriff's department and it was busy there as well. When I tried calling the Poth police department, the phone just clicked and gave me that annoying off-the-hook fast-busy signal; it was the same when I tried the San Antonio highway patrol." Ms. Sanchez combed her fingers through her hair; Marcus read the gesture as frustration. "I called the elementary school and spoke to the principal there. I tried, as best as I could, to explain the situation here and warn them to gather all the students, lock the doors and to keep away from the windows. She sounded sceptical so I don't know if they actually took the necessary measures."

"Smart." Mr. Hansfield sat in Marcus' chair and nodded.

"I tried calling 911 from my cell just after Mr. Tanners made the announcement but all of their circuits were busy as well," Suzanne Nettles, the computer sciences teacher said, holding up her personal cell phone. "Now I have no service."

Marcus frowned. "You have no service?" He hurried over to his desk, unlocking the filing cabinet beside it and pulled out his own phone. He stared at the depleted signal bars on the screen. "Shit, I don't have service either." He turned to Mr. Hansfield, motioning towards his computer, "May I?" he asked.

Mr. Hansfield, still in the chair, rolled away from Marcus' desk. Irritated by the principal's lack of courtesy, Marcus bent over his keyboard clicking furiously. Once the computer accepted his password, displaying his desktop, Marcus double clicked on the Firefox icon. The browser hung for several seconds before a 'Page cannot be displayed' error came up. "Oh please God," he murmured under his breath, as he clicked the connections icon. A small window popped up and read: Not connected - no connections available. Wide-eyed, Marcus turned to face the teachers. "We've been cut off."

Everyone turned to Suzanne. "Impossible!" she snorted. "Here let me take a look. I'll need that chair Bart," she said, glaring down at the principal who stood, waving at the chair with a sheepish grin.

The door burst open and Anita, the school nurse, stood framed in the doorway; her eyes wide and terrified. "We've just lost a student."

The horrifying answer...

By the time Marcus pushed out of his office and made his way to the bleachers, a small crowd was already gathered around one of the mats. Some students whispered behind their hands while some cried softly on one another's shoulders.

"Get back; all of you need to step away." The cluster of students looked up and slowly cleared a path as Marcus jogged towards them. With all of their eyes on Marcus, none of them saw the dead girl's hand twitch. *She's coming back!* His mind screamed but he couldn't say that aloud - it would cause too much panic.

He didn't know what he was going to do if all the students who died came back as zombies. Would the ones who'd been non-lethally bitten succumb to some sort of infection and come back to bite others? What would he do with them in the mean time? Marcus supposed he could dump the zombies in the storage area for the bleachers. With the bleachers extended, there was a large, secure space both beside and beneath them. He dismissed the idea. Not only would they end up with fifty of those things trapped behind the bleachers but they also ran the risk of the smaller students worming their way between the risers. *And they'd moan...* It would draw unwanted attention from outside while driving everyone trapped inside crazy.

A male student in the group yelled, "What the fuck?"

Marcus was pulled from his thoughts in time to watch the dead girl sit up. She leaned over the wounded student beside her and buried her face into his stomach. Blood splattered as skin tore; the boy, lying on the mat, screamed in agony as the zombie pulled a chunk of flesh away from his body. The cluster of students gathered around, tripping over one another in an attempt to distance themselves from the newly risen zombie. Marcus stood, paralyzed by fear, uncertainty and indecision.

The zombie's hand stabbed down into the boy's gut and he screamed again. The bloody hand was withdrawn, clutching a glistening rope of intestines; the zombie bent over and began to chew on the boy's innards. Gagging, followed by the sounds of the students retching, mingled with the boy's screams of agony.

"Marcus? Marcus!" Someone shook his arm violently. He turned and saw Anita standing by his side. "What are we going to do?" she asked, obviously panicked.

The students gave a collective gasp and Marcus and Anita turned in unison. The zombie lay sprawled across the boy unmoving - a javelin protruding from its head. They all turned and gaped at the boy, whose hair fell into his eyes concealing most of the thick black eye-liner he wore. Marcus recognized the kid but couldn't remember his name; he'd only taken Phys Ed for part of one semester before being excused for medical reasons.

"W-wh-wha..." Marcus stuttered, unable to speak.

The boy shrugged. "Everyone knows how to take care of a zombie. The movies are quite specific about destroying the brain." He motioned to the boy groaning beneath the dead-again zombie. "We'd better do him before he comes back too.

Volume 6: Apocalypse Storage

Bugging out...

Hefting his backpack and rifle further up on his shoulder, Cory slunk along the deserted streets. When the zombies first appeared in San Antonio, he'd shut himself up in his home to wait for the army, but after seven days, he realized help wasn't coming.

On the first day, his cell phone and home phone stopped working and then the internet went down. After boarding up the first-story windows of his home, Cory spent the remainder of the day watching the news, waiting for someone to break the story. None of the major news networks, however, seemed to know anything was amiss in San Antonio; for them it was politics, sports and the recovering economy. The second day, the news was more of the same with the exception of Houston's and Austin's news networks. They claimed there'd been a massive oil spill in San Antonio and troops had already begun evacuating the city. That no one was allowed to enter the city limits until the crisis had been resolved. For the first few days, Cory was content to stay in his home; he had food, electricity and running water. Two days ago, rolling brownouts began in his neighbourhood and his food stores ran dangerously low. He'd thought about sneaking over to his neighbours and looting their homes for more supplies, but after weighing his options, Cory decided he'd have a better chance of survival if he could find and join up with others. He packed his meager food rations, two changes of clothes, a canteen of water, and several other miscellaneous items, which included his two handguns along with their ammo. After waiting until dusk, Cory finally braved the outside world.

Four shots rang out from a nearby house, and Cory ducked into the bushes; a long string of curses preceded an agonized scream. Darting towards the house, Cory peeked through the cracks of the boards on the window, horrified when he realized what he was witnessing. Soft light filled the room of the home and he could see the shifting forms of several zombies, feasting on a prone figure. Smoke began to fill the room as the light brightened; the zombies, intent on their feast didn't notice the flames licking up the side of a couch.

A window above his head opened and Cory looked up just in time to see a shotgun appear through the opening.

"Down here," he called as quietly as possible.

A woman with chin-length hair poked her head out. "Who are you?" she snapped, pointing the barrel of the gun towards him.

Cory slowly raised his arms. "I heard the gunshots and came to see if I could help. I'm not one those things." He motioned towards the growing light of the window.

There was a bang and the woman's head disappeared back inside. "Watch out," she called, before tossing a backpack out the window. It landed with a thump and a clatter beside Cory, making him glad she hadn't been aiming for him - it sounded heavy.

Looking back up, Cory watched in amazement as the woman, now perched on the window ledge, reached for a drainpipe attached to the side of the house. *She's going to kill herself.*

With the rifle slung on her back, she shimmied down the pipe and was soon kneeling beside Cory, checking the contents of her pack.

"I'm Cory," he introduced himself.

The woman didn't look up from her backpack. "I'm Veronica. Ah! Here it is." She pulled out a large Maglite, setting it on the ground beside her rifle. Pulling on her backpack, she picked up the weapon and flashlight before finally standing to her feet, turning to look at Cory. "The fire will attract more. We have to get moving."

Cory didn't argue.

New friends...

"I was on my way into work when I first noticed them." Cory talked as he and Veronica walked along the bike trail. They'd decided it would be best to stay off the roads as much as possible. "The on ramp for the I-35 was backed up, so I went a little ways up the access road but traffic came to a dead stop there too. That's when I noticed the people, wandering between the cars - some banging on windows, while others crawled through openings. I didn't understand what was happening, until I saw a woman being pulled out of her car by the zombies. Of course, I didn't know what they were then, but when they started eating her, I knew something was very wrong. I knew with all that chaos that I wasn't going to make it to work, so I returned home." Cory shrugged, knowing Veronica couldn't see him in the darkness. "I feel like a coward for running and hiding."

"So why are you out now?" Veronica asked. "If Travis hadn't been such an idiot, I'd still be safe, hiding in his parent's home."

"I was low on food with limited ammo," he shrugged again, "but I guess I wanted to find others more than anything else. I have a stash of ammo, a few camping supplies, and several years' worth of MRE's at another location; if I can help some people survive along the way then maybe it would make up for my lack of action in the beginning."

Veronica snorted, "Lack of action? Even if you'd gone out the first day and tried to kill as many zombies as you could, you still couldn't have stopped the city from being overrun. You would have quickly died trying." There was a long pause before Veronica spoke again. "Travis was my boyfriend. When the shit hit the fan, we went to his parent's house since mine live in Florida; we figured safety in numbers... right? Well, it turned out that one of them bit Travis' dad before we got there. He told us that some maniac had tried to break into the house, and he'd gotten it while fending him off. It was only once on his forearm, but we soon realized once was enough."

Cory knew what she meant; he'd seen it a hundred times in the past week. The first time he fully realized what was happening was the afternoon of the second day. On the first day, he'd been standing in his upstairs window, picking off any zombies who wandered into his neighbourhood. His neighbour came home from work, cradling the bloody shoulder of his left arm and hurried into the house. Not thinking much of it at the time, Cory went back to his target practice until nightfall. He woke the next morning to someone banging rhythmically on his boarded up front door. Poking his head out the window, Cory looked down and into the face of his neighbour, standing with his arms raised and staring up at him with milky eyes. *That was the first one I knew.*

"When Travis' dad began to get sick, we knew it was because of the bite." Veronica went on, saving Cory from reliving the moment that his neighbour's head exploded from the buckshot. "We put his father in the basement, because neither of us could put a bullet in his head; I started moving everything up to the second floor while Travis boarded up the windows. He had this bright idea that we could break a few of the stairs so if some of them got into the house, they couldn't get to us on the second floor. When his dad died, Travis couldn't deal with killing him a second time, so we went up to the attic, hoping the two levels between us would block out his father's moans.

"Looking back, I wish I'd just gone downstairs and put a bullet in his head. His moaning brought a whole group of zombies to the house and for three days, they beat on the doors trying to get in. We knew we were safe upstairs, but when the back door finally gave way, Travis just had to go check out the zombies. Like an idiot, he wanted to see if he recognized any of his dad's neighbours. When they noticed Travis on the stairs, the zombies tried to get to him. They fell through the hole only to shuffle back to the stairs and try again." Even though they were walking in the dark, Cory could tell Veronica was getting choked up sharing her story; she cleared her throat. "I told him to stop taunting the zombies and to come back upstairs. I hoped that without us there to excite them, they'd wander off, looking for food elsewhere. I don't know how long we were in the attic for - a few days for sure.

"Then tonight, Travis decided to see if there were any zombies left in the house, saying he wanted to go secure the back door so looters didn't ransack the place." She shook her head. "Against my better judgement, I agreed, waiting at the top of the stairs, ready to shoot any zombies that appeared at the bottom, while Travis slid down the banister. It seemed clear at first; we didn't hear any moans from the other rooms, so off he went. I don't know exactly what happened after that. I heard the back door close; Travis hammered a few nails, and then started cursing and shooting. When he screamed I knew I needed to get the hell out, but I didn't realize the urgency until I smelled the smoke - the stupid idiot must have lit a candle to see what he was doing when he secured the door."

"And that's when you met me," Cory finished, deciding Veronica didn't need to know what he'd seen.

"And that's when I met you," she replied. It was too dark to see clearly, but he knew he heard the smile in her voice; it gave him hope that together they'd be able to survive.

A boy in a tree...

Dawn was rapidly approaching when Cory and Veronica turned off the bike path and back onto the city streets. Ahead, they saw a man standing on the cab of a truck, taking shots at a group of zombies clustered around the bottom of a tree.

"Over here," he whispered, pulling Veronica behind an abandoned FedEx delivery truck. He unslung his backpack, taking only his rifle. "I'm going to climb up to the roof and figure out what he's doing."

Veronica's eyes were wide with fear, but she nodded. "I'm going to poke through the boxes to see if there's anything useful," she said, pulling the back door open and peeking inside the dark interior.

Moving quickly, Cory stepped up on the back tire and pulled himself to the truck's roof. Crawling to the front of the vehicle, Cory readied his rifle and sighted down the scope. The man on the truck seemed so focused on the group of fifteen or so zombies beneath the tree that he hadn't noticed the growing crowd, wandering up behind him. He could help the man, but what if the man turned around and demanded their gear? Could he risk Veronica's survival to help one man he didn't even know? Did the man even need help or was he just driving around killing any zombies he came across? *He could be a total crazy.* Cory knew he had to make a choice - and quickly; the lead zombie was already trying to get into the man's truck bed.

He pulled the trigger and the zombie's head exploded. The man's gun whipped around, pointing in Cory's direction. Cory took another shot at the next closest zombie, and then lifted his hand in greeting. The man tipped his hat, before turning back to focus on the other group. Cory watched as he carefully and expertly sighted along his rifle before making another clean kill.

Finding another zombie in his sights, Cory pulled the trigger, but a shot from within the truck made his own shot go wide. *What the hell?*

He shuffled back to the door, hanging his head over the side trying to peer through the dark. "Are you okay Veronica?" He heard the panic in his voice. How could he have left her alone?

There was a grunt before Veronica called, "I'm okay. Just found the driver. Don't worry about me."

Cory wanted to get off the roof and check on his new companion, but another shot reminded him that the man needed help as well. Veronica said she was fine. He sighted along the barrel and pulled the trigger.

Once they'd put down the zombies, Cory climbed down from the roof to check on Veronica. "Find anything useful?" he asked, stepping over the top half of the unidentifiable FedEx man.

"No," Veronica replied, stomping through the packages. "But I did find this." She smiled brightly as she held up a glittery bracelet.

Cory glared at her. "Where's..." he pointed to the dead-again zombie beside the truck. Its' stomach was an eviscerated mess of torn intestines; he wasn't sure where the bottom half of his body was and wasn't sure he wanted to know.

She shrugged, dropping the bracelet into her shirt pocket. "I only found that half."

"I appreciate the help," a gravelly voice spoke from behind Cory; he spun around, rifle aimed. The man from the truck stood there with his hands held up - he had to be in his sixties. "I mean no harm; I just wanted to thank you for keeping my ass from being eaten." He held out his hand, "My names Bill. Nice to meet you both."

"No problem." Cory shook Bill's hand. "I'm Cory and this is Veronica."

"Why were you determined to kill all those zombies around that tree?" Veronica cocked her head, placed her hand on her hip, and scrutinized Bill intently.

Walking back to his truck, Bill motioned for them to follow. "Well why don't you come with me and I'll show you."

"I don't want to go along with some crazy old man who likes killing for the fun of it," Veronica whispered to Cory.

He shushed her, lowering his own voice. "I don't get the crazy vibe from him, do you?"

Handing him his pack, Veronica shook her head. "No, but it's weird right? Him standing on his truck shooting at a pack of zombies?"

"I suppose we'll just have to go find out why," Cory said, slinging his pack back over his shoulder.

"You two ride in the bed till we get to the tree," Bill said as they approached. "I'd rather not have to walk around in that mess," nodding to the bottom of the tree where the dead zombies lay in a heap. Turning, Bill opened his door and hoisted himself into the cab.

The engine started up with a rumble as Cory helped Veronica into the back of the truck, before climbing in himself. It was a short drive and the crunch of bones beneath the tires sickened him, but once beneath the low hanging branches, Cory knew he'd made the right choice in helping Bill. They stared up into the branches, and Veronica gasped when her flashlight beam illuminated the pale face of a scared little boy. He couldn't have been any older than five.

"Does he look bit?" Bill called from the cab.

Cory couldn't tell; the boy was covered in blood. "Are you okay kid?" The boy didn't answer, only stared from Cory to Veronica and back again.

Veronica held out her arms. "It's okay," she cooed, taking a step closer to the boy. "We're here to help you if you'll come down from the tree." Still the boy didn't speak, but Veronica had captured his full attention. "What's your name?" She made little come here gestures with her outstretched hands. "If you come down we can find somewhere safe to rest and get some food. You must be tired and hungry." With the mention of food, the boy's eyes went wide.

Cory wondered how long it had been since he'd eaten. Digging into his pocket, he pulled out a half-eaten energy bar. "Here try this," he said, handing it to Veronica.

The food worked like a charm and soon they had the boy in the truck, checking him over for bites. After determining the boy was clean, they all climbed into the cab; Veronica, with the boy on her lap, sat in the middle while Cory sat on the passenger side and Bill drove.

"Where are you two off to?" Bill asked, as they slowly made their way around the abandoned vehicles cluttering the street.

"My house wasn't safe, so I finally had to leave," Veronica answered first. "I didn't know where I was going when I climbed out the window tonight, but thankfully I ran into Cory."

"You two just met?" Bill took his eyes off the road, giving Cory and Veronica a look of disbelief. "Then it's serendipity that our paths crossed. What about you?" He nodded to Cory, "What made you pick tonight to leave the safety of wherever you'd holed up?"

Cory shrugged, "I was running low on food and ammo. I have a storage unit on the northern end of town with supplies and I figured if I could make it there then I'd figure out my next move after getting some rest."

"Sounds like you're the one with the plan then; mind if I tag along?" Bill smiled warmly, "I was just out gathering some supplies for myself when I noticed him," he nodded to the boy who had his arms wrapped tightly around Veronica's neck, "climbing that tree with a pack of those things not far behind. I couldn't very well leave him."

"I'd be happy to have you along," Cory said after Veronica gave him a slight nod of consent. "I've spent the past week thinking I was the only one left in this God forsaken city, and tonight I've found three more survivors. I don't think I could bear to be on my own again so soon."

Slapping the wheel of the truck, Bill grinned and said, "Then it seems we'd better make a stop at your storage facility. We won't get too far on what we have with four mouths to feed." With a nod, Cory gave directions.

The stupid woman...

"And thank God for my time served in the military," Bill was saying as they crossed over the highway; the storage facility was just ahead. "If I didn't have the army training that I do, I don't think I would have lasted that first day."

"Look!" Veronica pointed out the front window, at approaching headlights. The boy stirred in her arms, but didn't wake. "Someone's on the access road, heading this way."

"Damn fool," Bill spat. "Trying to get himself killed driving around with his lights on." Earlier, Bill explained that nighttime was the best for scavenging - provided you didn't turn on your headlights, which acted like a beacon for zombies to follow.

"Pull over and we'll see where they go." Bill did as Cory asked, and they watched the small blue car pull into the gas station on the corner.

"Now what in the hell are they doing?" Bill squinted through his window as Veronica and Cory craned their necks to see through the front.

"Getting gas?" Veronica asked, disbelievingly.

They watched as the car came to a stop in front of a pump and the door swung open; a woman with dark hair emerged from the car. She glanced around with a confused look on her face before hurrying around to the pump. Watching whatever her hand was doing, the

102

woman didn't look up as she reached for the pump and stuck it into the tank of the car.

"That ain't going to work for her and when she realizes that, she's going to go inside and try to get it running," Bill said, reaching for his ignition keys.

"Wait." Veronica put her hand on his arm. "She's doing something. Look."

They all looked and Cory felt his mouth fall open. The woman stood beside her car with a video camera in hand. She slowly panned the camera along the road before turning it to face herself. Saying something, she then put it on the roof of her car, facing the entrance of the store. Jogging across the parking lot, she slowly opened the door and called out to anyone inside. The door closed and the woman disappeared from view.

Bill cranked the key and the engine roared to life. "She's going to get herself eaten." Throwing the car into drive, Bill made a left hand turn at the intersection, and a right into the gas stations parking lot. The three survivors stared through the stores front window; there was no sign of the woman but they could see a zombie stumbling towards the register from the back.

"You two wait here, I'm going in." Cory pulled his pistol from the front of his backpack and before anyone could say a word, jumped out, slamming the door behind him.

He crept up to the door, searching for the woman through the window. Knowing she could already be dead, Cory opened it slowly and cringed when the bell above the door chimed.

"Who's there?" a quavering female voice asked from behind the counter.

Okay, not dead. The hallway zombie shuffled closer. Strangely, it hadn't moaned yet. "I'm here to help. It looked like you didn't bring any weapons in with you," Cory whispered.

"Weapons? I'm just trying to get this pump to work." The woman poked her head above the counter, ducking back when she noticed the gun. "You don't have to shoot me. I'll pay for the gas." She raised her hands.

Cory glanced down each aisle; checking to make sure, they were clear. "I'm not going to shoot you but your money's worthless here," he said, finally peering over the counter. "We need to go now."

The woman, still not noticing the approaching zombie, glanced up at Cory. "I need gas first," she said after reassuring herself that the gun was no longer pointed in her direction.

Cory cringed when she spoke, *Too loud*, his mind screamed.

The zombie moaned. Knowing it was now unavoidable, Cory turned and put a round into the zombies head. The shot echoed in the small building and the woman screamed.

"What the hell are you doing?" she poked her head up over the counter again.

"Saving your ass," Cory replied, motioning to the dead-again zombie. "What's your name?"

She stared at the zombie on the floor, fumbling in her pocket for something. "You just shot him!" Pulling out a cellphone, she began to take pictures of the heap on the floor.

"Better him than you," Cory replied, growing irritated with the woman. She was obviously in over her head and didn't know what she'd gotten herself into. "We really have to go." Just as he finished the sentence, a loud banging began from the back of the store and gunshots came from the front. "We have to go now!" He grabbed the woman by the arm but she wiggled free. Running behind the counter, she grabbed several cartons of smokes and stuffed them into her purse. As the zombies continued their assault in the rear, Cory could hear the door holding them back begin to splinter. "Now!" he growled, grabbing her arm again and propelling her out the front door.

"What the..." she began, stumbling out ahead of Cory.

Five, *No,* six zombies rounded the corner at the front of the store, moaning as they turned, noticing new, easier prey. *She's going to get me killed.* He pushed her towards the truck.

"Are these things everywhere?" The woman's voice had gone shrill, agitating the zombies even more.

Bill sat in the driver's seat, taking careful aim at the growing crowd. When he noticed Cory, he waved and shouted, "We have a problem. There's a whole group coming out of the mall and if we don't make tracks, we'll end up zombie chow."

A loud crash came from within the store and Cory knew they were about to have too many to deal with on their hands. "Into the truck."

"But my things," the woman tried to move towards her car.

"We have no time," Cory shouted.

A hand grabbed the back of his shirt; he shrieked, letting the woman go. A shot rang out and Cory felt the grip loosen, then it was gone. Ashamed for his girly scream, he turned to look for the woman, but caught Bill's smirk from the corner of his eye. She'd made it back to her car and was pulling a bag from the back seat.

"If she ain't gonna come, leave her," Bill shouted at Cory's back.

A zombie stumbled between the pumps, heading straight for the woman. He shouted, "Watch out!" Lifting his gun, he took aim and shot, dropping the zombie. She spun around, eyes wide and panicked. Cory looked to the truck then back to the woman; despite Bill's best efforts, the zombies were closing the gap between him and his new friends.

"Come on!" Veronica shouted.

Grabbing the video recorder off the roof of her car, the woman dashed back to Cory. "Thanks for shooting that thing," she panted; Cory wanted to smack her for being so dumb. She obviously didn't understand the urgency of their situation.

"We have to get to the truck," Cory said, shooting a zombie in his path. "Now."

They ran.

Upon reaching the truck, the woman threw her bag into the bed and Cory jumped in, turning to give her a hand up. "Hang on!" he shouted as he banged on the roof. The truck lurched forward and cleared a path through the zombies.

They peeled out of the parking lot and back onto the road. "Where are we going?" the woman asked as they sped north.

Cory pointed to the large white building just ahead. The building had a fenced perimeter, and he knew that once they were inside the gates, they'd have a minute to finally relax and regroup. Bill made the hard left into the parking lot and skidded to a halt. Jumping down, Cory jogged up to the gate, fishing the key card out of his back pocket, thankful this part of town still had electricity. The gate rattled open and the truck pulled through. With one last look to the gas station and the growing crowd moving in their direction, Cory slid the gate closed.

The passenger door swung open and Veronica jumped out, running to Cory and throwing herself into his arms. "I thought we were going to lose you!" she cried into his shoulder.

"You ignorant fool!" Bill was yelling at the woman as she climbed out of the back of the truck. "You almost got our friend killed because of your stupidity."

"Now Bill," Cory said, stepping away from Veronica and towards the growling old man, "we all got away. We're safely fenced in now and after clearing the building, we should be safe to spend a few day's here. No harm, no foul."

"What is this place?" Veronica sniffled from behind Cory.

The sun peeked over the eastern horizon and Cory turned, finally taking in the state of the storage facility; it was a disaster. There were tarps hung from the fences, blocking the view from the street. Appliances lined the interior of the fence, reinforcing the chain-link. The lower units stood open and empty; litter covered the driveway. "I think someone's already taken up residence here," he said, an uneasy feeling growing in the pit of his stomach.

"I can't believe this is really happening." Holding her camera, the woman turned in a slow circle.

"Who are you anyways?" Veronica snapped. Cory couldn't blame her - it would have been an easy trip if they hadn't stopped to help her.

The woman turned, gave Veronica a friendly smile, and held out her hand. "I'm Allegra Lozano, investigative journalist."

Resident survivors...

The door of the facility swung open and a man with a gun stood in the entryway. "You need to move on friends," he said flatly; the four survivors gaped at him.

"I just need into my storage unit." Cory walked forward, raising his hands. "As soon as I have my things we'll be on our way." He motioned back to the truck.

"We have a small boy with us, and if we could just rest here today..." Veronica began, but was cut off by a second voice from above.

"There's a large group moving this way from the Exxon station and drawing more from the mall."

The man with the gun sighed heavily and motioned for everyone to come inside. Cory got his backpack and helped Veronica

106

carry in the now sleeping boy they'd rescued; Bill and Allegra were already inside introducing themselves to the other survivors.

"...and I'm Allegra. I came here from Austin to do a piece on what's happening in San Antonio."

"Well my name is Mike; I used to work here pre-z." Mike pointed to each member of his group as he introduced them. "This is my sister Amanda, her daughter Robyn and this is my buddy Stu; he worked down the street at the gas station. Zach's up on the roof doing guard duty, so you'll have to meet him later."

"I'm Cory and this is Veronica. We're not too sure what the boy's name is because he hasn't spoken since we found him stuck in a tree."

Amanda walked forward slowly, with her arms held out and an expression of pity on her face. "Oh the poor little thing. Here, let me take him from you while Mike shows you guys around. If he wakes up, I'll radio and have Mike send you back down." After getting an almost imperceptible nod from Veronica, Cory handed the boy over to the plump woman. Amanda propped the sleeping boy over her shoulder and checked the back of his shirt.

"What are you doing?" Veronica immediately reached for the boy.

Laughing, Amanda replied, "I'm just checking the tag to see if his name is on it. I know that when Robyn was a few years younger, I had to put her name on every scrap of clothing if I ever wanted to see it again. See? Right here." She pulled out the tag, showing it to Veronica.

"Timmy," She read, shaking her head. "I should have checked."

"What's your unit number?" Stu spoke to Cory for the first time.

Cory wasn't sure if he wanted to give these strangers the location of his stash. If they proved untrustworthy, giving them access to all his guns, ammo and food rations would be very bad for him and his friends. "Second floor." He pulled a necklace out from his shirt, showing them the locker key. The last thing he wanted was a fight with this new group - all he wanted was to get what belonged to him and get the hell out of dodge. A startling, protective urge made Cory realize that sometime during the night, he'd begun to look at Bill, Veronica and Timmy as his responsibility; if it came down to it, Cory would protect his group at any cost - even at the cost of the other survivor's lives.

Mike smiled, patting Cory on the back. "Well you're in luck. We haven't started clearing out the lockers on B; we've only gotten through the outside lockers on the main level and half of the lockers on C."

The tension in Cory eased slightly by the man's easy-going demeanor, but he wasn't ready to let his guard down just yet. "Before I retrieve my things, would it be okay if we," he motioned to Bill, Veronica, and Allegra, "rest for an hour or so? We've been on the move all night and I, for one, need to take a break."

"Of course," Mike motioned for the others to follow as he made his way through the dark hallway. "If you'd like, I can radio up to Zach and ask him to put on some water. We can have coffee and discuss what's brought you all here."

"You've just become my new best friend." Bill slapped Mike on the back.

"I grabbed a few boxes of grounds before I skipped out on my job," Stu said from the rear of the group.

Mike opened the stairwell door and began to climb the three flights of stairs. "This way," he said once they'd reached the top floor.

They walked along another hallway lined with open storage units. Some still had random items in them, while others looked like bedrooms, complete with a mattress, a dresser of some kind, and a table. "You'd almost think there wasn't a zombie plague outside," Veronica leaned in and whispered to Cory.

"They've done well for themselves here," he replied, as he stared into the passing rooms.

Stu spoke up from behind them. "We've worked hard to get this place somewhat liveable." Indignantly, he pushed past Cory and Veronica. "Mike, Zach and I worked two whole days on emptying out the outside units and lining the fence. Then we spent another two days setting up the roof and these rooms."

"Now Stu," Mike said, "They didn't mean any harm. We have done well for ourselves here. We have food and comfort; we've built ourselves a home and other than scavenging, we've never had to run for our lives. I bet these three could tell you stories that would make your balls shrivel." Bill chuckled, nodding to no one in particular. Stopping at a ladder, Mike pointed up. "Last set of stairs - I promise."

The newcomers could have never imagined what they found on the roof. The first thing they noticed was the construction fencing, which created a safe perimeter around the building's edge. Then they noticed the old faded rugs, obviously pulled from a storage unit, which led to a camping awning. As they rounded the corner of the awning, they found a dining area set up that included a large wood burning barbecue made from a metal barrel, an outdoor patio set and a self-contained fire pit.

"You've set this up from things you found in the units?" Veronica walked around the space with her mouth hanging open.

Mike beamed with pride, "You got it. It's amazing what people put into storage."

"Mike," a teenage boy jogged towards the group, his face flushed, "we have incoming - a lot of incoming."

"Zach," Mike put his hand on the boy's shoulder, "get the guns ready and meet us downstairs." Zach turned and ran past Cory, giving him a nod as he went. Mike turned to Cory. "You said you have some supplies? I hope they include firepower; we're about to have a long day ahead of us."

Assault...

The storage room door rattled up, revealing the stash it contained. Mike let out a long whistle, "I think you're my new best friend." He smiled at Cory as he entered the unit, walking straight to the back where a row of high caliber rifles hung.

Cory's unit was neatly organized; shelves lined the walls and a worktable with boxes of MRE's beneath, sat in the middle. "I believe in being prepared." Cory shrugged, "This unit made it easy for me to get ready for my hunting trips and kept all of my toys safe in between. My buddy had a unit just down from this one - he was big into survival training and his locker should prove full of useful items as well."

"We've been searching the wrong floor," Stu snorted, pointing an unloaded handgun into the hallway. He pulled the trigger and the click of the hammer echoed in the small space. "I like this one." He ejected the clip, holding it out to Cory. "Do you have ammo?"

Nodding, Cory pointed to the locked cabinet in the corner. "The key is hanging on the back - help yourself."

Mike's radio crackled. Pulling it from the back of his pants, he pressed down on the transmit button. "What is it Amanda?"

"We've got a group of them at the gate Mike." Amanda's voice shook as she spoke.

Stu, Mike and Zach began grabbing guns and ammo; Cory cringed at the mess they were making in of his organized locker. "We're arming ourselves and we're on our way down. Make sure Robyn and Timmy are secure up on the third floor. Bill is already outside with Veronica and Allegra to make sure they don't breach the fence," Mike spoke in a commanding and calm tone; there was a long pause from the radio.

When Amanda responded, she sounded surer of herself. "I have the kids and am taking them upstairs now. If something happens and there is a breach, I'll make sure to follow your plan."

"That won't be necessary," Mike responded. "We've got this sis. We're going to make sure everyone's safe. Don't forget to barricade the third floor door and I'll radio when it's clear to come back down."

Cory grabbed several handguns, extra clips and the ammo for his rifle, "We've got to go." Armed, they filed downstairs.

The stench hit them when they opened the outer door of the facility. While Cory couldn't see the gathering horde beyond the fence, their moans were deafening and their smell overpowering. Bill and Veronica stood on washing machines, guns pointed beyond the fence; Allegra stood on top of a vending machine with her camera in hand.

Cory jogged up to Bill and asked, "How many do you think?"

Bill gave Cory a grim smile, holding out his hand to help Cory onto the machine. "Too many to count, but with all of us working together, we may just stand a chance of surviving today."

Mike jumped up beside Cory and nodded towards Allegra. "What's her story?"

Veronica answered. "We just found her. She'd have died at the gas station if we didn't stop and we haven't had a chance to find out since then."

Mike turned to Allegra, who still stood with her camera in hand. "I know they aren't sharing this on the news," Mike motioned towards the crowd of zombies pressing up against the fence, "so how did you find out there was something going on in San Antonio?"

Allegra didn't take her eyes from the camera as she panned over the zombies. "I received word from a contact within Synergy Pharmaceuticals that something far worse than an oil spill was going on here. No one outside of the city knows what's truly going on and I intend to show the rest of America what's being covered up - they need to understand that this won't be contained. That this will spread and they need to prepare themselves for what's coming."

"How did you get into the city?" Mike asked, studying Allegra, "The military has fallen back and they've set up road blocks, not allowing anyone in or out." Cory turned to the crowd and began picking off the zombies while listening into Allegra and Mike's conversation; he hadn't realized the US army was keeping those already in San Antonio from escaping.

"How do you know that?" Bill asked, sighting down his rifle and taking another shot - the zombie's head snapped back and his decaying body disappeared beneath the mob.

"When I tried to get out of the city on the second day, they blew the tires out of my truck, and if I hadn't gotten out and into the brush beside the road, I'd have been killed when my truck exploded." Mike sighted and shot; his shot hit the shoulder of a zombie but it did little to stop the lumbering creature. The zombies moaned in chorus, reaching up with bloody, grasping hands. "I don't know what they used, but there wasn't much left after the fire died down." He looked at Allegra with an unspoken question.

"When I came up to the blockade, they told me a very plausible story about the contamination caused by the oil spill and how the city was uninhabitable for the time being. That anyone coming out needed to be tested for life-threatening toxins because the contamination had made its way into the water table." Cory realized that Allegra was recounting her experience for the camera as much as for them. "I drove west until I found a road with an unmanned barricade, and then I turned south."

"So you can show us a way out of this hellhole?" Mike seemed eager but Cory didn't think that getting out would be as easy as getting in.

Allegra shook her head. "I don't think I can remember all the turns I had to make to detour around car accidents and other military blockades. There are spike strips on some of the roads and when I tried to move them, I realized they couldn't be tampered with. The strips are wired to explosives and I wasn't about to blow myself up by messing with them. Besides, I have to get to Synergy. The answers I need are there." Allegra moved from the top of the vending machine to the concrete block wall, surrounding the garbage area.

"What the hell are you doing?" Cory shouted, waving for her to come back to the safety of the enclosure.

"I'm just looking for a better angle," she called back, walking further onto the wall. Fingers reached up and curled around the top, but it didn't appear that any of the zombies could reach Allegra.

Shaking his head, Cory turned back to the mass of zombies in front of him, and resumed shooting. They'd been out for over an hour and the group had made little difference in the horde pressing up against the fence. There had to be well over one hundred standing below him and still stragglers from the mall wandered across the parking lot.

He studied the zombies as he shot them. A woman with tangled blond hair had a chunk missing from her cheek; after a moment, she had a new hole in her head as she slumped, disappearing into the crowd. Another, this one a man, had multiple chunks of skin torn from the flesh on his arms - he too received a new, tidy little hole between the eyes. The zombies, while obviously dead, still looked like humans for the most part. Cory wondered what they'd look like after a month had passed - after a year had passed - and prayed that eventually, it wouldn't feel like killing human beings.

A shout pulled him from his concentration. He turned and saw Zach jumping up and down on his washing machine, pointing into the crowd. Cory made his way over to the boy. "What are you shouting about?"

Zach looked down with an excited gleam in his eyes. "His shirt says fifteen. It has to be him. He's so big!"

Cory didn't understand. He jumped up beside the boy and looked in the direction he was pointing. Standing in the crowd, a full head and shoulders taller than the mob, stood a man wearing a white basketball jersey with black detailing; the number fifteen clear between the heads of the other zombies. "Holy fuck! He can reach over the fence." Cory took aim.

"Wait!" Zach grabbed for Cory's arm. The shot went wide, hitting another zombie right in the side of the head; Zach stepped in front of him. "You can't shoot him!"

112

"He's a zombie Zach and one that could threaten our survival here." Cory tried to explain, but Zach wouldn't move from Cory's line of sight.

"You aren't shooting him!" Zach reached for Cory's gun.

Cory lifted it, leveling the gun at his chest. "Get out of the way."

"No!" Zach lifted his chin and stared at Cory, his look daring him to pull the trigger.

"What's going on over here?" Mike demanded, walking over to where Cory and Zach stood in a stalemate. Of course, he wasn't going to shoot the boy but something needed to be done about the six-foot-ten zombie wandering in the mob.

"He's going to shoot my favourite basketball player." Zach's voice had turned shrill as he argued.

"He's a fucking zombie Zach!" Cory argued back.

Mike hopped up beside them. "If he's a zombie then he's no longer a basketball player." He rested a hand on the boy's shoulder. "You need to understand that whoever they were in life is gone. The zombie that rises after the body dies isn't the same as they were in life. That one especially poses a threat to us." Catching Zach's eye, Mike gave him a sad look and squeezed his shoulder. "You understand, right?" Zach's head dropped and his shoulders slumped; after a long moment, he nodded. "Good, now you don't have to shoot him but you can't stop us from..."

There was a long shrill scream. The three of them turned just in time to watch the basketball player pull Allegra off the wall and into the mob; her screams quickly fell silent. The others stopped shooting and turned to stare wide-eyed at Cory and Mike. Allegra's video camera lay in the trash heap but that was all that remained of the reporter. Cory took aim and this time Zach didn't stop him from putting a bullet through the player's head.

The sun was setting by the time the last zombie fell; it had been an emotionally draining day. The survivors were too tired to clean up the piles of bodies littering the ground, so they filed inside to get some much needed food and rest. Plans for the cleanup and cremation of the bodies were set for the following day.

"You guys did good work out there today," Mike said, sighing as he slumped against the wall of his room.

"Thanks - same to you and your group." Cory slid down, sitting beside Mike. "I was hoping that after what we all accomplished together today, you guys would agree to let us stay for a while. We'll help out wherever needed and I have my MRE's to keep us fed, so we won't be using your resources, but I don't think that I can handle another day like today again so soon."

"We'll figure something out," Mike replied; his eyes closed and his head resting against the wall. "The only way we're all going to make it is if we stick together. There are other groups out there and some aren't as friendly as we are. Run into the wrong group and you won't have to worry about being eaten by zombies."

Cory studied Mike as they sat in comfortable silence. If there were more threats than just the zombies, he was glad to have found this group of survivors. Here they could make their stand and maybe, just maybe they could all survive the apocalypse together.

Volume 7: Escape from SA

Plan of action...
Eleven days had passed since the first zombie was seen in Pecan Valley - to Ruth, it seemed more like a lifetime. In those eleven days, she'd seen humans at their worst, doing unimaginable things to those they'd once held dear. She'd seen her neighbours caught unaware and eaten right before her eyes, people fighting amongst themselves instead of the new threat they faced, and she realized how strangers could come together, each with a common goal: survival.

Sitting on the bed of the small motel room, Ruth rocked Paige in her arms, praying they'd find a safe place for their group. Travelling with six adults and two children under the age of ten, Ruth found that it was difficult for them to move quickly through the infested city. They often needed to stop and rest for the sake of the little ones, but stopping had its own set of dangers and staying in the same place for too long attracted unwanted attention from the undead. Fortunately, those left in their group had been smart about their movements, and even now, were making plans in the adjoining room. Their immediate goal was to get past the army barricade outside of Seguin and escape the plague-ridden city.

The first day of the outbreak, Ruth's husband Ron had been in their backyard when one of their neighbours attacked the mail carrier. He watched, helpless, as she proceeded to strip the flesh from the man's exposed arm. Realizing something was very wrong, Ron secured their home and began rescuing as many people as possible from the nightmares on their street.

They'd even helped a cop who'd come searching for a neighbourhood girl. *I wonder whatever became of them,* she thought and sent up a quick prayer for their safety.

During that first week, they took in anyone without a safe place to go; their numbers swelled to almost twenty survivors. Ruth and Ron tried to reassure their growing group that help was on the way - that their government hadn't abandoned them - but when a group of zombies finally overran their home, they realized that if they were to survive, they needed to do it on their own. Out of the nineteen people staying with them, only ten of the adults and the two children made it out of the house before it was too late. Four people in their group decided they needed to look for other survivors in the city and Ruth knew, as she watched them walk away, that she'd never see them again.

When Paige stirred in Ruth's arms, mumbling something in her sleep, Ruth stood and gently placed her on the bed beside Caleb - the nine-year-old boy who they'd found hiding in a garage. After making sure both children were sleeping, Ruth made her way to the strategy meeting in-progress in the adjoining room.

"Another survivor told me that the army opened fire on his group, killing most of them before they could get close enough to explain their situation," Paula was saying as Ruth entered.

Ron looked up and gave her a tired smile, patting the bed beside him. She hurried over to her husband and was comforted when his strong arm wrapped around her shoulder, pulling her close to him. "Well we'll just have to find a way around the army's barricade when we get that far, but in the meantime, walking straight up the highway is the quickest way to Houston," Ron replied.

"I still don't understand why we have to go all that way to find Steven's wife." Mark was nineteen and believed that nothing could kill him - that he'd never become one of the undead simply because he'd managed to survive those chaotic first days. Ruth constantly worried for the recklessly fearless boy. "I say we head straight to the cottage and hope to find a working phone on the way; they can't all be out of service." He crossed his arms defiantly over his thin chest.

Steven straightened in his chair. "I've already lost my son and Paige needs her mother as much as I need my wife. How am I supposed to explain to Paige that I don't know if her mother survived after the zombies reached Houston?" He looked to each member of the group as he spoke, "You all know that this won't be stopped by a few blockades."

"It doesn't matter," Ron said with a sigh. "We all agreed to go with Steven, in exchange for him letting us stay at his cottage. If his cottage has all he says it does, we could thrive there without worrying about zombies overrunning us again." Ron looked from Harris to Megan, who'd been silent up until now. "Stone walls surrounding the property, a cast iron gate at the road, a room for each of us..." he turned to Paula, "a garden for you to plant all those seeds you carry around with you and solar power so we can live comfortably." He shifted to face Mark, "All of this in exchange for traveling to Houston first to get Steven's wife. Can you tell me you'd rather be on the run than make a small detour?"

The room was silent as everyone in the group stared at one another - they all knew Ron was right; making the trip to Houston was a small price to pay.

"It seems there are no further objections." Ruth stood, taking Ron's hand in hers. "Now if you don't mind, we all have several long days ahead of us, and I for one am exhausted. We set out at dawn, so I suggest you all get some rest."

First light...

The following morning, the group started down the highway just as the sun peeked over the eastern horizon. Ron, Megan and Mark took the lead, clearing any of the zombies wandering between the abandoned cars. Harris and Paula walked at the rear of the group to make sure they weren't attacked from behind. Between Ron's group and Harris's, Steven walked carrying Caleb on his shoulders while Ruth carried Paige. They'd been walking for an hour and a half, talking to the children about their favourite TV shows, when Mark jogged back to them.

"The west-bound lanes are clear up ahead and Ron thinks we should get out from this line of cars. He says it will be safer for all of us if we walk on the open road instead of picking our way through this mess." He motioned to the stalled traffic around them. Ruth tried not to stare at the front of his shirt, which was splattered with black blood and at the crowbar, dripping with gore, gripped loosely in his right hand. Ruth saw the gleam of exhilaration in his eyes; the boy seemed to enjoy his task of disposing of any undead they came across.

Their situation had changed each of them, some fitting better into this new reality than others, and Mark thrived on the carnage. She felt relieved that they wouldn't have to continue walking past the undead trapped in the cars. In an effort to ease the burning pain in her arms, Ruth hoisted Paige further up onto her hip. "We need to find a place to stop and rest first." For a small girl of four, Paige was deceptively heavy.

"I agree," Steven said, stretching his neck. "I say we take five minutes to sit and get some food and water passed around before moving on." Mark began to protest.

Ruth spoke up before the boy could say much of anything. "Go talk to Ron and see what he thinks about Steven's suggestion. My arms could use a break." She smiled, hoping he wouldn't argue.

Mark's eyes flashed in irritation as his gaze flicked from one child to the other. Ruth could read his thoughts - leave them; they're only slowing us down. "I'll talk to Ron, but I'm sure he'll side with you two." Before Ruth could say more, the boy spun, jogging back to Ron and Megan.

"There's something wrong with that boy." Steven shook his head. "I feel like I need to sleep with one eye open for fear he'll bash my head in during the night. He enjoys killing the zombies a little too much in my opinion."

"I'd like killing a zombie." Caleb spoke with a serious tone from Steven's shoulders. "I'd like to kill all the zombies for hurting my mom."

Ruth's heart broke a little more at the boy's words, but knew he shouldn't be encouraged. "Now Caleb, you can't seriously..." Ruth said but was interrupted by Paige.

"I want to serially kill a zbombi too." Page's eyes were wide but Ruth didn't see fear in their blue depths.

"When I get big enough, I'm going to bash in their heads just like Mark." Now Caleb was smiling.

"I'm going to chop off their heads." Paige tried to one-up Caleb, smiling just as widely; to Ruth's dismay, they'd found a new game.

"Well, I'm going to get a whole bunch together and tie them up and burn them."

"I'm going to squish them with cars I drop on their heads."

"You can't move a car so that's just silly," Caleb snorted. "I'm going to blow them all up." He threw his arms in the air and shouted, "Ka-boom!"

"Keep it down," Steven warned, glancing around to make sure their new game wasn't drawing unwanted attention.

"I'm going to do that too. Blow all the zbombies up so we don't have to walk anymore." Paige wiggled in Ruth's tired arms, straining to see around her to Caleb; she almost lost her grip on the girl.

"Copycat."

"Am not."

"Are too."

Already tired from the hour's walk, Ruth snapped, "Enough!" and both children fell silent. It was hard enough caring for the children while on the run without having to deal with their bickering.

"And it's zombies not zbombies, stupid." Ruth heard Caleb mutter beneath his breath and was thankful when Paige didn't seem to notice the boy's snide remark.

She cast a quick glance to Steven and was surprised to find a wistful smile on his lips. "You're enjoying this?"

Steven nodded. "Paige and her brother used to squabble like this all the time." There was a long pause as they walked on; Ruth assumed Steven was lost in his memories. His son, almost ten years older than Paige, had been lost during the first days of the outbreak. Ruth couldn't imagine the pain of losing a child - especially in such a horrific way.

She was about to ask why the kids bickering made Steven happy when Mark jogged back to them. "Ron says there's a truck station a quarter mile up. We're going to clear the building and rest inside for fifteen minutes or so," Mark said, obviously irritated by Ron's decision.

A moan came from beneath the transport truck beside them and Paige squealed, pointing behind Mark. "Zbombi!" she wriggled in Ruth's arms, making her lose her grip on the child. Paige hit the ground and scuttled behind her father, peeking around his legs.

Mark turned, raised his crowbar over his head and brought it down on the top of the zombie's skull. There was a sickening crunch and the zombie crumpled to the ground.

"Scaredy-cat," Caleb snorted.

Kicking the zombie to make sure he was dead-again, Mark turned to Paige with a wide smile. "Want to come hit it a few times?" he extended the crowbar to her and both Ruth and Steven stepped forward.

"Hell no she's not," Steven barked. He pointed to the dead heap on the ground, "You guys are supposed to make sure the way is clear for us. What if you hadn't been here?"

"Why are we stopped?" Harris spoke from behind them. Mark's face went a deep red as the group turned to see Harris and Paula walking up behind them.

"The zombie crawled out from under the truck, and Mark bashed his head in," Caleb said, not taking his eyes off the corpse.

Harris chuckled. "Paula noticed a filling station a little ways up. I think we should make a quick stop and check for supplies."

"We've already talked to Ron about it." Ruth said, scooping Paige back into her arms. "I need to give my arms a break and Steven's neck is sore." She motioned to Caleb, sitting on Steven's shoulders as he swung his legs back and forth.

"We're hoping we can find some bottles of water and maybe some food," Paula said, extending her arms towards Ruth. "I can take her if you don't mind zombie duty for a few minutes."

Paige clung to Ruth's neck, burying her face in her shoulder. "I don't want you on zbombi duty."

"I'll do it." Caleb swung one leg over Steven's shoulder, hanging from his neck. Steven gurgled, clawing at the boy's hands around his throat; Harris stepped forward and helped the boy to the ground.

"I think you're too little to be of any use in killing the zombies." Harris ruffled the boy's hair as Steven stretched out his neck, taking in deep breaths.

"We'd better get moving," Mark snapped, obviously irritated.

"I'll take Paige if Caleb wants to walk." Steven lifted his daughter from Ruth's arms.

"Thanks," Ruth smiled relieved her arms could rest. Taking Caleb's hand in her own, Ruth motioned for Harris to lead the way. "I think we'd better stay close together. If Mark hadn't been here, that zombie would have been a problem for Steven and me." She of course had a pistol tucked into the back of her pants, but the group had decided before setting out that morning that they'd limit the use of firearms so as not to draw in unwanted attention. The group walked in silence and soon caught up to Ron and Megan, without further incident.

Pit stop...

"What's the situation?" Harris stopped beside Ron, who stood watching the service station through a pair of binoculars.

"I see a handful wandering around the parking lot and at least two in the store," Ron said, not taking his eyes from their goal. "If we're careful we can eliminate the wanderers outside then open the door and let the ones inside come out. There's a lot of movement in vehicles, but those seem to be trapped and we shouldn't have to worry about them."

Harris glanced from Paula, to Megan and finally to Mark, who stood bouncing from foot to foot, eager to get going. "Ron and I will start on the far side of the parking lot while Mark and Megan start on this side. Paula, I'd like you to stay here with the others and make sure nothing catches us unaware."

Mark started down the steep incline, not waiting for further instruction. Megan turned to Ron, grimacing. "Do I really have to go with the suicidal maniac?"

Ron chuckled, checking his gun before putting it back in its holster. He turned, resting his hands on the young girl's slender shoulders. "I need you with him to keep him from getting himself killed. You're smart and he listens to you... well more than he listens to anyone else." He nodded after Mark, "You'd better catch up. Once you have your side cleared, meet us at the store but don't go in until we're all together."

Megan nodded, took a deep breath and set out after Mark, who'd already reached the parking lot. Ron turned to Ruth; she stared up into her husband's weary eyes, giving him a small, encouraging smile. "You're doing just fine," she said softly, lifting up on her toes to give him a quick kiss. "Eyes wide."

Ron nodded and turned to Harris, patting his back. "Let's do it."

Ruth watched as the men made their way to the far end of the parking lot; each armed with machetes and short homemade spears.

She prayed that the four of them didn't come upon more zombies than they could handle.

Caleb tugged on her shirt. "Can I stand on the roof of the car to watch?"

Ruth squatted beside the boy, taking both of his hands in her own. "You don't want to watch them get rid of the zombies Caleb. It isn't something a little boy should see."

"But I'm going to have to know eventually," Caleb pouted, glancing up to where Paige now sat on her father's shoulders, watching the scene below. "And Paige gets to watch and she's littler than I am."

Sighing, Ruth knew the boy was right. He would have to learn how to defend himself against zombies if he hoped to survive in this new world. She'd hoped to keep his childhood innocence intact a little while longer, but that seemed impossible now that they were on the open road. "Okay, I'll help you get up on the roof of the car, but we need you to keep very quiet." Caleb nodded, eager to watch.

Noticing the living creeping through the parking lot, the zombies began to wander towards them. Ruth wanted to shout for Ron to be careful, but knew she couldn't distract him from his task - Harris was watching his back and Ruth had to trust he'd take care of her husband. Having already killed one of the zombies, Mark and Megan were moving on to the next; Megan acting as bait while Mark manoeuvered behind the undead creature to bash in its skull.

"Yes!" Caleb whispered from his perch on the roof of the car, when Mark's crowbar ended another zombie's existence.

"He's being reckless," Paula said from beside Ruth.

"He's never been anything but reckless," Steven replied in disgust. "He's the weak link in the group and I'm willing to bet he'll be the death of us all. We'd be better off if he got himself bitten."

"Steven!" Ruth gasped, shocked at the man's callous attitude. "Mark is an asset. Yes, he might be reckless, but that doesn't mean he should die because of it. He's young and given time, I believe he'll become invaluable to our group. He's not afraid to get up close with those things, which has already proven useful."

Paula looked at Ruth and gave a small shake of her head. "I have to agree with Steven on this one. Mark is mentally unstable. Not only did he have to kill his parents and his baby sister, but he also had to do his girlfriend, her parents, and three of his friends. That's got to take its toll."

"They've cleared the lot and are getting ready to open the doors to the store." Caleb turned briefly to Ruth before turning back to watch. "I hope there aren't too many inside." Ruth hoped the same.

A low moan came from behind them and Ruth turned to see a fat zombie stumble from behind a van. The zombie's express delivery shirt hung in tatters, exposing his fleshy belly; dried gore plastered what was left of his shirt to his chest.

"Shit!" Paula squealed. She lifted her hatchet and walked towards the creature.

Ruth could see the bites on his left arm and shoulder; sadness filled her. This poor man was probably on a delivery run, complaining about the stalled traffic when the zombies caught up with him. In his condition, Ruth doubted he'd stood much of a chance in escaping.

"Get him Paula!" Paige cried, pulling on her dad's hair, as if that would get him to back away from the enormous zombie.

"Don't let him grab you," Steven warned, moving back as the zombie stumbled towards them, flailing his arms and gnashing his teeth.

Paula swung the hatchet but the blade became embedded in the fleshy side of the zombies head. The zombie snapped at her arm, "Now what?" she squeaked, backing away from the creature; she'd lost her only weapon.

"Wow!" Caleb said in amazement as they all stared at the hatchet protruding from the side of the zombies head.

The zombie moaned and swiped at Paula again. "We need to do something fast."

Realizing they had little choice, Ruth pulled her pistol, pointed it at the zombies head and pulled the trigger. It was impossible to miss at such a close range. The back of the zombies head exploded and the massive lump of dead flesh thumped to the ground. A moan floated down the highway from ahead of them and several shadows between the vehicles began to shift and move.

The gun was too loud! Ruth began to shake as she realized they'd just given away their presence to every undead in the area - they hadn't cleared much further up the road and who knew how many zombies lurked between the cars.

"You didn't have a choice." Paula shook Ruth. "But we can't stay here."

Ruth tore her eyes from the shadows and glanced from Paula to Steven, who'd gone pale and wide-eyed. "We have to get down to the parking lot and hope they don't notice us."

Paula put her foot on the side of the zombies head and bent, pulling at her hatchet; the squelch from the blade as it pulled free from the dead flesh turned Ruth's stomach. She pulled Caleb, who now sat crouched on the car's hood, into her arms and hurried down the embankment towards the service station; Ron and Harris were already weaving through the cars towards them.

Harris waved them over to the cover of a large truck. "We heard the gunshot. What happened?" he hissed.

Ruth fell into her husband's waiting arms. "I'm sorry," she whispered as Ron gently stroked her hair.

"A big fat one with a thick skull happened," Paula retorted, nodding in the direction of the building. "What's the situation in there?"

Harris shook his head, dismayed. "Everything's been looted. We're going to check some of the trailers to see if there's anything salvageable inside them, but we won't have much time. That gunshot's drawn a lot of unwanted attention."

Steven cleared his throat. "I think we'd better move on." His voice shook as he spoke. They all turned, following his gaze - six zombies stumbled down the embankment. One lost its footing and fell, rolling down the hill landing hard on the paved access road. Caleb and Ruth giggled as the zombie struggled back to its feet. It continued stumbling towards them; they fell silent when it stretched out its arms and moaned, exciting the others.

They quickly wound their way through the vehicles, trying to stay low and out of sight. Upon reaching the building, they crept along the side of it, quietly calling for Mark and Megan. When they reached the lot where all the transport trucks had parked, they began to make their way through them carefully searching for signs of their two other companions. Ruth saw zombies stuck in truck cabs, wildly thrashing at the windows, trying to get to the fresh feast walking by. One of the trailers rocked and loud thumping sounds echoed in the silence.

"A group of survivors must have locked themselves in the trailer," Ron spoke in low tones, bending to see beneath the line of trucks. He moved away from the rocking trailer, not wanting to risk drawing additional unwanted attention to them.

"Shouldn't we let them out?" Paige asked innocently.

Ron turned and sadly shook his head. "By the sounds of it, they aren't survivors anymore."

A bloody hand with two missing fingers suddenly reached out from behind the truck they were standing beside and dead fingers gripped onto Ron's shoulder. Ruth cried out a warning as Ron spun. He tried to back away from the clicking teeth but the zombie held on, stumbling after him.

"Shit!" Harris moved with lightening reflexes. Grabbing a knife from its sheath at his side he deftly pulled back on the zombies head and buried it to the hilt in the zombies chin.

The clacking stopped and the limp body slumped to the ground, tearing the sleeve of Ron's shirt as it fell. "That was too close," he breathed.

Someone behind Ruth retched and she turned, still in shock, to Steven hunched over with his hands braced on his knees, emptying the contents of his stomach. Paige stood beside her dad, gently patting his shoulder and making soft comforting sounds. Caleb stood beside Paula, mimicking Harris' movements as he watched the dead-again zombie twitch on the ground at Ron's feet. Ruth marveled at how resilient the children had become - adjusting to their new reality so quickly. If only she could be so lucky.

"This guy was fresh." Harris nudged the body with the toe of his boot. "Couldn't be more than a few hours old, which means there may be other survivors in the area."

A crack of a rifle cut through the silence and everyone turned in unison to the rear of the property.

"We've got to go Mark." They heard Megan shout just before another shot echoed through the maze of transport trucks.

"Just a few more," Mark shouted back as two more shots rang out.

"Head towards the pumps," Ron hissed, pointing in the general direction. "Hopefully the shots draw the zombies towards them and away from us. I'll meet you there with the others." He turned and jogged off without a backwards glance. Ruth wanted to call after her husband, to warn him to be careful, but in a moment, he'd disappeared from sight, lost in the maze of trucks.

"Paula, take the rear. Ruth, keep the kids between you and Steven." When they all nodded their understanding, Harris motioned for them to follow. The roar of two truck engines spurred them into action. "Let's go." They moved quickly and quietly, checking for undead between the trailers before moving forward to the next, and were soon at the edge of the parking lot.

Before them stood the abandoned gas pumps, tattered signs hung from the displays informing patrons that diesel was no longer available. The ground around the pumps was littered with bodies; the four adults stood stunned by the scene. Ruth pulled Caleb to her in an attempt to shield the boy from the grisly sight, but he pulled away, straining to take in every detail.

"There's Ron," Steven said, pointing down the line of trailers.

Relief washed over Ruth as she turned to watch her husband, followed by Mark and Megan, jog towards them. Mark was holding something in his arms and Megan was carrying both hers and Mark's backpacks, which appeared to be filled to capacity.

"What's all that?" Harris asked as the three approached.

"We don't have time to explain," Megan huffed, handing one of the packs to Harris.

"She's right," Ron said, glancing back over his shoulder. "There is a group of survivors in a warehouse at the rear of the property and they apparently didn't like that we found several trucks with supplies and helped ourselves. Let's get out of the immediate area, and then we'll find a place to stop and divide up what we've found."

A little slice of normal...

Mark and Megan filled the group in on what happened as they cautiously made their way out of the area. Apparently while Harris and Ron came back to find the others, Mark and Megan began searching the trucks behind the store. There they'd found a truck carrying a load of bottled water, another filled with beef jerky and pepperettes from one of the stores suppliers and a third, half-filled with cigarettes. While no one in their group smoked, Mark insisted they'd be a good item to have if their group ever needed to trade for supplies.

After grabbing several cartons of smokes, and while Megan had been filling their packs with the beef products, Mark went to check

126

out the truck with the water logo -that's when the group from the warehouse opened fire without warning. While Megan quickly finished filling their backpacks, Mark grabbed two cases of bottled water and together they made a dash for the cover of the tractor-trailer parking lot.

That's where Ron found them, discussing how they'd find the others in the maze of trucks. They filled Ron in on what happened and were surprised when five armed men exited the warehouse, carrying two gas cans. He'd overheard two of the men talking about how they'd have to spend the next several days searching trailer by trailer to make sure they got everything of use out of the trucks. After moving the cigarettes from the third truck into the trailer of the other, and closing the doors on the bottled water truck, the men drove back to the warehouse. Ron supposed they hadn't known the contents of the trucks or expected anyone to start searching them, so they'd left them there until their supplies ran low. However, when Mark showed up, they realized the need to secure the now precious commodities so no other passers-by would come along with the same idea.

The story shocked Ruth. They were all survivors - all in need of supplies. It wasn't enough that the men had a secure place to stay; they also wanted to hoard what was left, so they wouldn't have to go without - no matter the cost to others. She wasn't sure if she could live by this new world's rules... wasn't sure she wanted to. Mark and Megan wouldn't have been able to take all the food or water - they wouldn't have been able to carry even a quarter of what must have been there, but the men hadn't wanted them to take what little they'd been able to carry. Ruth was just glad they'd made it back safe and with what provisions they'd found.

After a brief stop to rest and eat, the group continued east along Frontage Road since it had far fewer cars than the highway. Finally, just before the sun began its daily descent, they reached the outskirts of Sequin. Six miles from town, the traffic on the highway abruptly stopped at a concrete barricade, which ran the width of the road. While human remains littered the ground, Ruth hadn't seen a single undead since crossing the barrier; apparently, the army had been clearing the area regularly.

"We're going to need to clear one of these houses," Ron motioned to a house, "and I'm voting on that one." It was a ranch style home with a ridiculous-looking second story addition, sticking out of the middle of the roof. There were large, boarded-up windows along the front and a tall fence ran that around both sides of the house, enclosing the backyard. To the survivors, it looked like Fort Knox.

"I don't care where we stay, I just need to sleep," Ruth sighed, setting Paige down. Her back ached from the day's long walk. The rest of the group nodded their agreement; they all needed to unwind from the day's trek.

They slipped into the backyard, closing and securing the gate behind them, intently listening for any signs or sounds of the undead. It didn't take long for Harris to pick the lock on the side door and soon, the group was clearing the house room by room. Ruth waited with the children in the kitchen. Luckily, the house still had power.

Ruth opened the fridge. "There's food in the fridge that's still good..." she opened the freezer to see what it held, "and the freezer is full, so we can defrost something and have a home cooked meal tonight," she told the kids, who cheered.

Wanting to keep herself occupied, she began to look for some grounds and filters after spotting a coffee pot in the corner of the counter. It had been twelve days since she'd had a good cup of coffee and wasn't sure when any of them would get another opportunity for some time to come. The cupboards hung open with piles of non-perishables stacked haphazardly on the counter tops, children's pictures drooped from the fridge and several lay scattered across the tile floor, legal-looking papers had been dumped on the table and carelessly rummaged through - the family had obviously left in a hurry. Going through the cupboards, Ruth felt like an intruder as she searched the scattered remains of a family's life.

The coffee pot was half-full by the time Paula returned to the kitchen. "They must have been evacuated when the blockade went up." Paula inhaled deeply. "Mmmmm, there's coffee?!" She glanced around the kitchen, looking for the source of the tantalizing smell. "It looks like they packed some of their clothing and took a few of the pictures hanging on walls. They were probably only allowed to take whatever they could fit into their car."

"I'm just glad to have electricity and running water." Steven came in with a huge grin on his face. Taking a glass from the cupboard, he filled it to the brim with tap water. "The showers are working and there are enough beds we can all sleep in comfort tonight." He drained the glass, sighing in contentment.

A loud beep made the three adults jump and quickly scan the room for the source. Caleb stood at an answering machine with a sheepish look on his face; he and Paige had sat so quietly that Ruth almost forgot they were there. "It was blinking," he shrugged. They all fell silent when a woman's worried voice filled the kitchen.

"Kat, I just got your voicemail and was hoping to catch you before they evacuated the family; I must have just missed you. The news up here hasn't reported any oil spills in Texas, which is strange because I found online reports in both the Houston and Austin newspapers. Maybe it's already under control and they don't want people making a big deal of it? I tried to call your cell but the message said you were out of the service area - where's the FEMA camp they took you to? The moon? We're praying for you and the family. That everyone's safe and being well taken care of. Call me as soon as you get home." The answering machine beeped again and an automated voice announced that the call came in a week earlier.

"Hey Ruth?" Mark poked his head in the room, breaking the silence that had fallen after the answering machine clicked off. "Ron asked me to come get you. He's upstairs." He bounced over to the coffee pot, "Hey, is this coffee for us?"

Ruth nodded, turning to get two mugs from the cupboard. "I'll take a coffee up to Ron. Mark, go find Megan and Harris, tell them there's coffee and once you're all here, you can figure out what we're going to have for dinner. Defrost it and when I come back down, I'll get dinner started. Oh," she said, as she poured the steaming liquid into the mugs, "make sure to start another pot of coffee once this one's empty." She pointed to the grounds she'd left on the counter. *I hope he does as asked...* she thought, *I worry about him.* She picked up the two steaming mugs and went in search of her husband.

Ruth found him on the second floor, standing in what she suspected was the master suite. The room had large windows, allowing them a clear view from the western horizon, where the sun's last rays of light colored the sky a deep orange, all the way to the east, where bright spotlights illuminated the road and surrounding area. *The blockade.* She wasn't sure why, but the sight of it made her shiver.

"I've brought you some coffee," Ruth said, holding out the mug for Ron.

He turned with a weary smile. "I was hoping we'd find some once I realized the electricity was on." He held the mug beneath his nose, inhaling deeply. "I miss freshly brewed coffee the most I think."

"So what do you think our best course of action is for getting around the blockade?" she asked, sipping her steaming coffee; the taste was heavenly.

Ron shrugged, "I'm not sure. We'll have to watch their patrol patterns tonight and see what makes the most sense in the morning. I can't decide if we're better off trying it in the daylight or at night. I'm sure they have night vision goggles, but we'd be just as easy to spot in the daylight as well... and with all the farm fields surrounding us, we'll have little cover no matter when we go."

Ruth nodded, not taking her eyes off the movements of the soldiers behind the concrete wall. From this distance, they looked little more than dots on the horizon. "We'll need to keep our use of lights to a minimum so as not to draw attention from the military, but I figure we can safely use the showers and make a hot meal."

"Someone will have to stay on watch, but I think a little normalcy would do all of us some good."

At the end of the night, they all went to bed clean and with full stomachs; a sense of safety they hadn't felt since the dead began to rise, filling their hearts with hope.

The first, last stand...

"Holy fucking shit!"

Ruth started awake at the outburst and turned to make sure it hadn't woken the kids; they still lay asleep beside her. Ron insisted that Ruth sleep with Paige and Caleb in the master suite since it had the king size bed, but she hadn't expected to be woken in the middle of the night by whoever was on guard duty.

Gunshots rang through the night bringing Ruth to full consciousness. She sat bolt upright, and as her eyes focused on Mark she asked, "What's going on?"

Footsteps thundered up the stairs and a moment later Steven and Harris stumbled through the door. "We heard some moaning coming from the front of the house... then the guns - what's happening?"

Mark turned and looked to each of them; his face was drawn, his eyes were wide, and his mouth moved but no words came out. When he realized he couldn't explain, he simply pointed out the window.

Automatic gunfire began to go off at the barricade; the men bolted to the window and as they looked out, their jaws dropped. Frightened by the men's reaction, Ruth got up to look for herself, and as she gazed into the night, felt her stomach drop to her feet. The dinner they'd all worked so hard in preparing, tried to jump up her throat.

Outside the window was a sea of undead.

The lights from the barricade illuminated the front of the crowd. They stumbled forward in a jagged line as wide as both the east and westbound lanes, spilling down the embankments and filling both frontage roads as well. When Ruth turned to look west to see how deep the horde was, she could no longer hold back the bile. She turned and vomited. She closed her eyes tight; willing away the image burned into her brain.

With the little light cast by the moon, Ruth saw that the horde extended further back than she could see. There were hundreds of thousands of undead marching past their hiding spot and if even one decided to investigate the house for living, they didn't stand a chance at survival. The sheer number of undead could easily level the house with enough incentive.

"Go get everyone upstairs right now. Tell them to bring some bottles of water from the kitchen but to be as quiet as possible; one wrong sound and we're joining that horde," Harris hissed to Mark. When he didn't move, Harris shook his shoulder until the boy tore his eyes from the outside and focused on the man. "Go." He pointed out the bedroom door.

As Mark disappeared down the steps, a loud boom shook the windows and light illuminated the room. At the noise, both Paige and Caleb began to cry; Ruth hurried to quiet them. "What was that?" she asked Steven when he came to the bedside, holding out his arms for Paige.

"I think someone threw a grenade," he replied quietly, a grim expression on his face. He focused back on Paige and began to rock her back and forth, murmuring softly.

"What was that loud noise?" Caleb said, looking up at Ruth as he knuckled away his startled tears.

"Shhh," Ruth pressed her finger to her lips, "there are a lot of zombies outside and we need to keep very quiet. That loud boom was the army fighting, trying to kill them." The room slowly filled with the members of their group who'd been sleeping downstairs; each carried several bottles of water and some leftovers, not that anyone wanted to eat. Screams from the military unit could be heard in between explosions, and over the moans of the undead, but Ruth knew that nothing could be done to help. Soon enough the gunfire, explosions and screams ceased. Ruth knew there was no one left alive at the barricade, because even the moans of the undead faded into silence.

The night wore on and the horde continued to pass, traveling into the unsuspecting town of Seguin as the survivors sat, huddled together in silence. Several times, Ruth nodded off into an uneasy sleep, only to start awake when the slightest noise emanated from the main floor. She finally decided to stretch her legs when she noticed the soft orange glow coming from the eastern horizon. The sun was rising and they would be able to see the full extent of their situation. Upon looking out the window, she wished she hadn't moved from her spot on the floor; her sore back and knees be damned.

While the sky to the east was turning a soft pinkish purple, the orange glow she's noticed emanated from Seguin - from the fires spreading across the town, backlighting the horde as it continued east. There were still a few stragglers wandering past the house, but the largest part of the mass had already moved beyond the barricade. Ruth could see the devastation the horde had inflicted on the blockade. The concrete barriers were pushed aside and dismembered bodies lay strewn about the highway. Just beyond the barrier, it appeared the horde had split into two; a majority of the zombies continued along the highway, while a portion followed the access road into town.

"They didn't stand a chance," a voice spoke softly from beside Ruth. She hadn't noticed Mark's approach; she'd been too lost in the destruction beyond the window. She turned towards him, noticing the haunted expression and the dark circles beneath his eyes. His bravado from the day before was gone, replaced by fear and uncertainty. "There were so many," he went on, not taking his eyes off the town, "nothing could have stopped them, and the people in that town were completely unprepared for what happened." He turned haunted eyes on Ruth, searching her face - for what, she wasn't sure. "Is this what's going to happen everywhere? Will we ever truly be safe again?"

Ruth put her arm around Mark and was surprised when he buried his face in her shoulder, his body shaking in silent sobs. His usually callous attitude made it easy to forget that he was still just a teenager. "We made it through the night," she whispered softly. "We're safe here for the time being and once we get to Buchanan Lake, we'll be even safer." She wasn't sure she believed her own words, but knew Mark needed reassurances. Movement to her right caught her eye, and she glanced over to where Ron sat watching the two of them, sorrow and pity filling his expression, knowing they'd never be truly safe ever again.

Once the sun rose, Ron assembled the group in the kitchen to discuss their next course of action. "I'm sorry Steven," Ron addressed him first, "I don't think we can follow the horde to Houston and there is no way for us to get around it now." Steven's shoulders slumped, but Ruth knew he'd already come to that conclusion for himself. "We need to get north and hope we don't run into another horde along the way. If the zombies are moving out of San Antonio, something must be attracting them to other areas and we can't take the chance of being cut off from the only place we know we can fortify.

"We'll stay here for one more day and head out early tomorrow morning. We need to search the house and the surrounding houses for supplies because we may not get another chance. We need to be looking for medicine, first aid supplies, non-perishable food, water and transportation."

Everyone nodded their agreement and began to disperse throughout the house, searching for items they would need in the future.

Ron rubbed his hand over his face and Ruth walked to her husband's side. "We'll make it," she said, squeezing his hand. "We have to believe that we'll survive and that others will as well. The army may not be able to stop them and life may never be the same again, but we'll adjust and make a new life."

Ron looked into Ruth's eyes, smiling weakly. "I hope you're right Ruth." He leaned down and gently kissed the top of her head. "I hope you're right."

Volume 8: Black Horizon

Workday's end...

The excavator rumbled to a stop and Aisha killed the engine. She'd put in her twelve hours for the day and was looking forward to returning to her motel room with a bag of greasy takeout. She couldn't wait to take a steaming hot shower, call her mom and veg in front of the TV with a beer or two before heading to bed; she was exhausted.

She climbed down from the excavator, closing the door firmly behind her. "Hey Aisha," Rudy called from his truck, waving her over.

Aisha pulled off her hardhat, tucking it under her arm. Jogging towards her co-worker, she smiled brightly. "Hey Rudy, packing it in for the night?"

"Yup," Rudy nodded with a chuckle. He leaned out of his truck and ruffled the top of Aisha's hair. "Parts of your bangs were sticking straight up." They laughed as she raked her fingers through the sweaty, tangled mess.

During her first week, most of the men had barely spoken to her but not Rudy. He'd treated Aisha like a little sister right from the start. Being the only woman on a road-crew, she'd started work knowing there would be comments and jibes; Rudy was never a contributor. In the beginning, the macho men teased her about how a woman should be taking care of her home and family. Rudy just told the men to shut their mouths and pay attention, that the farm girl could teach them all a thing or two about driving. Most of the jokes were good-natured, but a few men still didn't like the fact that a woman worked on their site - doing a job that was perceived as 'men's work'. Rudy just flipped them off, reminding Aisha that she'd proven her adeptness and put them all to shame. How she shouldn't worry about the chauvinist pigs who gave all men a bad rep; that most of them accepted her as part of the crew. He was a good guy and someone she was proud to call a friend.

"What are your plans for tonight?" Aisha leaned against the truck and closed her eyes. A breeze blew in from the west, cooling her skin. There was a strange, faint odour in the air. *Smells a little like the composers back home,* she thought, dismissing it as quickly as the thought came.

"We're headed back to the motel to get cleaned up, and then a bunch of us are headed to T.G.I. Friday's for some grub and a few beers; wanna join us?"

Aisha shook her head. "No, I'm staying in tonight. I need to call my mom and see how she's doing, so I figured I'd just grab something and eat in my room."

Nodding in understanding, Rudy's gaze drifted over the site. "Less than a month left here. Boss said we're starting the paving next week and then from there it's just the little things left." His green eyes slid back to her. "He mentioned the next job is in Missouri but doesn't start until mid-June. Are you going to head home for a few weeks to visit your mom? Make sure that farmhand you hired isn't taking advantage of her?"

Aisha wasn't native to Texas; she'd been raised on a farm in Iowa and her mother still lived in the old farmhouse she'd grown up in. She shook her head, "I don't know if I can handle three weeks on the farm. She says Sven is doing a great job so I'll trust her judgement on that. She did mention needing one of the tractors fixed so I may stop in for a few days to take care of it, but that's all I can take." Uncomfortable with the turn in conversation, Aisha patted the side of the truck, "Well, I'm headed back to my room Rudy. Tell the others I'm sorry I couldn't make it and to have a good night." Rudy waved as he put the truck into drive and rolled away.

Aisha stood gazing down the empty highway, lost in thought. She'd left home close to fifteen years earlier and the prospect of going back left a queasy, sick feeling in the pit of her stomach. When she'd been fifteen, her father and older brother had been in a fatal car accident. With their deaths, her mother had become a different woman. Once cheerful and warm-hearted, Aisha's mother became closed-off and bitter, ever mourning the loss of her husband and eldest child. Turning the farmhouse into a shrine for the dead, Aisha's mother withdrew, leaving her to fend for herself. By her eighteenth birthday, Aisha knew she had to leave - get out of the oppressive atmosphere of the home she'd grown up in, but with limited skills outside of the farm, she found herself driving for a road construction crew.

Aisha turned towards her SUV, ready to head to her motel and saw Saul, the sites supervisor, running back to the trailer he used as an office. She didn't think she'd ever seen the large man move so fast. In the distance, Aisha heard the telltale whump whump whump of a helicopter and the rumble of large trucks approaching on the highway. Considering how light the traffic on the I10 had been over the past several weeks, and the sketchy reports from San Antonio about the oil spill, a bad feeling crept into Aisha's gut. She adjusted her heading, turning away from her SUV and towards Saul's office, unsure of why she felt so uneasy.

"... not sure how long they'll need the crew for, but they say it's a matter of urgency" Saul was saying as Aisha made her way up the three steps to the open trailer door. "No, I don't think they'll be covering the OT." There was a long pause, causing Aisha stop at the top step. "No, I don't know what the emergency is, he wouldn't tell me over the phone." Another pause, "As soon as the work is done, the crew's free to leave again." Saul let out a long gusty sigh. "It will put the job behind by a day at least and no, they won't be reimbursing us for that either." Aisha shifted, suddenly uncomfortable with her eavesdropping. She turned to go back down the steps but stopped when Saul shouted, "Either we do it or they use our machines to do it and personally, I'd prefer a few of my own driving. We aren't being given much of a choice here."

The rumble from the highway grew louder. Aisha quietly made her way back down the steps and around the corner of the trailer; the six covered army trucks rolling to a stop just outside of the construction zone made her stop abruptly. A helicopter flew overhead but continued west, following the highway. What was going on? Aisha had a sinking feeling her plans for the evening were about to change.

The army's orders...

"Aisha! Thank God you're still here," Saul said from the doorway of his trailer.

"What's going on?" she asked, turning to her supervisor. His face was pale and drawn; now she regretted lingering on the site past shift's end.

The supervisor wiped his brow with a hanky before stuffing it into his back pocket. "I need you to get at least five others back to the site - more if they'll agree to come." He waddled down the steps, hurrying as fast as a large man could towards her. "Tell them that anyone who agrees to work for a few extra hours will be paid overtime. That they are not to ask questions nor are they to disturb the army personnel. They are only to do as asked."

"What are we supposed to be doing?"

Saul glanced behind Aisha before responding, "We need to move all the concrete barriers. Stack them in a wall beneath the overpass to barricade the way through."

Aisha felt her mouth fall open. "The ones surrounding the site? What about traffic trying to get through? Will we be paid overtime to take down the barrier once the army's done?"

Saul's face tightened. "Yes the one's surrounding the site and as for the traffic," he pointed to the empty westbound lane of the I10, "when was the last time you saw a car headed in or out of Houston?" He turned away, walking towards the waiting army trucks.

"What am I supposed to tell the guys when they have questions?" She yelled after him. She hadn't agreed to stay or work the OT he was offering; the extra money, however, would be nice come payday and she was already onsite.

"Tell them they aren't to ask questions if they want the overtime pay. The address book with everyone's contact info is on my desk," he called to Aisha without looking back.

Stomping back up the steps of the trailer, Aisha grumbled to herself. Saul didn't understand what he was asking. Dragging the concrete barriers to beneath the overpass wasn't going to be a simple task, not to mention the extra work that would have to be done the following day to get the site back as it was. Riffling through the scattered papers on the desk, Aisha finally found the spiral notebook Saul mentioned. It listed everyone's room, their cell phone numbers and emergency contact info.

She picked up the phone and dialed Rudy. After telling him what little she knew, he promised to round up the guys and be back to the site within the next fifteen minutes. She'd just hung up the phone when a short man in a pristine uniform marched in; for someone so small, he had a big voice.

"This will be command. We'll have several units stationed on the overpass with the heavy artillery and two units beneath. We'll need..." Looking up, he was momentarily silenced by Aisha's presence. He recovered quickly, removing his hat and extending his hand in greeting. "I'm Lieutenant Howard and this is Staff Sergeant Jenkins." He indicated the tall dark-skinned man standing rigidly behind him. "You must be the one who'll be operating the excavator; Saul mentioned that the best operator he had was a woman."

Aisha bristled at the skeptical look Staff Sergeant Jenkins gave her - she tried to ignore it as she shook the Lieutenant's hand. "I'm Aisha."

He smiled brightly, but Aisha could see his underlying fear. It concerned her. "I'll need someone directing the others when they get here. Can I trust that you'll be able to coordinate with Sergeant Jenkins and your co-workers to complete the task? I have other duties to tend to and will be unable to provide the appropriate direction."

Aisha looked to Jenkins, who appeared to be displeased with the turn in events. "If we can get radios then I can coordinate them." She said with a shrug, inwardly pleased with the scowl on Jenkins' face.

"Sergeant Jenkins will see to it that you have everything you need to get this done ASAP," he said with a distracted wave of his hand. Jenkins nodded to someone outside beyond Aisha's line of sight, and within moments, the trailer was filled with men carrying armloads of radios, wires and maps.

"Let's step outside," Jenkins said coolly, motioning out the open trailer door.

Aisha walked out, noticing the helicopter was back and attempting to land on the overpass. A man knelt on top of the trailer, inserting wires into a small mobile satellite antenna. Soldiers moved about with purpose both on top and beneath the bridge, carrying large black containers from the trucks. She noticed several mortars in the process of being assembled. It was beginning to look more like a warzone than a construction zone... *What is all the fuss about?*

"What we need from you guys," Jenkins said as they moved away from the trailer, "is to move the concrete barriers lining the highway and stack them on the west side of the bridge. We want it to

139

enclose the area beneath the bridge but also allow for periodic openings, only wide enough for my men to shoot through."

Frowning, Aisha turned to face Jenkins. "So you want it blocked off so your men are safe, but still want to be able to shoot whatever's on the other side. What are you expecting... an army of undead?" She laughed but Jenkins' face grew stonier.

"No questions," he replied curtly, moving towards Aisha's excavator. "Is this thing fueled?"

"It has enough to get the job done," she snapped, flinging the door open. "I'll get it into place, but I can't start getting the medians moved until the others arrive; I'll need two chains and a radio..." she paused, glancing over Jenkins' shoulder to the growing number of canvas covered trucks. "You guys don't happen to have a proper crane in one of those trucks, do you? Because if you do, this will go a lot faster."

A small smile flickered across Jenkins' lips, "I'll make sure you have what you need."

Aisha climbed over the tracks and into the cab with ease. The engine rumbled to life and after a quick check of the controls, she turned back to Jenkins; the sergeant wore a look of surprise as he watched her. "What?" she shouted over the engine's rumble, knowing full well that the sergeant's surprise was due to her comfort with the large machine.

"Nothing," he shook his head, "do you need anything else in the meantime?"

"Just have one of the guys flag me down once they're all here and I'll give everyone their tasks."

With a nod, Jenkins turned and walked away.

Aisha's crew assembled around her less than fifteen minutes later. After moving the excavator into place, she'd switched to the forklift in order to get started immediately, but it was slow going since the lift could only carry one median at a time. In order to properly secure the area beneath the bridge, Aisha calculated the span and height of the overpass, deciding that a minimum of one hundred and thirty four medians were needed to complete the barricade. Stacking them three high would give the soldiers almost eight feet of protection against whatever they were preparing to face, but this also meant they had to ensure the barriers stability as they built it.

"Kev," Aisha said as she hurried over to the huddled group of men, surprised that Rudy had been able to round up so many with such short notice. Noticing a pile of heavy chains and box of radio's sitting at Rudy's feet, Aisha spoke to the group. "Everyone grab a radio; this is how we'll make sure everything goes smoothly." They handed out the radios, turning back to Aisha in silence. Used to the men giving her a hard time when she asked them to do anything, their sudden rapt attention unnerved her; never had they looked to her for direction. "Kev," she said again, turning to the young man.

"What's up?" Kev, the newest member of the crew said, fiddling with one of the handheld radios.

"I want you on the forklift." She jerked her finger over her shoulder to the still idling machine. "I need you to drive around the outskirts of the site, gathering the medians into the dump truck and unloading them there." She indicated the small pile she'd already started. Kev nodded, but didn't move. She took a deep, steadying breath, "You can get started now... we're short on time."

With a nod, Kev jogged off; Aisha turned to Carl, a huge man known to most of the crew as Tiny. "Tiny, I need you to stick with Kev in the dump truck. Load up as many medians as you can at a time, but try to keep an eye on how many we have left. Just make sure we don't run out and are sitting around waiting for more."

"Sure thing!" Tiny said, saluting Aisha before he made his way to the truck.

"Chris, I want you in one of the bulldozers and Bert you're in the other; I'll be operating the excavator. Rudy, you can coordinate between the three of us and you six," she motioned to half of the remaining men, "make sure that we're moving at an even pace and not getting backed up."

The helicopter lifted off the overpass and everyone turned to watch it fly overhead, headed west once again. "What the hell is going on?" someone asked.

"I've been told we're not to ask questions. That we're to get the barricade built as quickly as possible and then we're free to leave," Aisha said, turning back to the men. "As for the rest of you, I want you at the barricade. We need to get the medians in place and secured so they don't topple once we start stacking them. I'll get the sergeant to come give you directions for spacing once we get to that point." She looked around the group, waiting for questions, but when they remained silent, Aisha clapped her hands. "If any questions come up, just call on the radio; we can't waste time running around. We've got a lot to do before sunset, but I know we can get it done."

The group broke apart, leaving Aisha and Rudy standing alone. "Good job boss." He winked.

Snorting, Aisha replied, "I'm not the boss. I'm just the one who was unfortunate enough to still be here when the army arrived."

Approaching horizon...

"Can you hear that?" someone whispered.

Having worked for close to an hour, they'd gotten the first level of the barricade in place. Not want to miscalculate the spacing needed between the barriers; Aisha called for a five-minute break while they waited for the sergeant.

Aisha paused and listened; her ears still hummed from being in the excavator for so long, but she could definitely hear something - she just wasn't sure what.

"Why are you all standing around?" Jenkins shouted from behind them; they all turned in unison. "We need to have that barrier up before nightfall." Obviously irritated by the delay, he studied the group around him before looking to the setting sun. "We have less than an hour left of daylight and while we do have lights set up for after sunset, I'd hoped to have you evacuated from the area by then."

"Um," Kev spoke up, "I know we aren't supposed to ask questions, but what the hell is that noise?"

"Trouble," was Jenkins reply. He turned to Aisha, "Now, what's causing this delay?"

Rudy stepped forward, eying Jenkins. "We need to know how far apart you want the barriers on the next two levels."

Giving Aisha a withering look, Jenkins snapped, "I told you that we need only enough space for the gun barrels."

Tiny stepped in front of Aisha, crossing his barrel arms over his huge chest. "Does that mean an inch or a foot?" the big man growled. "Construction is pretty precise and we're not going to half-ass our work just to save time. If we aren't precise, and something goes wrong, it'll be on us." Aisha suppressed a smile when the sergeant's face paled.

"Uh... Um..." he stuttered, glancing down at his hands, measuring out approximately four inches. "About this big?"

Tiny snorted, not backing down.

"Four inches it is." Aisha placed a hand on Tiny's arm. The big man looked down at her with a raised eyebrow as if to say, 'you're going to let him off that easy?' She nodded almost imperceptibly and Tiny dropped his arms, stepping back behind her. "We'll get back to it and hopefully have this done within the hour." The men dispersed, returning to their work.

"ETA in one-point-two-five hours," the radio on Jenkins' belt squawked; he immediately turned down the volume, cutting off whatever the responder said. "Just get it done before dark," he sighed and walked away.

By the time they'd completed their task the sun had set, the last of its rays still illuminated the horizon in gold's, red's and oranges; it appeared as if the sky was on fire.

So beautiful, and yet, somehow ominous. Pushing her apprehension aside, Aisha smiled at her team. "Thanks for all the hard work guys." They'd all come together and worked quickly and efficiently, completing the barricade before dusk.

"When this is over I'll buy you all a round of drinks." Jenkins' offer was rewarded by cheering from the men. He turned to face Aisha, smiling sheepishly, "I'm sorry for questioning your ability to get all this done in time. You've done a great job in motivating your people and coordinating their work." She waved his comment off, but inside she knew she'd made a breakthrough, finally gaining the respect and loyalty of her crew.

"Look there." Kev pointed down the I10 towards western horizon.

They all turned and a collective gasp went up from the group. On the hill, less than a mile down the road, a black line began to form on the horizon, contrasting with the bright skyline.

Jenkins whipped out his radio. "Command, I have a visual; they're earlier than expected. Over."

"Get the construction crew behind the barrier, and we'll move onto the next phase. Over and out." The radio crackled back a moment later.

A cold chill crept up Aisha's back as the faint, eerie chorus of moans reached her ears.

"What the hell's all of that?" Rudy whispered to Aisha, so the other wouldn't overhear. She only shrugged in response, unable to take her eyes from the growing line of dense shadow.

"What is that smell?" Kev said, covering his nose. "It smells like death." The others around Aisha sniffed the air, making disgusted faces at one another; whispers rippled through the group.

"We've got to get behind the barrier," Jenkins barked, pointing to the exit ramps.

"Wait!" Aisha grabbed Jenkins arm, holding him back as the others quickly made their way across the grassy expanse between the highway and exit. Jenkins' jaw tightened, but he remained silent. "We've blocked off the underpass, but the ramps are still open. Do you think that whatever this is will simply ignore the easy off-ramps?"

Concern crossed Jenkins strong features and then resolve. He nodded curtly, "You don't know what we're up against, but you're right. They'll push up against the barrier and spread out, eventually finding their way over the guard rails."

"There isn't anything I can do about a proper blockade, but I can at least push the rails so Pin Oak isn't as easily accessible as it is now."

Jenkins shook his head, pulling out his radio. "Come in command."

The radio hissed, "Go ahead Sergeant."

"I'd like to request that the tanks be repositioned to the ramp exits; the crew lead has pointed out the oversight and I agree with her assessment. Over."

"Copy that; Lieutenant Howard has acknowledged and will take your suggestion into advisement. Command out." The radio hissed again then fell silent.

"You have tanks here?" Astonished, Aisha gazed at Jenkins with wide eyes. "Can I look at them afterwards?"

The rumbling sounds of engines were soon followed by the appearance of two tanks - one at either exit. Aisha gaped and Jenkins chuckled. "You know, given your obsession with heavy machinery and obvious talent, I think you'd like being in the army. We have some pretty big toys."

Aisha snorted, but didn't take her eyes off the tanks, watching as the massive barrels swung westwards. "I don't think the army can handle me." They stood in silence, watching the tanks adjust their angles. She peered up at Jenkins, unsure if he'd give her answers now that the threat was upon them. "What's really happening here Sergeant? I've never seen anything like this before." Bright spotlights suddenly illuminated the highway, blinding them both.

"Here." Jenkins handed her a set of binoculars, turning to face away from the bright lights.

After a hesitant moment, Aisha took the binoculars. In the dim light, she could make out tiny, shadowy figures walking down the highway in a clumsy, staggering line. The line spanned the width of the east and west bound highways as well as both access roads. "What's going on?"

Jenkins cleared his throat. "It's a horde from San Antonio."

Aisha lowered the binoculars, confused by the sergeant's words. "A horde of what?" A sick feeling started in the pit of her stomach as she took in the approaching group, their moans and the intensifying smell of rot.

After a long pause, Jenkins sighed, "there is no oil spill in San Antonio." He scrutinized her for a moment before continuing. "Earlier, when you joked about us preparing for an army of undead, you were actually right on the money."

A small gasp slipped past Aisha's lips and her stomach clenched in fear. It was a dream... it was a drill... it couldn't be real... shit like this only happened in movies and zombies sure as hell didn't exist in real life.

Jenkins went on, oblivious to Aisha's inner turmoil. "Several days ago, we lost contact with our barricades surrounding San Antonio. We sent out three helicopters to investigate and quickly realized that we had two hordes on the move - one is approaching Houston and the other hit Austin yesterday. We don't know why they're moving in herds out of San Antonio, nor do we know why they're traveling along the highways to the major cities. We do know that the horde has swelled in numbers as it's traveled down the interstate - that the one headed here is approximately two hundred thousand strong."

They stood in silence for a long moment, neither sure what to say next. Jenkins radio broke the silence, "Sergeant, we need you behind the barrier. Our eye in the sky has just informed us that the horde's speed has increased. It appears they've caught the scent of fresh meat and are in a bit of a frenzy. We have reports that members of the horde have broken ahead of the large body and will make contact within the next ten minutes. The Lieutenant wants the area clear, so we can begin launching mortars. Over."

"Roger," Jenkins said, keying the radio. He turned, jerking his head to the newly constructed barricade. "Let's get behind the line of fire."

"I think that you need to talk to your Lieutenant, and convince him to let me in front of the barricade with the tandem roller and a bulldozer," Aisha called after Jenkins.

He jerked to a halt, glancing back with a thoughtful expression. "We have enough firepower; sitting in those machines in front of the barricade will only get you killed."

"Think about it." Aisha caught up to him but went on knowing she had to give him a reason his superior couldn't refute. "You'll have all those bodies pressed up against the barrier and it won't hold forever - not with how little time we had to put it up. Besides, the ones who fall will just begin to pile up. The bulldozer can easily clear away the bodies."

Chuckling, Jenkins shook his head, "and the tandem roller? Where does that fit in?"

"That's the best part," Aisha smiled, "a tandem roller won't leave much more than a smear behind."

Long night...

Gunshots rang out from the barricade as mortar rounds exploded in the distance; Aisha dialed her cell phone. She sat in the tandem roller with Tiny in the bulldozer beside her, surrounded by the moaning undead while waiting for the order to clear the road.

The phone rang once, and her friend Sarah answered with a perky, "Hey Aisha, I thought you were staying in tonight."

"Change of plans," Aisha half shouted.

"What? I can barely hear you. Are you watching an action movie?"

"I feel like I'm in an action movie," Aisha replied, rubbing her weary eyes with the back of her hand. "Listen Sarah, there's something going on at the construction site. The army's here..."

"The army?" Sarah shouted back to be heard over the loud boom. "What's the army doing there?"

"Listen to me." Aisha didn't have time to answer inconsequential questions. "You need to get as many supplies as you can and however many people you can gather and head for Curt's place on the gulf. Something really bad is about to hit Houston and you need to get out."

"What are you talking about Aisha?" Sarah snorted, not understanding the gravity of the situation. "Curt just got back yesterday from being out on the water for a month and Heather doesn't want any company for a few days."

"Just fucking do it," Aisha snapped, her patience running thin. "Gather who and what you can. Make sure everyone has enough food and water to last at least a month and get to Curt's. I'll try to get there within the next twenty-four hours."

"Whoa, hold on a minute." Sarah sounded irritated by Aisha's outburst. "Why do you want me to do this?"

"There's a horde of fucking zombies headed into Houston and if you don't get out now, you may never be able to."

Sarah snorted, "Zombies? Make sure to bring some of whatever you're on next time you come over."

"I'm not on anything Sarah. Please just do as I say." A grenade exploded a little too close to the roller; shaking the vehicle. Aisha grabbed the radio and shouted into it, "Whoever just threw that fucking grenade is going to lose their balls."

The cellphone clutched in Aisha's other hand buzzed faintly; she put it back to her ear. Sarah was shouting on the other end of the line. "Aisha... Aisha!"

"Please, please just do as I ask," she pleaded with her friend.

"Okay fine," Sarah huffed, "but if this turns out to be some kind of sick joke, you can be the one to explain it to the others."

"I wish it were a joke." Another grenade, this one further away, exploded. Dismembered limbs and miscellaneous body parts showered the cab; the thwack of flesh hitting metal turned Aisha's stomach. "I've got to go Sarah but please do as I ask."

Sarah's voice began to shake, "This is real isn't it? It's not a joke."

With a sigh of relief, Aisha said, "No joke. Get friends, get supplies and get to Curt and Heather's. Tell the others I'll meet them there as soon as I can."

"You better show up." Now Sarah sounded like she was crying.

"I will," Aisha promised, before hanging up. She sat for a long moment, staring blankly at the cellphone clutched in her hands; the buzz of the radio pulled her from her dark thoughts.

"Aisha? Tiny? We're going to cease-fire while you guys take care of the mess out there. Over."

"We should be less than five minutes," Aisha responded, glancing over to Tiny who nodded his agreement.

Putting the roller into gear, Aisha crossed the highway just in front of the barricade they'd erected only hours earlier; it was standing up surprisingly well. The zombies pushed against the side of the big machine but it didn't stop moving forward. The dead zombies, which lay piled at the base of the barricade, crunched and popped as they were crushed beneath the rollers weight. When the walking corpses who were trying to climb over the pile of bodies disappeared from view, Aisha couldn't help the feeling of satisfaction. The grinding of metal on pavement echoed above the zombie's moans as Tiny cleared the road of the pulpy debris behind her.

"As soon as you're clear we're opening fire again," Jenkins said through the radio, but Aisha didn't bother to respond.

Once clear of the barricade, Aisha turned back to see their handiwork, but the zombies had already filled in the space they'd cleared, once again pressing up against the concrete divider between the living and the dead.

The zombies were hideous, she'd decided early on. Some of the zombies no longer resembled human beings but at least those ones were easy to kill. For the most part, they still looked like people with only bites and small chunks of flesh missing. Every time she watched one of the more human looking zombie's heads snap back or one explode into pieces, she couldn't help but think that she'd just watched someone die. Regardless of what they looked like, whatever had made them human was gone, leaving only a monster in its place and she continually had to remind herself of that.

More than an hour later, Aisha realized the tandem roller was running low on fuel. She was about to radio Jenkins when her radio burst to life with shouts and gunfire.

"The northern side of the bridge has been breached and we're unable to hold them off much longer." There was more gunfire and

Aisha watched in horror as a ball of fire lit the night, illuminating the flood of zombies streaming onto the bridge.

"Don't throw any more grenades," someone was shouting into the radio; Aisha thought it might have been Jenkins but wasn't sure. "We have men beneath and don't have the manpower to deal with a collapse. Fallback to the south side and reinforce the teams there. We cannot lose both sides of the..." The radio cut off when the screams began.

A fire, started by the grenade, created macabre backlighting to the death scene unfolding atop the bridge. The zombies fell onto the soldiers, devouring all in their path. A flaming zombie hit the rail and toppled into the crowd below; several others in the vicinity quickly became walking torches. New zombies, dressed in fatigues, appeared on the overpass, quickly turning on those who'd once fought alongside them. Anyone witnessing the massacre now understood the unwavering determination of the undead.

The bridge exploded and the lights flickered out. Aisha threw her arms protectively over her head and tucked her chin to her knees, her mind reeling with what had just happened. Confused and disorientated, she groped for the radio. "Tiny!" She shouted over the ringing in her ears.

"We need to get the fuck out of here and far, far away." She heard the big man reply.

"I don't have enough fuel."

"I'll come get you." It wasn't a question - Tiny was coming for her.

Thank god, I'm not going to die in here. Looking at the zombies pressing against all sides of the roller, however, she wasn't sure she'd make it to the cab of the bulldozer even if he get to the roller. "There are too many," she said, resigned to waiting until the crowd was thin enough for her to make a break for it.

"Then I'll go get fuel and come back for you." She began to protest but Tiny cut her off, "it's not a question Aisha. Shut down the engine and conserve what you have left. I'll try to get back as soon as I can." The radio fell silent and the bulldozer pulled away.

Aisha killed the engine and stared out at the sea of zombies surrounding her.

Early morning...

The zombies moaned all through the night and those trapped in the rubble of the collapsed bridge screamed while they were devoured. Aisha hadn't dared to sleep. Dead hands continuously banged against all sides of the roller, but thankfully, the zombies didn't appear to have enough dexterity to climb on top of it. They shuffled around moaning and clawing at the sides of Aisha's tiny refuge, in an attempt to get to the living within.

The night seemed to drag on forever. With the barricade destroyed, the bulk of the horde continued their march into Houston. Unfortunately, some of the zombies lingered around the construction site, hoping to find more of the living stuck in the debris. Trapped in the tandem roller for what seemed like an eternity, Aisha watched the gradual lightening of the eastern sky. From further within the city, she could see smoke lazily drifting skyward; an unnatural hush had fallen over Houston. The cities residents hadn't stood a chance of survival. She only hoped that Sarah and her friends had made it out of the city in time. Throughout the night, she'd tried to use her cell phone to confirm her friend's safety, but only received an automated message saying that all circuits were busy and to try her call again later.

The sun, having risen just above the cityscape, began to heat the cab and Aisha knew she couldn't linger for much longer - she needed to make a decision and get on the move. Being short on fuel and having no supplies, a change in transportation would be necessary. Scanning the top of the collapsed overpass, Aisha noticed a small grouping of army trucks on the southern side of the bridge. If she could make it there, then she should be able to make it to the gulf, and hopefully, locate her friends before it was too late.

With new determination, Aisha started the engine and realized too late that its loud rumble drew the attention of all zombies in the area. They swarmed around the roller with rotting arms stretched out; thankfully, the engine drowned out their moans.

The radio on the floor squawked. "Is someone out there? Can anyone hear me?" It was Rudy. She reached down, searching the floor for the abandoned radio. "We can hear the engine and if anyone's out there, we desperately need help. We're trapped in the trailer on the east side of the bridge and there are too many of them outside for us to make an escape." There was a long pause. Aisha's face pressed against the controls as her fingers frantically searched the floor beneath her. "Please, if you're out there and can hear us, we desperately need assistance. One of our men was injured last night and we need to get him to a hospital."

Aisha's heart sank, but only for a moment; her fingers brushed against plastic and she snatched up the radio, quickly depressing the respond button. "Rudy, its Aisha. Thank God you're still alive!"

"I knew you made it through the night." Rudy sounded relieved and a little choked up.

"Who's all with you in the trailer?" she asked, shifting the roller into drive; a few zombies didn't stand a chance against the pressing weight of the two rollers.

"It's just me, Kev and Jenkins. Kev's hurt pretty bad; he caught some shrapnel in his calf and can't walk. I think the things outside can smell his blood because they haven't stopped beating on the walls of the trailer. I'm worried they're going to break through at any minute."

"I'm on my way." Aisha gunned the engine and was satisfied with the crunch as she rolled forward.

"They got Tiny and Saul but I think the others made it off the site before the shit really hit the fan." Rudy talked as Aisha navigated her way across the highway, squishing every zombie in her path. "The Lieutenant was airlifted out of here when they lost the bridge. I think it was their missiles that blew the thing to kingdom come." A zombie wearing camo stumbled into her path. Aisha thought she remembered seeing him speaking to Jenkins the night before. Now, half of his face was gone and burn marks ran down his right side. The burns didn't hide the bite marks on his arms, chest and neck.

Rudy kept talking, "Army personnel were trapped in the bridge collapse. Jenkins and I attempted to dig them out, but there was no time - the zombies overwhelmed us and we had to fall back to the trailer." There was a slight bump as the army zombie fell beneath the front roller and Aisha whispered a prayer for the dead soldier. "We were running for cover and noticed Tiny running down the hill shouting something about fuel. That's when a mortar went off behind us... when Kev got hit. One minute he was running beside me, and the next he wasn't. Jenkins was the one who found him in the ruble and pulled him out. I didn't see Tiny again."

Aisha pushed the engine as it started up the incline to Pin Oak road, easily knocking over the guardrail once it reached the top; Rudy fell silent. To her right, Aisha could see the crater where the bridge once stood, and to her left, the ground littered with bodies - some still twitching. The bulldozer sat abandoned. Crossing the road Aisha paused, surveying the trailer that stood just clear of the bridge's debris. Rudy was right - a group of thirty or so zombies crowded around it, but as Aisha began to descend, they all turned and wandered towards her.

Stopping, Aisha reached for her radio. "Rudy?"

"I'm still here. Whatever you are doing is drawing them away from the trailer."

"I can see that," she replied dryly. "I'm going to need you guys to come out when I get there. There's enough room in the cab for the three of you to fit in but it will be tight until I can get us to the south side of the bridge. There are a few trucks there and I'm hoping we can find one that runs." She paused, realizing that getting Kev into the cab would be a feat with him badly injured and so many zombies in tow.

"If the zombies aren't crowded around out there I think we can manage." Rudy's tone had changed from despair to hope, but Aisha wasn't so optimistic.

After a quick glance at the fuel gage, she knew that they didn't have time to waste. "I'm worried about Kev," she finally said, trying to lower her voice.

"Me too," Rudy replied quietly. "He's lost a lot of blood Aisha. He needs medical attention."

"Hospitals are out of the question Rudy. The zombies have made it to Houston and I doubt anywhere within the city limits is safe. Will he survive being moved?" She hated to ask, but they needed this to go as quickly and smoothly as possible. There was no response for a long moment.

When the radio crackled, Jenkins was the one to respond, "Hey Aisha, glad that you're okay."

"You too." She tried to smile, but was far too exhausted.

"I was listening to you and Rudy and I'm positive we won't be able to get Kev into the cab. I don't think we can move him Aisha; I'm worried that the bleeding will start up again or worse."

"Can we get the truck, drive back to the trailer and put him in the back?" she asked, hoping they could find a quick solution.

"If we come back, we run the risk of getting trapped again. I'm out of ammo and neither Kev nor Rudy have weapons. I hate to say this but I think we should put him out of his misery." Aisha gasped at his words. "Even if we were able to get him to a hospital, I doubt there is much they would be able to do for him - I'm not even sure how he made it thought the night."

"You can't just leave him!" Panic finally set in. Was this the world they were now living in? Where you'd just leave your friends behind because they wouldn't survive?

"Aisha," Jenkins' voice was soft and sorrowful, "I'm sorry but I don't think we have any other option. He's been unconscious for hours now and lost excessive amounts blood. This isn't easy for me either but given the situation, I don't see what other options we have."

"Well you have five minutes to figure out another option," Aisha snapped, dropping the radio into her lap and shoving the roller into drive.

The zombies, who were once crowded around the trailer, were now closing in on her location. With no remorse, Aisha rolled over the zombies in front of her and stopped, waiting for more to gather around. She put the roller into reverse and backed over the few zombies unfortunate enough to be in the way; she waited a moment before putting it into drive. Several more times she drove back and forth until most of the zombies were unrecognizable smears on the road and bloody streaks on the rollers.

By the time she made it down to the trailer, the fuel gauge was dangerously low but there weren't many zombies left stumbling around. "I hope you've figured it out because I'm outside, and we're low on fuel," Aisha snapped into the radio.

The door cracked open and Jenkins head popped out, glancing around the area, assessing for threats. Upon deciding it was clear, he nodded and exited with Rudy close behind; Kev wasn't with them. The two men didn't look at one another as they clambered up the side of the roller and squished themselves into the cab beside her. Jenkins cheek was swollen and red, Aisha noticed, and Rudy wore an expression of resigned defeat.

"Where is Kev?" she barked, not wanting to move forward until someone explained.

Rudy glared at Jenkins who sighed and shook his head. "He'd gone into shock."

"What did you do?" she almost lunged out of her seat at the sergeant.

"He shot him in the head," Rudy said flatly, not moving to help Jenkins.

Holding up his hands in an attempt to fend her off, Jenkins tried to explain, "His pulse was too fast and too weak, his skin was moist and clammy, he'd been unconscious for over two hours and his lips were turning blue. He wasn't going to get the immediate medical help he needed, and if we tried to move him, it would have caused his heart to fail."

"I should make you get out," Aisha hissed.

"I punched him for even making the suggestion, but he was right Aisha." Rudy looked out the window, focusing on something far away. "I doubt Kev would have survived the trip. It was the merciful thing to do."

"I thought you were out of bullets." She turned on Jenkins again.

"You always save one for yourself." Jenkins didn't look her in the eye when he spoke. "We'd better get to the south side of the bridge if we're going." He nodded towards the rubble of the collapsed bridge; zombies were already crawling out of the wreckage and advancing on the survivors.

"You'd better hope two of the trucks work because you sure as hell aren't coming with me." Shifting the roller into drive one last time, Aisha drove away from the remnants of the battle they'd fought... and lost.

Volume 9: Final Layover

Gate A26...

Pharmaceutical sales rep Stewart Witt hated layovers, but as a man who traveled for his job, he often found himself stuck in airports. While traveling from Chicago to Miami, he disembarked at the Dallas/Fort Worth International Airport, thankful that he had a relatively short, hour and a half layover.

Throughout his travels, he'd become accustomed to airport security practices but upon disembarking in Dallas, he recognized the signs of heightened security protocols. Men in uniform walked amongst the travelers, watching the passengers with wary expressions. Security, with a fleet of dogs, weren't allowing anyone to enter the city, guarding the doors that led out of the secure area and into the main terminal. A voice, repeating the same message every five minutes, droned over the loudspeakers.

"Due to the civil unrest growing in the southern end of Dallas, no passengers will be allowed to leave the airport premises. For those passengers who are on a layover, we ask that you please wait patiently at your gate; all other passengers must speak with their airline to make alternate arrangements. All inbound flights are currently being diverted to Will Rogers World Airport in Oklahoma City until this matter is resolved. We are sorry for any inconvenience this may cause."

Every television in the airport was tuned to the news. Blaming the rioting in Austin and Houston on several major oil spills, the reporters repeatedly urged those with family or friends out of state, to leave the area until the matter could be resolved. That if people were unable to stay with family, they should travel north to Stillwater Oklahoma where FEMA had set up a relief camp. Video footage taken from a helicopter showed swarms of people fighting amongst one another in Dallas' streets, but there was little else in the reports detailing the spills and the nature of the riots. Texas' governor gave a speech about people needing to work together throughout the crisis and assist others in need wherever possible. Stewart regretted his choice of layover locations.

In the airport, large groups of angry people crowded around the ticket desks, shouting about the injustice of not being allowed into the city while a steady stream of panicked people flowed in from the check-in area. Fear, irritation, and anger were the most prevalent emotions amongst the travelers and Stewart was thankful he didn't have long to wait. Knowing he didn't have time for his usual routine, he settled into a seat by his gate and pulled a journal out of his carry-on. The chaos around him fed his imagination.

Throughout his travels, Stewart had grown accustomed to waiting for his connecting flight, and over the years, he'd learned a few tricks to pass the time. It was his routine, after disembarking, to find a restaurant nearest to his connecting flight, sit at a table overlooking the crowds, and order a sandwich with a beer. While waiting for his food, he'd review his next stop - what doctors he was visiting and which drugs he would promote. After his food came, he'd turn his attention to the crowded walkways and filled seats, waiting for someone to catch his attention. Upon finding an individual who interested him, Stewart would then make up a story about who they were, where they were going, and why.

For example, if Stewart saw a harried mother totting two screaming children, he'd come up with a story like: the woman is on the run after kidnapping her children from their father. He was a high-level mobster who gave them whatever they asked for, but his position within the mob meant they could easily become targets to rival groups. She's taking them away to protect them, but they fight against her - they want to go back, not understanding the dangers. The woman, however, knows that if she returns she'll be the one to pay, and probably with her life. Disappearing is her only remaining option.

As he sat and watched people interact, Stewart scribbled down notes in his journal; the appearance of the people involved, the motivation of his characters, the fictional events which lead up to their being in the airport, and the outcome of their imagined situations. While he'd always dreamt of becoming a writer and was very good with character building, his attempts always fell short when it came to putting fingers to keys. He lacked the skills to develop his ideas into a full-length manuscript. Instead, he contented himself with filling the journal with his observations and imaginings.

Watching the group of impatient and haggard people waiting for the flight to Miami, Stewart's mind began to fill with stories; one man in particular caught his attention. Sitting in the corner alone, he cast paranoid glances at those passing him by; flinching away from anyone who came too close. A sheen of sweat glistened on his brow, emphasising his sickly pallor and his body shook with chills. The man seemed to be suffering from the flu given his quiet coughing and heavy breathing, but he also favored his left side, puzzling Stewart with the strange combination of symptoms. The man looked up and noticed Stewart watching him; he flipped Stewart off. Quickly averting his eyes, Stewart's face heated with embarrassment that he'd been caught staring. Letting his gaze drift over the growing crowd around the gate, he made notes about the panicked state of the people, all the while wondering about the cause of the civil unrest in the area. When a man sat down next to him with a weary sigh, Stewart set down his journal and struck up a conversation, determined to find out what was really going on in the city.

"Are you from this area?" Stewart asked; the man nodded his reply. "What's happening out there?"

"People are attacking one another," the man said with a shaky voice. Stewart frowned, not understanding what the man meant; he just shrugged and went on, "I live in Arlington and this morning I woke up to my neighbour screaming bloody murder. When I looked out the window, I saw people wandering in the street. They seemed confused - taking a few steps in one direction before turning and stumbling in another. Some were banging on doors and windows and whenever a car drove down the road, they all swarmed after it making these hideous moaning noises." The man shuddered as if the moans still echoed in his head.

"So are you going on a trip or did you just decide to up and leave because of what's happening?" Stewart nodded to the carry-on sitting at the man's feet. Given his rumpled appearance, it seemed that he'd grabbed whatever clothes had been lying around and threw them on before rushing out of the house. From his left came a loud, rattling cough, but the man went on with his tale and Stewart dismissed it.

"I was supposed to work today, but as I was getting out of the shower I saw a group of people break through the patio door of the house behind mine. I'm friends with the family who lives there so I called to warn them but didn't get an answer. I heard three gunshots and then I thought I heard screaming, but by that point, I knew I had to get far, far away." The man chewed on his nail and Stewart noticed that he'd chewed them down to the quick; they looked painful. "Lately we've been seeing all sorts of reports on the television about rioting in San Antonio, Austin, and the surrounding area. That every time the rioting spreads, the army arrives and starts moving people to that camp in Oklahoma. I didn't want to end up in some camp, so I packed my bag and called to reserve a seat - I didn't care where just so long as I was out of Texas. They had a few seats left on the flight to Miami and I figured that while anywhere would be better than here, the beach would be a nice bonus."

"Did you talk to any of your neighbours when you left?" Stewart's curiosity was piqued. He hadn't really paid attention to the news lately, but he'd at least heard of the rioting spreading through Texas.

There was another fit of coughing and Stewart couldn't help but look over at the man he'd noticed earlier; he looked even more ill than before if that was at all possible. People walking by gave the man a wide berth and those who'd been sitting in his section earlier, had now found seats elsewhere. How could the airline allow someone so obviously sick onto a crowded plane where the contagion could easily spread and infect the other passengers?

"...seemed to be chewing on something." The man was saying when Stewart returned his attention to him; he thought for a moment, trying to remember the context. He was about to ask the man to repeat what he'd just said, but the man continued, not noticing the lapse in Stewart's attention. "I called to her but she didn't respond and then someone slammed into the passenger side of my car," the man's face had gone pale as he spoke and his clasped hands began to shake. "It was the teenager who mowed my lawn. He was covered in blood - like he'd bathed in it or something - and his eyes weren't right either." He leaned in close and Stewart bent forward to hear his hushed words. "I don't think it's rioting over oil spills, happening out there. I think that something is making people sick and causing them act this way; that's why they're telling people to leave the area and only drink bottled water until they're out of state."

Leaning back in his chair, Stewart contemplated everything he'd been told. As a pharmaceutical rep, he knew a little about communicable diseases but not enough to determine what was plaguing the Texan population. He'd have to ask one of the doctors at his home office once he'd returned. After jotting down a few notes in his journal, he turned back to the man and said, "I have to use the facilities. Would you hold my seat for me?"

While Stewart washed his hands, the sick man from his gate stumbled into the bathroom gasping for breath; he dashed into a stall and promptly vomited. The sickly-sweet scent of bile permeated the men's room, but beneath it, Stewart noticed something else - something close to putrefaction. Not wanting to linger in the bathroom, Stewart finished washing his hands, wiping them on the trousers of his eight hundred dollar suit. Not only would drying would take too long but the odours were also growing more intense with each passing minute; he couldn't stomach another second in the small room and his pants could always be cleaned.

Hurrying out of the men's room, Stewart made his way to the gate's desk. The attendant acknowledged him with a nod and he stepped up, ready to demand a seat change if the sickly man proved to be near him on the flight. When he opened his mouth to speak, however, he changed his mind on how he'd approach the situation - the poor woman standing behind the desk looked as if she'd pulled a double shift. She appeared fatigued with dark circles beneath her eyes.

"How may I assist you sir?" she said, trying to smile; it appeared more like a grimace to Stewart.

"There is a very sick gentleman in the bathroom." He chose his words carefully, knowing he'd fare far better if he didn't immediately get the woman's defenses up. "I noticed him sitting over there," he pointed to the area he'd seen the man in earlier, "and was wondering if I could possibly change my seat to the front of the plane. I'd like to put as much distance as possible between us."

The attendant's smile faltered, but she held out her hand for his boarding pass. She typed for a moment before looking up from her monitor. "I'm sorry sir, but you are already booked for seat B5 in business class; we don't have any seats available closer to the cockpit. The flight is almost fully booked and I'm unable to determine where the man you are speaking of is sitting without his boarding pass."

"How are you even allowing him onto a plane full of healthy people?" Stewart demanded, his pleasant demeanor slipping into irritation. "Do you not understand how his germs will spread in such close quarters? What if he's in first-class? Will I be able to move my seat to economy once we board?"

"Sir," the attendant's shoulders slumped as she looked up at Stewart with a weary expression, "due to the rioting, we have an increase in requests for flights out of the area. Your flight is almost entirely booked and I'm anticipating that it will be fully booked by takeoff. We are trying to accommodate all of our passengers, including flying in several more empty planes. I can put you on another flight to Miami if you'd like, but it won't be departing for another two and a half hours."

Stewart bristled, "I have an important client meeting I cannot be late for. Why can't you move the sick man to that flight instead?" Although he hadn't meant to, he realized he was shouting at the poor woman.

"Sir," she said again, this time with exasperation, "I cannot request that he remain behind and wait for the next flight when there is room for him on the one he's currently booked on. I'm sorry sir, but there isn't anything I can do."

"If I come down with whatever he has, I'm suing this airline," Stewart growled, snatching his boarding pass from the attendant and marching back to his seat in a huff.

Flopping into the chair, Stewart realized he wouldn't be making his dinner appointment. Upon arriving in Miami, he'd have to stop at his hotel and shower before meeting with his client; otherwise, he'd spend the evening feeling contaminated. Typing furiously on his smartphone, he sent a message to the doctor, asking to move their appointment to an early breakfast instead. Slipping his phone back into his carryon, Stewart eyed the man who'd saved him his seat. He wanted to write down all he'd told him but instead Stewart asked, "What's your name?"

"Peter Ferris," he replied, extending his hand to Stewart.

"Stewart Witt," Stewart said in turn and shook Peter's hand. "What seat are you in?" he asked, watching the bathroom door as it swung open and the sickly man stumbled back to his seat, wiping his mouth on his sleeve.

"Umm," Peter looked at his boarding pass before saying, "seat D11. Why?"

"Because, they won't move that man to another flight." Stewart nodded towards the man who'd once again begun to clear out the seats around him with his coughing.

"There is a widow who lives alone on my street; I think she came down with the same flu," Peter said in hushed tones. "Two days ago my neighbour's wife told me that she took soup over to her and tried to get her to go to the hospital, but the old woman refused." He shivered, "Now that I think back on it, I believe I saw Mrs. Robertson wandering in the street with the others."

"There's more than just rioting going on here," Stewart said, knowing in his gut that his assumption was right - he just wasn't sure what the 'more' could possibly be.

Boarding passes please...

"Flight 1028 is now boarding at gate A26." A calm voice spoke over the chatter of the crowd. "We will begin boarding those with seats in business class along with any passengers requiring assistance; all other passengers will be called to board in the order of their seating. Thank you for choosing American Airlines and have a good flight."

When the speaker finished, Stewart gathered his belongings, tucking them into his carryon; he turned to Peter, "We should grab dinner once we're in Miami; I had to cancel my plans for tonight."

Peter genuinely smiled for the first time since he'd sat down next to Stewart. "Count me in."

"See you on the other side." Stewart saluted before walking away.

Getting into line, Stewart pulled out his boarding pass and was about to hand it over to the attendant when a sickly-sweet smell permeated the air around him. Glancing over his shoulder, Stewart felt his skin begin to prickle; the sick man stood in the line only two people behind him. His eyes were sunken in their sockets and Stewart could swear the man seemed worse than before. Why was he already in line? Did he have a business class seat? Stewart didn't think he could deal with the man's coughing and horrible smell for the entire flight.

"You'll find seat B5 on your right hand side." The attendant said after pulling the boarding pass from Stewart's hand.

He turned back to the woman, "Thank you." He gave her a tight smile as she handed the ticket back to him; he hurried down the jetway, eager to get into his seat.

Stewart had just stowed his carryon when the now familiar rattle of the man's cough echoed down the jetway. Watching the doorway with trepidation, he lowered himself into his seat. Relief filled him when the man came into the plane, leaning heavily on an attendant, and the two walked slowly past Stewart heading back to the rear of the plane. Finally at ease, Stewart put his head back and closed his eyes, determined to get some sleep.

Stewart drifted in and out of consciousness while the plane boarded and after an indeterminate amount of time, he felt the plane being taxied out to the runway. They began to pick up speed and the last thought Stewart had before sleep took him was how glad he was to be on his way out of Dallas.

Rude awakening...

"Oh my God!" someone shrieked, dragging Stewart back to consciousness. "Heather, come help me get him off of her." There was a crash in the galley and a flight attendant brushed past Stewart.

"What is he doing?" someone asked loudly, just before a scream filled the plane's cabin.

Thundering footsteps approached business class and Stewart turned to see what all the commotion was about in the rear of the cabin. An attendant, with splashes of blood on her crisp uniform, brushed aside the curtain that separated economy from business and ran for the cockpit door. Stewart gaped at the sight of the woman and wondered what could possibly be happening in economy to cause such a mess.

"Captain," she shouted as she pounded on the door, leaving bloody handprints behind, "Captain, there's a situation out here and we need to make an emergency landing." The cockpit door swung open and the attendant collapsed inside; the door closed again with a soft click, preventing Stewart from overhearing whatever she'd been about to say regarding the unfolding emergency.

A muffled voice from the rear of the plane shouted over the growing hysteria of the passengers. "Everyone, please take your seats. Anyone who needs to use the facilities please go to the front of the plane until we have this matter resolved."

"I'm a doctor." Another voice, this one clearly male, spoke over the clamor.

There was a moment of silence and Stewart imagined all the passengers turning to see who'd stepped up to assist. "Clear the aisle and let him pass." The first voice said in an authoritative tone.

Stewart could hear indistinct murmurs and shuffling from the rear of the plane. Curious about what has happening, he leaned out of his seat and attempted to see around the curtain. The woman sitting beside him asked, "What's going on?"

"I'm not sure," Stewart replied. "All I can see is people moving around." He was about to get out of his seat and see for himself when the speakers overhead crackled and the voice of a man began to speak.

"This is the captain speaking," the disembodied voice said. His tone was commanding and reassuring; the cabin fell into silence as all listened to what the captain had to say. "Due to the nature of the disturbance in economy, we will be making an unscheduled stop in Slidell. The runway is shorter than normally recommended for a plane this size and weight, so it will be a rough landing. I'll ask that all passengers please take their seat and fasten their seatbelts until we've safely landed. Once we're on the runway, we'll be able to determine..." Another scream echoed from the back of the plane, drowning out whatever the captain had been saying; several more screams of fear quickly followed the first.

Jumping to his feet, Stewart hurried back to the curtain separating business and economy. He flung the curtain aside and rushed down the aisle, searching the seats for Peter - his new friend would know what was happening. At the rear of the cabin, just outside of the lavatory, several attendants struggled to subdue a thrashing passenger while the others knelt on their seats, watching the struggle but doing nothing to assist. Upon spotting Peter sitting quietly in his seat, staring forward with wide, terrified eyes, Stewart rushed over to him and knelt down.

"Peter!" When he got no acknowledgement in response, he gently shook the man's shoulder. "Peter, what happened?"

"Sir," a soft feminine voice spoke from beside Stewart.

"What?" he snapped, not taking his eyes off Peter, whose glassy gaze slowly began to focus on Stewart.

"I'll need you to return to your seat and fasten your seatbelt. The captain has requested that all passengers..."

"I'll go sit once I've spoken to my friend and made sure he's okay." He cut the woman short; he was out of patience. "Go do whatever you need to do. I won't cause problems and I'll return to my seat as soon as I know my friend here isn't going into shock." He looked back to Peter, whose eyes seemed to have regained some of their clarity, and dismissed the attendant.

"Kimmy," someone called from the back of the plane.

Stewart was relieved when the attendant hurried away, leaving him alone with Peter. He turned back to his friend, "Buddy, what's going on?"

Peter's lips moved but no sound came out. Stewart placed a hand on Peter's shoulder and the human contact seemed to revive him somewhat. "I... I saw the guy who was sick back at the terminal." His gaze became distant once again; Stewart gently shook his shoulder, trying to get Peter to tell the story in a coherent manner.

"What about the sick guy?" Stewart asked, trying not to grow impatient with him.

"I noticed him when he began to cause a scene in front of the bathroom. He looked really sick - delirious almost - and I think he began to beat on the door because it was occupied. An attendant came to see what he was causing a fuss about and then he just collapsed... he just fell into the attendant's arms, limp. His weight must have been too much for her because she fell with him. I think his weight pinned her to the floor." Peter's eyes flicked to the other passengers sitting around him and he lowered his voice so only Stewart could hear. "Another attendant went to assist, to see what the matter was, but as she approached he began twitching..."

A long moan came from the rear of the cabin followed by another scream. The passengers sitting in the rear of the plane surged out of their seats with renewed panic. Peter shrunk lower into his seat and his eyes darted towards the back of the plane. People pushed past Stewart, not caring that he was squatting in the aisle and blocking their path.

"He... he bit..." Peter's voice broke, "there was so much blood, and she screamed and he moaned." Peter visibly shook as he tried to retell what he'd witnessed and Stewart had to strain to hear him over the commotion caused by the other passengers around them. "I don't understand." He grabbed Stewarts arm, squeezing tightly; his eyes had a wild look about them, "another attendant tased him and he began to convulse and then laid still. They got him off the poor girl, but she'd had a huge chunk of skin torn from the side of her face." Peter shivered, remembering what he'd witnessed. "Then they sent another attendant to speak to the captain; or at least I assumed that's what she was doing. They tried to get everyone settled and they did for the most part - that was until the man came out of the bathroom. We all thought the flight attendant had died from shock and blood loss... the doctor stopped attending to her wounds you know, like she was dead... but as soon as the man came out of the restroom she turned to her side and bit the man on the leg." His voice shook when he turned to see the carnage behind him. "That's when you came." Peter took a shuddering breath, "Thank god you came; I thought I was going to lose my shit."

Stewart glanced to the rear of the plane, now vacated of all its passengers, and for the first time noticed the sick man squirming on the floor beside the open lavatory door. While his hands had been bound with a white zip-strip, his head still swiveled from side to side, clacking his teeth at anything that moved near him. Beside him lay the flight attendant; she too was restrained but Stewart could still see the missing portion of her cheek. Beneath the blood, he could see a glint of bone and her gnashing teeth. Behind the two squirming people on the floor, knelt a man bent over the prone figure of another twitching flight attendant. Stewart couldn't see what the man was doing to the poor woman, but he felt the sudden urge to vomit.

"That's the guy who was in the bathroom." Peter whispered breathily. "See the bite on his ankle?"

Stewart's gaze shifted to the man's foot and he couldn't help but gasp. The man's left pant leg was torn, revealing the extent of the wound. Beneath the slick of blood and the tattered fabric, the flesh on the man's ankle was gone, revealing bone. "She did that to him?" he indicated the restrained flight attendant still struggling on the floor.

Peter only nodded, watching with wide eyes as the prone attendant beneath the man began to twitch.

A passenger in the crowd of people, trying to get away from the chaos at the back of the cabin, shrieked when the attendant's hand spasmed. The man kneeling over her suddenly lost interest and turned to face the cabin's occupants. Horrified gasps rippled through the huddled passengers as they took in the man's gore covered face and the gaping hole in the twitching attendant's stomach.

When the woman sat up Stewart heard several thumps behind him and turned to the crowd, stunned to realize some of the passengers had fainted dead away. Chaos erupted a moment later when both the man and the woman struggled to their feet.

"How can she be standing?" Stewart overheard someone say in disbelief.

He looked around for an exit and was ready to lunge for the door, when he realized the full extent of their situation - they were thirty-thousand-plus feet in the air, and opening the door would destabilize the pressure in the cabin, probably causing catastrophic system failure. For a moment, the thought that crashing would be far preferable to being eaten crossed Stewart's mind, but when a male attendant stepped forward calling for silence, he quelled his suicidal thoughts.

"I need two volunteers to help me restrain and secure the inflicted individuals." Two men raised their hands and Stewart was thankful he didn't have to offer his assistance. At that moment, the plane began to descend and the sudden change seemed to startle everyone aboard. The attendant whistled loudly but didn't speak until the passengers quieted down. "We must be approaching the airstrip for the emergency landing. I'll need everyone, other than the two volunteers, to return to their seats in an orderly fashion and put on their seatbelts."

The two men and the attendant made their way to the back of the plane, using a pole they'd found to push the two mangled people back into the galley, all the while discussing how exactly they were going to subdue them. The other passengers slowly made their way back to their seats, trusting everything was finally under control. Stewart was furious because an unscheduled stop meant he'd have to move his business meeting yet again.

"I'll see you when we land." He patted Peter's shoulder before turning to make his way back to his own seat; as he turned away, Stewart noted the glaze in Peter's eyes had returned.

"What's going on back there?" the woman sitting next to Stewart asked when he flopped into his seat.

Laying his head back against the headrest, Stewart mumbled, "They're attacking one another... eating each other."

"What? Who's eating whom?"

She cringed back when Stewart turned a furious glare on her. "Several of the attendants and two passengers; they aren't acting like sane people." The plane adjusted its altitude once again, making Stewart's stomach heave. "Excuse me" he said to his neighbour and hurried to the front of the plane. Once he'd locked himself in the lavatory, Stewart finally gave in to the urges of his churning stomach.

The end of flight 1028...

Stewart hadn't been in the bathroom for more than ten minutes when the screams started anew. Suddenly, Stewart couldn't imagine leaving the safety of the bathroom; he sat down and listened to the chaos unfolding in the cramped plane, wishing he'd paid the extra fare for a direct flight. If he hadn't been so concerned with cost savings, he could have already been sitting poolside with a cocktail.

"Get him off," someone shrieked before another scream ripped through the cabin; any replies were quickly drown out by the panicked cries of the other passengers.

Someone pounded on a nearby door and Stewart assumed another attendant was trying to speak with the captain - he hoped they'd land soon and he could get off the worst flight of his life.

The pounding ceased, "What?" a deep voice demand and Stewart imagined the Captain standing in the doorway with a scowl.

The screams from the cabin had reached an all-time high but Stewart still couldn't resist a peek; he needed to know what was happening. He cracked the door open and peeked out, just in time to watch the disembowelled attendant wrap her bloody arms around the neck of a man wearing a captain's uniform. The man struggled to disentangle himself from the woman's grasp, but she held on as the captain stumbled backwards into the cockpit.

The floor beneath Stewart's feet suddenly tilted, causing him to lose his balance and slam into the lavatory door; it closed with a thump beneath his weight. Stunned, he struggled to right himself, but the odd tilt of the plane made it impossible. He lay back against the door as his heart thundered in his chest; dawning horror filled him as he realized that the plane was going to crash. He'd seen the attendant's teeth break the captain's skin, but it hadn't appeared to be a fatal bite - just a nibble really. The plane had been in a dive for only a few seconds, but Stewart suspected that if he'd been capable of correcting the angle of decent, the captain would have already done so. His mind wandered to the co-pilot; wouldn't he be able to regain control over the plane?

Bracing himself against the wall, Stewart carefully lifted the door. Bloody, searching fingers poked through the crack and Stewart slammed the door closed again. The bones in the fingers snapped but their owner didn't try to pull back, instead there was a thump and the door hit Stewart's back.

"Occupied," he shouted as he braced to close the door again.

There was another thump and again the door cracked open. The airplane banked wildly to the left, causing Stewart to lose his footing and the door to fly open. Peter stood bracing himself against the wall, or at least that was Stewart's first thought. He looked carefully at the man he'd only met a few hours earlier, and knew that his new friend was no longer present in his body. What he was, Stewart wasn't sure; he was sure he wasn't looking at Peter.

There was an awful bite on the side of Peter's neck, exposing torn muscle and his severed trachea. His eyes were pale, with a milky film coating them and his teeth clacked together making the most unsettling sound. Part of his nose had been bitten off and Stewart noted with disgust that a portion of his tongue also seemed to be missing. Bile rose in his throat as he stared into the vacant eyes of the man he'd come to like only a few short hours earlier.

How had things spiraled so quickly out of control and what was really plaguing the state of Texas? Stewart didn't think it was just a few oil spills and rioting. He thought back to the footage he'd seen earlier and suddenly understood why all of it had been taken from a helicopter. No one in their right mind would willingly go shoot ground level footage if these things were the cause of the rioting. He also had a sneaking suspicion that the government was trying to cover up the true reason for the rioting until they could get it under control - but would they be able to? Stewart was witnessing firsthand how quickly this thing could spread and he doubted the army would be able to stand against them for long.

The plane tilted again and the screams coming from the cabin amplified. Peter's corpse was knocked back against the galley doors and several bloody figures crashed down the aisle and through the open cockpit door. An attendant flew past, hitting the doorframe with a sickening crunch. Her limp body lay half on the galley doors while her legs dangled into the cockpit; within moments grasping hands pulled at her and she disappeared through the doorway.

Stewart, now kneeling on the bathroom wall, knew there was no way he was getting off this plane alive. Tears streamed down his face as unbidden thoughts of his estranged wife and son filled his mind. They'd have to face this horror without him. He wouldn't be there to protect them because now Stewart understood that this plague could not be stopped. He wished for his phone, wanting to hear his family's voices one last time and tell them how much he loved them. Not being a religious man Stewart wasn't sure if his prayers would be heard, but he still sent up a silent plea that they'd survive what was coming.

Having regained its footing on the wall of the galley, the Peter-monster poked its head into the bathroom. He raised his arms and let out a long, pitiful moan. Stewart pressed himself into a corner of the small room, wishing he wasn't about to die in the lavatory. The Peter-monster's fingers closed around Stewart's ankle and he whispered a goodbye to his family. For a split second, the plane shook violently and a moment later went up in a ball of flame.

Aftermath...

A blackened figure stumbled from the smouldering wreckage of the fuselage; its hair was gone, burned away along with its clothes and the remaining arm hung limply at its side. Movement in the nearby bushes caught its attention.

"That plane crashed somewhere around here" a man said in the growing darkness; the burned corpse awkwardly turned and shuffled towards the sound of the voice.

"We've called the police," said another voice; this time the speaker was female, "we should let them handle it."

The first voice responded "What if there are survivors?" there was more rustling of bushes, closer now. The corpse paused, swiveling its head back and forth before letting out a long low moan.

"What's that?" a third voice squeaked.

"Over here. Someone's alive!" the rustling of the underbrush quickened; the corpse paused behind a large tree as a light danced through the shadows.

"What if we can't find them?" There was a long pause and the corpse shuffled forward.

"Then we'll tell the rescue crew that we heard someone moaning in this area, but for now we should keep searching." The brush began to rustle again, coming ever closer. The zombie moaned, shuffling towards the approaching searchers. Soon a beam of light found the walking corpse and someone gasped.

"You shouldn't be walking around," one of the disembodied voices said, aghast.

The light grew as the group hurried towards the zombie, not understanding the situation they'd found themselves in. The zombie blinked, not seeing as much as sensing the approaching meal. Hunger was too small of a word for the gnawing pit in the monsters stomach; it was ravenous, and only wanted to consume one thing - the warm flesh that was quickly approaching. The moment it felt an arm wrapped around its charred shoulders, the zombie pivoted and bit down on the tender flesh and for a split-second, it was satisfied.

Volume 10: A Boat to Nowhere

24 hours earlier...

Sarah was watching TV when her cell phone rang; the caller ID read Aisha Peterson. While she hadn't been expecting the call, she was always happy to hear from her BFF. Snatching her phone off the table, Sarah muted the TV and answered with a cheerful, "Hey Aisha, I thought you were staying in tonight."

"Change of plans." Aisha shouted into her ear.

Sarah pulled the phone away from the side of her head with a frown; there was a cacophony of noise in the background, making it difficult to hear Aisha's words. "What? I can barely hear you," she shouted back. "Are you watching an action movie?"

"I feel like I'm in an action movie," there was a moment's pause and Sarah could make out the sounds of automatic gunfire in the background. Aisha continued, "Listen Sarah, there's something going on at the construction site. The army's here..."

There was another loud boom. *What the hell is going on there?* Sarah raised her voice in order for Aisha to hear her. "The army? What's the army doing there?"

Rather than answering, Aisha quickly went on, "Listen to me. You need to get as many supplies as you can and however many people you can gather and head for Curt's place on the Gulf. Something really bad is about to hit Houston and you need to get out."

"What are you talking about Aisha?" Sarah snorted, "Curt just got back yesterday from being out on the water for a month and Heather doesn't want any company for a few days."

"Just fucking do it," Aisha snapped; Sarah pressed her lips together so as not to say something she'd later regret. "Gather who and what you can. Make sure everyone has enough food and water to last at least a month and get to Curt's. I'll try to get there within the next twenty-four hours."

Still irritated by Aisha's outburst and not understanding what her friend was telling her to do Sarah said, "Whoa, hold on a minute. Why do you want me to do this?"

"There's a horde of fucking zombies headed into Houston and if you don't get out now, you may never be able to."

There was another long pause, as Sarah's mouth fell open. *Has she lost her mind?* She snorted, "Zombies?" Maybe Aisha was high..."Make sure to bring some of whatever you're on, next time you come over."

Taking a deep breath, Aisha responded and said slowly, "I'm not on anything Sarah. Please just do as I say." Another boom, this one seemingly right next to Aisha, made Sarah pull the phone away again. Even with it three feet from her ear, she clearly heard Aisha shout, "Whoever just threw that fucking grenade is going to lose their balls."

Fear flooded Sarah. "Aisha?" Who was she talking to and what was her friend doing messing around with grenades? When there was no response, she shouted her friends name with more urgency, "Aisha!" *What have you gotten yourself into now?*

Sounding exhausted, Aisha finally replied, "Please, please just do as I ask."

"Okay fine," Sarah huffed, "but if this turns out to be some kind of sick joke, you can be the one to explain it to the others."

"I wish it were a joke." A sick thwacking sound followed another explosion. "I've got to go Sarah but please do as I ask." Aisha said with urgency.

Sarah's stomach churned and despite her best efforts, her voice still shook when she asked, "This is real, isn't it? It's not a joke."

Aisha sighed in relief, "No joke. Get friends, get supplies and get to Curt and Heather's. Tell the others I'll meet them there as soon as I can."

Choking back a sob, Sarah said, "You better show up."

"I will." Aisha promised and hung up.

Still clutching the phone to her ear, Sarah sat for another minute listening to dead air. She set it down with shaking hands, unsure how she was going to convince her friends to pack up and leave. As Sarah hurried into her room to pack the necessities, a growing sense of dread filled her. Aisha wouldn't have been so adamant, nor sounded so scared when she called, if they weren't all in grave danger.

Out of time...

Sirens sounded in the distance but the boatyard seemed eerily silent. Sarah had been pacing the length of the deck for the better part of two hours, and still there was no sign of Aisha. Her cell phone hadn't worked since arriving in Galveston twenty-two hours earlier so she had no way of contacting Aisha and her BFF was already running an hour late.

"She'll be here," Heather said gently from behind Sarah, making her start.

Sarah took a steadying breath; her hand pressed to her heart, "You scared me." Nothing felt real for Sarah since she'd answered that call, but she was eternally grateful that Aisha had thought to warn them.

Smiling sheepishly, Heather apologized and placed a hand on Sarah's arm. "You've been up here since before the sun set. Your dinner's gotten cold."

"I'm not hungry." Sarah folded her arms over her chest, turning back to watch the empty boatyard for signs of Aisha's arrival. *I don't know if I'll ever be hungry again.*

Only twenty-four hours earlier, she'd been trying to convince her friends she wasn't joking and now everyone was in full-on survival mode. They'd refused to believe her at first - that was until Carmen, who lived on the west side of Houston, confirmed Aisha's story via texts with image attachments; within the hour, they were packed and ready to leave. During the hour drive to Galveston, Carmen shared what she'd seen and what they were dealing with. For her, it had started with explosions lighting the horizon, then the ragged people staggering down the streets. Finally she shared how she'd seen them attack; how ignorant people went out into the street to help, and in return were torn apart.

"The guys should be back by now," Heather said, referring to Tomos and Quinn. They'd volunteered to pick up a few last minute supplies in Galveston while the group waited for Aisha's arrival.

"Maybe they got caught up in the mayhem." An uneasy feeling settled into the pit of Sarah's stomach. "The sirens have been going non-stop for the past few hours."

"I still can't believe this is happening." Beside Sarah, Heather shivered. "Just yesterday Curt and I were cuddled up on the couch, watching a zombie movie and laughing at the absurdity of it."

Sarah and Carmen, along with Tomos and Quinn, had shown up on Heather and Curt's doorstep, telling their irritated friends about the horrible things they'd heard on the radio as they'd left the city. Before they were finished telling their story in its entirety, Curt was on his feet packing, while on the phone warning others. His plan was to get to his one-hundred foot fishing trawler, A-Fishy-Nado, and head out for the open water of the Gulf, believing they'd be safe far away from land. Still disbelieving, Heather didn't want to hear any of it - even after Carmen took out her phone and showed her the proof. Sarah still wasn't entirely sure that Heather believed the dead were rising and eating the living.

"It's not so funny now." Sarah shivered despite the night's warmth. Lights flashed in the boatyard and she heard the distant sound of an engine drawing closer. "Please let it be Aisha," she whispered beneath her breath.

Heather turned away from the rails, "I'll go tell Curt that Tomos and Quinn are back. He can get the engine started and we'll be ready to leave by the time they arrive and unload."

"Wait." Sarah grabbed Heather's arm; Heather glanced back at her with a look of sympathy. "What if it's Aisha? We can't leave yet."

Heather slowly shook her head. "I'd recognize the sound of Tomos' car anywhere." She wrapped her arm around Sarah's shoulder, pulling her in for an embrace. "I'm sorry but we can't wait for Aisha any longer. She's had a full day to get to us, and as much as I don't want to say it, she may never make it no matter how long we wait."

"Don't say that," Sarah sobbed, knowing in her heart that if her BFF had been able to get south, out of Houston, that she would have arrived already.

"Maybe she couldn't get across the bridge." Heather offered the alternative in an effort to comfort Sarah. "Maybe the roads were too jammed up with traffic and she decided to head north instead."

Sarah nodded, swiping her arm across her tear-streaked face. "Maybe."

Headlights suddenly illuminated the women; they both turned as a car fishtailed off the paved road and onto the dirt road of the parking lot. It skidded to a halt at the bottom of the gangplank and the door flew open. Quinn spilled out of the driver's side and clumsily ran around to the passenger side door. "Get Curt," he panted, "I need help getting Tomos onto the boat."

"What happened?" Sarah asked, leaning over the rail. Behind her, Heather dashed for the stairs that lead up to the boat's bridge where Curt was performing the final checks.

"We ran into a crowd of people with the same idea as us." Quinn jerked the passenger door open, catching the lump that sagged out. "A fight broke out over the remaining water bottles and Tomos got beat up pretty bad. What we managed to get is in the trunk." He grunted as he propped the lump against the side of the car. "Can you help unload it while I check out Tomos?" Sarah nodded, hurrying down the gangplank to the rear of the car; Quinn kept talking. "While everyone was throwing punches at one another, a group of those things joined the fray and then things got really interesting."

"You saw them in Galveston?" Sarah gasped as she pulled out several bags packed with supplies. She glanced over her shoulder, suddenly convinced that zombies were creeping up behind her, but the immediate area was still and silent.

"Yeah," Quinn said, coming around to the trunk and helping Sarah lift out the three large water jugs, "we saw masses of those things crossing the causeway on our way back." For the first time, Sarah noticed Quinn's swollen and red cheek.

She was about to ask who'd hit him when Curt's deep voice boomed from the deck of the boat. "What were you doing all the way over there?" Sarah wondered the same thing.

Quinn looked up, and sighed. "Most of the stores have been cleaned out already. We had a hard time finding water and Tomos knew of a place over on Harborside Drive, so we went to check it out." He shook his head, "it was a bad call on our part - we almost didn't make it back."

"Other than being beat up, did either of you come into close contact with those things?" Curt now stood over Tomos, looking down at him with cool detachment.

Not liking the calculating look, Sarah went to Tomos' side, checking for any wounds that weren't from the fight. He was badly beaten and blood covered most of his face, but she guessed most of it was from the gashes on his head.

"If you're wondering if he got bitten by those things," Quinn snapped, "no, he didn't. He got hit over the head with a bottle, which is where I think most of the blood is coming from but I didn't see any of those things near him when I pulled him out of the pileup."

Curt scowled, muttering a curse. "He's my friend and I don't want to leave him here, but if he's been bitten, he's as good as dead and bringing him aboard will only put the rest of us in danger."

Quinn grabbed Curt by the front of his shirt, pulling him close so they were standing nose to nose. "He's just beat up; we're not leaving him." He growled, releasing Curt with a shove, "and besides, you have no clue about how this thing is spread. For all we know its air born and we're all infected."

Curt shook his head and Sarah found herself shaking hers as well. "Zombies one-o-one - if someone is bitten they'll become a zombie; it's just a matter of time."

Quinn barked out a harsh laugh, "and you're the expert on zombies now? Hollywood and real life are very different things my friend. We have no idea what is causing this or how it's transmitted."

"Now, now boys." Heather interjected; she turned to Curt, "We can't just leave him here babe; I've looked for bite marks and haven't found anything that even remotely looks like one. Tomos has just been beat up and badly - we need to get him inside so I can clean up his wounds." Curt began to protest but Heather simply held up her hand, silencing him. "If it will make you feel better, we can put him in the other stateroom and secure the door. I'm sure the rest of our friends won't mind sharing the other berths in the aft."

"Fine," Curt growled through clenched teeth, "all aboard."

As the others moved the supplies onto the boat, Sarah stood, watching intently for a sign that Aisha was close by - other than the distant sirens, everything was quiet. They'd all agreed that if Aisha wasn't there by the time the guys returned from the last minute supply run, they were outward bound without her. Now that the time was at hand, Sarah couldn't bring herself to leave. Maybe she could convince Curt to wait for another forty-five minutes. What could another hour possibly cost them?

"We can't wait Sarah," Curt said softly, from behind her.

"But what if she's almost here?"

"What ifs will only get you killed. Look at how fast this has already spread and tell me you want to risk waiting a little longer." Curt sighed, "We can no longer be who we were yesterday. When we found out about the zombies, our old lives were gone - lost forever. The world will never be the same again and if you want to survive, you'll have to accept that. Become someone whose number one priority is survival at any cost - even if it's at the cost of another; people too weak to realize that won't survive."

Sarah turned and smiled weakly at Curt, "how did you become the resident expert?"

Curt laughed, "I was a zombie fanatic long before this and I've always known what I'd do if the zombie apocalypse ever came about." He sobered, taking Sarah by the shoulders and turning her towards the boat. "Aisha sent you to me for a reason - she and I spent a lot of time theorizing plans for survival while watching zombie movies. If she wasn't able to get here, I'm sure she's found another way to survive."

They were outward bound less than twenty minutes later. Sarah remained on the deck, watching for signs Aisha until the slip was out of sight. The last thing she saw on land was several figures, stumbling out of the shadows.

Seasick...

"I saw her swing the bottle and then everything went black." Chagrined, Tomos ducked his head as the rest of the table laughed good-naturedly. Seven of them sat in the galley playing poker while Tomos, who'd woken up twelve hours earlier, regaled them with the story of his trip into the chaos of Galveston.

"Taken out by an angry old lady," Carmen ribbed him. "It's a good thing Quinn was there to rescue your sorry ass." They all laughed again.

"Speaking of Quinn..." Sarah glanced around the room, her eyes settling on Heather who was curled up with her nose in a book. "Heather, have you had a chance to check in on him lately?" Not long after setting sail, Quinn began to complain about being seasick and retired to the bunk above Tomos' in the stateroom; he hadn't come out since.

Heather looked up from her book, shaking her head. "No. The last time I was in to check on him he didn't want to wake up. When I finally roused him enough to get him to talk, he just told me to get out and leave him be."

"Men can be such bears to wake up." Tina giggled, casting a knowing look at her boyfriend, Caden. Sarah didn't know the two well since they were friends of Heather and Curt's, but the couple seemed nice enough. She knew Caden worked for Curt's fishing company, but knew little else about the two.

As most of them had been up for over twenty-four hours, the first thing they'd done after setting out was to get some sleep. After their naps, they'd worked at storing their previsions in the galley's pantry while discussing how to divvy up the daily chores and keep themselves from going stir-crazy. Since they weren't sure how far the contagion would spread or how long they'd be on the boat, Curt explained he'd charted a course for the Florida Keys, hoping the zombies hadn't yet reached the area. His plan was to stop, refuel the boat and pick up additional provisions so they could stay on A-Fishy-Nado indefinitely - no one disagreed. Now, after eighteen hours on the boat, they'd settled in and Sarah, Tomos and Carmen were getting to know Tina and Caden a little better.

"I suppose I should go check on Quinn since he did pull my ass out of that brawl." Tomos stood and stretched his lanky body; the boat swayed beneath him causing him to stumble as he walked towards the galley doors. "It's going to be hard adjusting to life on a boat," he said with a chuckle after catching himself on a nearby table.

"You'll get your sea legs soon enough," Heather said, not taking her nose from her book.

"I'll be back in a few," Tomos said as he rounded the corner and disappeared down the corridor.

"He's so thin," Sarah overheard Tina whisper to Caden, "Like scary skinny for a guy."

Caden hushed her with a look that Sarah couldn't read. "I'm going to check on Curt and see if he needs anything," he said, getting to his feet.

Sarah watched as Scott pushed through the galley doors and waited until they'd swung closed before saying, "Tomos is so skinny because last year he was diagnosed with Graves disease."

Tina flushed a deep red as she asked, "What's that?"

"It's an autoimmune disease where the immune system over stimulates the thyroid gland, causing hyperthyroidism. I don't understand the specifics, but I know it's rare for men to get it and causes severe weight loss. He's been on medication and it's seemed to help with his other symptoms, but he hasn't been able to regain the weight he lost before being diagnosed." Embarrassed, Tina got to her feet and walked over to stare out the porthole without another word. Sarah absently shuffled through the deck of cards she'd been holding. When the king of spades caught her attention, she pulled it from the deck and handed it to Carmen.

"She's fine Sarah." Carmen assured her after seeing the card.

Everyone in their small group knew that the king of spades was bad luck for Aisha; every time she lost big while playing, the king had always been in play. Seeing it now, Sarah's mind wandered to her BFF and she prayed that Aisha had somehow found safety. "You don't know that," she mumbled.

Carmen reached out, resting her hand on Sarah's, "she's hard-headed and stubborn. I doubt a few zombies could get the best of her."

A loud crash from the aft of the boat had all four women trying to look through the closed galley doors. "Tomos!" Sarah said, jumping to her feet. "I'm going to go check on him."

They heard something splinter and then everything fell silent. "I'm coming with you," said Carmen, hurrying after Sarah.

The two of them jogged down the corridor, listening for any indication of what had happened, but the only sound they could hear was the purr of the boat's engine. When they reached the stateroom Quinn had been sleeping in, Sarah stopped abruptly, making Carmen bump into her from behind.

"Why did you..." Carmen began, but stopped abruptly as she too noticed what Sarah had. Quinn lay sprawled at the foot of the bed, a chair spindle sticking out of his left eye socket. The room was a mess. Blankets from the bed were sprawled across the floor and the desk chair lay in smashed pieces. Books from the single shelf were scattered across the desktop. "Tomos?" Carmen whispered.

"Here," Tomos wheezed from their left.

Sarah and Carmen walked further into the room, careful to avoid Quinn's body.

"What happened?" Sarah asked as Tomos' legs came into view. He sat on the floor concealed by the wardrobe. She wasn't sure if she really wanted his answer.

"He... he was one of those things."

Carmen gasped and rushed towards Tomos when his blood-streaked arms became visible. "One of those things? What do you mean?"

Sarah glanced down at Quinn, really looking at him despite her churning stomach. His pallor was gray and his untouched right eye was a pale, milky white. To her horror, his bloody fingers still twitched erratically, but the rest of Quinn's corpse lay still and silent.

"He must have got bitten before he pulled me from beneath all those people." Tomos' thin frame shook as he spoke, his scratched and bloody arms held tightly to his chest. "I came in to check on him and Quinn was tangled in his blankets on the floor." He looked at Carmen with tears in his eyes. "He was thrashing around, so I figured he'd just fallen out of bed in his sleep. I tried to talk to him but he just moaned and kept struggling against the blankets wrapped around him. I managed to get him free, but when he turned to look at me I knew something wasn't right; his eyes were white and his skin was really pale."

"What the hell happened?" Curt boomed from the doorway.

"That's what we're trying to find out," Carmen snapped, not looking up from Tomos. "Aren't you supposed to be piloting this floating metal box?"

Curt waved her off as he knelt and felt for Quinn's pulse - as if the wooden spindle sticking out from his eye socket wasn't enough of an indication that Quinn was dead. "Heather called up to me on the bridge, said something was going on and that I needed to check on Quinn."

"He was already dead when I got here," Tomos said, refusing to look at his friend's body. "He was one of those things Curt. He grabbed my arm and before I knew what was happening, he was pulling my fingers towards his open mouth. I-I managed to pull free but he had a really good grip and his nails scratched me." Tomos held out his arm as proof. Sarah could see that beneath the blood, he had long nail marks gouged into his forearm and hand. "As I backed away, I bumped into the chair. I didn't see anything else I could use as a weapon, so I smashed the chair over Quinn's back." His voice went shrill, "It didn't even faze him. I grabbed a piece of the chair back from the floor and I... I..." Tomos' voice broke; his head dropped into his hands and his body shook with silent sobs.

"He didn't bite you did he?" Sarah asked, afraid to hear the answer; Tomos only shook his head. She looked to Curt who wore an expression somewhere between wariness and apprehension.

Turning to Carmen, Curt asked her to check Quinn's body for a bite mark. With a look of disgust Carmen did as asked and soon pointed out the infected area on his side. "We didn't even think to check Quinn for bites." Carmen finally said, flopping back against the open door.

Curt rubbed his fingers over his eyes and looked back to Tomos. "And you're sure he didn't bite you."

Tomos finally glanced up, his eyes bloodshot and his face tear-streaked. "I pulled my hand out of his mouth before he could bite down." Sarah wasn't sure, but she thought she heard him add, "His teeth only grazed the tip of my fingers," under his breath.

A dark and stormy day...

Sarah awoke sometime in the early morning, just as the eastern horizon was beginning to turn from a light purple to a pale pink; she hadn't slept much that night. After discovering Quinn's body, Carmen took Tomos to the galley, where she'd cleaned and bandaged his wounds. Curt and Caden carried Quinn's body up to the deck and threw it overboard. Tina freaked out when Sarah explained what happened to Quinn and Heather locked herself in her stateroom. After having his wounds cleaned and wrapped, Tomos retired to his berth for the night. During dinner everyone had been uncomfortably silent, no one willing to say aloud what was on everyone's mind - that even on A-Fishy-Nado, none of them were safe.

Making her way to the galley for a glass of water, Sarah's mind wandered to Aisha. She hoped for the gazillionth time that her BFF evaded the zombie plague sweeping across the state of Texas and had somehow found safety; for the first time, she was glad Aisha hadn't made it to Galveston. Most of the night she'd tossed and turned with Tomos' whispered words ringing in her ears: *'his teeth only grazed the tip of my fingers'*. Had Tomos been infected? *Will we lose another friend to this new, horrific plague? Should I have told Curt*

181

about what I thought I'd heard? By not telling anyone had she put them all at risk?

Shaking the questions from her head, Sarah filled a glass and leaned against the counter, staring out the porthole at the approaching dawn. She watched as the horizon began to brighten with the rising sun, but the ominous feeling that had continuously disrupted her sleep didn't subside. Feeling like she needed some fresh air, Sarah made her way up to the deck where she found Curt staring over the vast expanse of the gulf.

"You can't sleep either?" she asked, smirking when Curt jumped at the sound of her voice.

"There's a storm blowing in," he pointed to the dark clouds moving in from the south, "and I find this time of the morning to be peaceful. When I'm out on the water, I enjoy having my morning coffee here." He patted the deck beside him, but Sarah just shook her head.

Glancing up at the dark clouds moving in, she asked, "Think we're in for a bad storm?" A flash of lightening backlit the dark clouds and Sarah shivered.

Without taking his eyes off the approaching storm, Curt replied, "Well, it's not a hurricane but I don't think it's just a spring shower either; I hope you guys don't get too seasick - I'd hate to have to clean up the mess." He laughed and Sarah's stomach gave a nervous little flip. Curt got to his feet, "Well I'd better check our heading and give Caden a break."

"I'm going to head back to the galley and get some coffee; I think I'll skip breakfast..." The rest of Sarah's sentence was cut off by a shrill scream from below decks.

"Heather!" Curt shouted as he raced for the ladder, which led into the belly of the boat.

Sarah followed close behind, but couldn't take the ladder as quickly as Curt had. Upon reaching the bottom, she glanced up and down the corridor but couldn't see which way Curt went. Another scream ripped through the air and Sarah took off at a run, towards the berths. Cory was shouting by the time she rounded the corner of the corridor; Sarah slid to a halt. Bloody handprints led down the hall and half way between her and Curt, who stood banging on his stateroom door shouting Heather's name, lay the body of Tomos - an axe protruding from the top of his skull.

"Where's Heather?" Sarah asked, approaching the open door to the room where she'd left Carmen and Tomos sleeping only an hour earlier. The room was empty. "Where's Carmen?"

Curt continued to beat on the closed stateroom door, ignoring Sarah's questions. "Heather, please unlock the door." A loud thump came from within the room. Backing up, Curt raised his foot and kicked in the door; he stopped in the doorway, unmoving.

Running footsteps sounded in the corridor behind Sarah. "What's going on?" Caden, out of breath, slowed to a stop beside Sarah. When he saw the body of Tomos, he shouted, "Tina!" and ran to the closed door opposite the one she'd shared with Carmen and Tomos.

Flinging open the door, Caden glanced into the empty room. Turning back to Sarah, he asked with panic, "Did you see Tina?"

Sarah shook her head. She turned back to Curt, who stood in the doorway of his stateroom and saw movement behind him. "Is Heather okay?" she asked, stepping forward. Something in the room made a wet, slurping sound.

Curt waved her back, "Don't move. Carmen's distracted right now and I don't think we want to draw attention to ourselves."

Sarah looked down at Tomos, who lay on the floor, dead eyes staring at the ceiling. For the first time, she noticed the blood running down his chin, covering his bare chest with red streaks. Running up his finger and spreading in a web-like pattern across the back of his hand were the same dark brown lines she'd seen around Quinn's bite. He had been infected and she should have told Curt - it was her fault this was happening. She wasn't sure how he'd turned so fast from such a small bite but quickly realized that, with the autoimmune disease he'd struggled with for the past year, his body hadn't stood much of a chance of fighting off a virus.

"I have to go find Tina." Caden's voice shook when he spoke. Sarah heard his footsteps retreat down the corridor, calling Tina's name in quiet whispers.

Suddenly Curt's large frame came into Sarah's view and Tomos' body jerked when he bent down and pulled the axe free. Sarah stared up into Curt's shining eyes and knew that whatever was happening in his stateroom wasn't good. "Heather and Carmen?" she asked quietly, her own voice shaking.

Curt shook his head. "Go to the galley and barricade yourself in. Once I've taken care of Heather and Carmen, I'll come and get you."

"What happened?" Sarah tried to look around Curt, but he blocked her view.

"You don't want to look. I think Tomos bit Carmen and she went to Heather's room to get help before she bled out. Heather stupidly let her in and when Carmen died, she turned on Heather." Thunder sounded in the distance and behind Curt, something moaned. "Go," he commanded.

Gooseflesh prickled on Sarah's arms as she began to back down the corridor. "The galley... right." She paused before turning to leave, "and you'll be right behind me - you'll come as soon as you've taken care of those two." She jerked her head down the corridor, towards the busted open door.

Curt hefted the axe in his hand, nodding with grim determination. "I'll come to the galley as soon as I'm done - we'll go up to the bridge together and head for land. I'm going to help Caden look for Tina if he hasn't found her by the time I'm done here." Something bumped in the stateroom, making Curt look over his shoulder. "You need to go Sarah. I promise I won't be long."

After barricading herself in the galley as instructed, Sarah spent the next hour pacing back and forth, as the storm raged overhead. The boat rolled in the waves, making Sarah's stomach heave, but after some peppermint tea, she was at least able to calm her stomach if not her nerves.

When someone pounded on the galley door, Sarah jumped. "Who's there?" she called out, praying Curt was finally there to take her to the bridge.

"It's Caden and Tina." Caden called back, panic evident in his voice. "Hurry up and let us in," the doors rattled, "I don't want to be eaten."

Sarah made her way over to the door. She'd just been about to pull the two-by-four from behind the handles, when she remembered what Curt said to her before they'd set sail, *'Become someone whose number one priority is survival at any cost'*. She paused, her hand hovering over the wood, securing the doors and asked instead, "Are either of you bitten?" There was a long pause then hushed whispers, giving Sarah her answer.

184

The doors rattled again, "You fucking bitch, let us in!" Caden shouted, pounding his fist when Sarah didn't respond.

"At least give us a weapon." Tina, sounding frantic, pleaded.

"Which one of you is bitten?" Sarah responded, not wanting to arm a potential zombie.

There was another long pause and Tina finally said, "Me. Tomos managed to get me when I tried to get past."

"Where's Curt?" she asked, knowing in her gut that he wasn't going to be coming for her. She didn't know how to operate the boat and having Caden with her would give them both a chance to get off the floating disaster known as A-Fishy-Nado. Coming out onto the water had been a terrible idea.

"He's one of those things. He's the one we're trying to get away from." The door rattled so hard, Sarah was worried Caden would pull it from its hinges.

"Oh God," Tina squeaked, "he's almost here Caden, we have to keep moving."

"Caden, you can come in if you aren't bitten but I can't let Tina in. She can go lock herself into the fish freezer and wait there to die. At least then we won't have to worry about her sneaking up on us later." Sarah pressed her ear up against the door, trying to make out what the two were arguing about beneath their breath. She thought she heard Tina try to convince Caden to take Sarah up on the offer, but apparently, he'd refused.

"You'll rot in hell for this," he shouted and then they were gone, running down the corridor.

Nowhere to go, nothing to do...

The storm passed; the boat's engine died; the sun rose and set, rose and set, rose and set. All the while, Sarah remained in the galley, surviving on the provisions they'd gathered before setting out, as the boat drifted aimlessly on the Gulf. She'd become bored with playing solitaire, read the three books on the shelf, took stock of the food, re-took stock of the food and organized it; now she was resorting to conversing with her deceased friends... who weren't even in the room with her. On several occasions, something would bump into the galley door but soon moved aimlessly on. Her clothes reeked of days old sweat and her hair hung in limp tatters around her face;

she desperately wanted a shower, but contented herself with sponge baths in the tiny galley sink.

Gathering up her courage, Sarah finally made up her mind to make a dash for the room she'd shared with Carmen and Tomos to get her bag and some books she'd seen in their room. Taking a deep breath, she quietly removed the two-by-four from the door and opened it a crack, listening for any movement. When all remained quiet, she slipped through the door and dashed for the end of the corridor.

The stench hit her before she rounded the corner. There was a soft thump, thump, thump and Sarah stopped to listen for what direction it was coming from. When she realized the thumping matched the rocking of the boat, she stepped into the corridor, holding out the broom pole she'd brought with her. It wouldn't kill a zombie, but with it, she could keep one out of arms reach.

Soft light filtered from the rooms, but most of the corridor lay in shadows. Sarah could see Tomos' corpse lying where it had fallen days earlier. Carmen's body lay several feet beyond and Sarah realized the soft thumps came from Carmen's decapitated head rolling back and forth with the boat's swells. There was no sign of Heather's remains.

Slipping into her room, she closed the door so no to be caught unaware and began to gather her things. Thankfully, she found her bag still mostly packed, allowing her the opportunity to search through her friend's bags for anything useful. In Tomos' bag, she found a butterfly knife and in Carmen's she found a group picture of her friends, taken the previous summer. Guilt stabbed through her chest at the reminder of everything she'd lost and the part she'd played in their demises. Ever since locking herself in the galley, Sarah had berated herself for not taking action - for not telling Curt that Quinn had in fact bitten Tomos. Putting the guilt aside for later, Sarah shoved the six books from the shelf into her bag, not bothering to look at the titles, and grabbed the blanket and pillow from her bed. She looked around, one last time, to make sure there wasn't anything else of use, left in the room.

Satisfied with her haul, Sarah slowly opened the door and peeked into the corridor; a shadow to her left, shifted then let out a long low moan. Not willing to allow herself to be trapped in her room without food or water, Sarah grabbed the broomstick and stepped out into the hall. Heather stood before her with a gaping hole in her stomach and entrails spilling out. Sarah felt bile rise in her throat, but when Heather took a step towards her, she quickly braced the pole against her chest and pushed her back. The zombies stumbled but didn't fall, regaining its balance and shuffling towards the fresh meat it craved. Sarah placed the pole again but this time, maneuvered Heather back little by little until she had a clear shot up the adjacent corridor. Just before making a run for the galley, Sarah thought she saw Curt, shuffling towards her from further down the corridor. She ran.

Sarah dashed through the doors of the galley, fumbling with the two-by-four for a moment before it slid back into place. Her heart racing, Sarah rested her head against the door and closed her eyes, concentrating on her labored breathing. Several heartbeats later Heather crashed into the door; Sarah fell backwards, sprawling across the floor. There was another bump on the door, but the barricade held fast and soon Heather moved on.

Sarah flopped back on the floor and lay unmoving, staring at the ceiling. She was safe. Heather couldn't get in. Someone would see the boat adrift and come to investigate. She could shout out the porthole to let them know of the dangers on board. They would have weapons and they'd come rescue her - maybe then she could go search for Aisha.

A can fell from the shelf in the pantry with a crash; Sarah sat up, her heart skipping a beat.

"Is anyone there?" she called out, listening for other sounds of movement over the thundering of her own heart. The boat listed with the waves and a can of corn rolled into view. Sarah chuckled. She'd freaked herself out for nothing. How many times had that can fallen off the shelf in the past few days? She'd had to pick it up more than once.

Getting to her feet, Sarah opened the nearest porthole to let some fresh air into the room. Walking back to the door, she picked up her belongings, listing what she'd do next aloud. "I'm going to put my books away and make my bed," she placed the blanket and pillow on the couch, "then I'll unpack," she put her duffle on the coffee table in front of the couch, "and then I'll make myself something to eat and maybe have a nap." Now that she was back safely in the galley, the rush of adrenaline was draining from her body, leaving her feeling exhausted. Pulling the books from her bag, Sarah walked over to the shelf and arranged them in order of their spine's colour - she'd probably rearrange them again later.

Sarah's mind wandered as she placed the books; she didn't hear the shuffle of feet behind her. She registered the rancid scent a moment before cold, dead arms wrapped around her from behind. Letting out a shriek of terror, Sarah squirmed, trying to break the grip the zombie had on her. She managed a half turn in the zombies embrace, only to stare up into the deadly pale face of Caden.

His eyes were milky and his skin was cold against hers; there was a nasty-looking bite mark on his jaw. She squirmed again, trying to break free, but he held on with a vice-like grip. She hadn't cleared the galley when she'd come back in - she hadn't thought it was necessary. She cursed herself for being so stupid. Apparently, Caden slipped in while she was getting her bag and the can falling to the floor hadn't been because of the boat's movement.

The zombie's teeth clacked together once, and Sarah struggled to free herself, but he held on tight. Leaning down, the zombie buried his face into her neck. Pain shot through Sarah's body as she fell back; the collision with the floor barely registering with her overwhelmed pain sensors. Caden pulled back, rending her flesh with his teeth and Sarah screamed in agony.

Warmth spread across Sarah's back and she knew if she didn't stop it she'd bleed out, but her arms were still pinned at her sides and the room around her was growing fuzzy. When the zombie tore into her breast with its teeth, she forgot about stopping the flow of blood. Her mind detached from her body and the pain eased into numbness. Sarah's consciousness seemed to float through a heavy mist and her last thought was of Aisha - she hoped her BFF was having better luck than she did.

Volume 11: The Crash's Survivors

Aftermath...

Todd crashed through the brush, feeling the finger-like branches catch at his clothes and scrape along his skin. He imagined burnt fingers wrapping around his arm, and pushed his body to run faster. His chest heaved as he gasped for air; he had to get as far away from the nightmare as possible. While he grew up in the small town of Covington and knew the area well, between the dark and his panicked run through the woods, Todd wasn't quite sure where he was. *I need to get back to Misty's, grab my truck and get home to pack a few things. I need to get to the cabin. I'll be safe there until they get whatever this is under control.*

Having seen the plane explode in the thick bush behind Misty's house, Misty, Todd and Dennis went to investigate and search for any survivors. When they'd come upon the charred person stumbling away from the inferno of the plane, they'd immediately gone to help. Little did they know that they were about to encounter their first walking corpse. *It just turned on Dennis. It wrapped its burnt arms around him and wouldn't let go. It bit him and then...* the sound of Dennis' screams echoed through Todd's head, *and then I ran.*

Slowing to a stop in a small clearing, Todd braced his hands on his knees and tried to catch his breath. He glanced around, trying to figure out where he was, and soon spotted the huge trunk of a familiar sycamore; when they were young, Todd and his friends built a clubhouse in the large tree. Something in the underbrush rustled, making him jump. As images of burnt corpses flashed through his mind, he realized he needed to get away from the area - as far away as possible. Now that he had his bearings, Todd turned east and jogged towards Misty's, trying to avoid his guilty thoughts over abandoning Dennis.

Upon arriving at the small house Misty called home, Todd noticed light pouring from every window. He blew out a relieved breath, as he climbed the three steps to the porch, "Misty. She'd made it home. Before the plane crashed, they'd been sitting by the fire pit in the side yard, enjoying the beautiful night.

Todd reached for the door handle and turned; it was locked. "Misty!" he pounded on the door with his fist, "Misty, come open the door."

After a long moment, the curtain fluttered and Misty's pale, scared face filled the tiny opening. "You ran away," she said, wiping a hand over her cheek. She didn't move to unlock the door. "You ran away and left me and Dennis there with that thing."

"I'm sorry," Todd motioned to the doorknob, "let me in and we can talk."

Misty shook her head, "what if that thing followed you back here?" Her eyes flicked over Todd's shoulder, scanning the yard. "I don't want to be eaten, like Dennis was."

"I promise, I won't let that happen," Todd raised his hand, placing it on the glass in a silent apology. "What happened to Dennis..." he trailed off, not sure if anything he said could excuse his actions. "I was scared; it surprised me when that thing attacked him so viciously. I wasn't thinking straight. My first and only instinct was to get as far away as I could." His head bowed in shame, "I should have never left you like that."

There was a long moment where Misty just stared at Todd. Finally, she unlocked the door and opened it, motioning him inside. "Come in, but I'm packing," she turned towards the kitchen, "I can't stay here knowing that thing's so close to my house." Closing the door behind him, Todd followed her into the house.

In the kitchen, every door was flung open; cans of food sat in piles on the counter, and a large duffle bag sat by the back door, stuffed to capacity. *Sure, I'd been turned around in the bush, but she couldn't have gotten home much before I got here.* Amazed, Todd stared around the chaotic room, "I'm going home to pack, before heading to the cabin. There's plenty of room if you want to come with me."

Misty turned away from the cupboard she'd been ransacking, "You're going to Mississippi?"

Todd shrugged, "You know of a better place to go?"

190

"I'm going to my grandmothers," she said, stuffing a pack of pasta into a bag, "she lives in Georgia - I can make it there in less than seven hours. Your cabin's only two hours away," Misty gave Todd a skeptical look, "do you really think eighty-five miles is enough distance?"

Todd snorted, "Soon, the response team will be here and they'll take that delirious person to the hospital for treatment. They'll get the plane crash cleared up and life will go back to normal."

The sound Misty made was somewhere between a laugh and a sob, "that thing that attacked Dennis, it wasn't alive. How do you know they'll even find it in the woods?" She pointed out the dark window, "After what it did to Dennis, do you really think that it will be contained by a few responders?" He slowly nodded, but a sudden sinking feeling filled the pit of Todd's stomach. He somehow knew that nothing would be the same again. "Then you're not just a coward," she spat, "you're an idiot too." Misty turned back to the cupboard she was rummaging through, "now, I really need to finish packing; you know your way out."

Three days after the plane crash...

Todd stood on the second story walkway of the Covington library. His thoughts drifted over the events of the past several days, as he stared out at the zombies absently shuffling down the street. *I can't believe how quickly its spread,* he thought to himself, watching the mail carrier stumble over a discarded suitcase. It fell, landing face-first on the pavement; he'd swear it took half the skin off its cheek. The zombie lay still for a moment, before awkwardly picking itself up and continuing down the street, unaffected by the fall.

Dawn, three days earlier, Todd tried to leave town after packing his Land Rover with all of his food, clothing and camping supplies. On his way out of town, he found the army, with a blockade already set up. When he asked why he couldn't leave, the soldiers gave him some bullshit story about a terrorist on the plane, and containment of the situation. After trying several other routes, and after a threat at the third barricade, Todd returned home and went to sleep. Waking in the late afternoon, he decided to stay indoors, terrified of the faint screams coming from outside. If what happened to

Dennis was happening to his neighbours, he didn't want to get involved.

The following morning, reminded of Misty's words and ashamed of his twice-over cowardice in as many days, Todd went out and found his neighborhood crawling with the walking dead. His friends, his neighbours - people he'd known all his life - turned into ravenous flesh-eating monsters. No one warned them to stay in their homes, and the town went about its usual business. Attacked sometime throughout the first day, people went home to their families, not understanding the ramifications.

It's an awful cycle, Todd thought, remembering the little girl from three houses down as she'd stumbled across her lawn in her nightdress. After realizing the army wasn't coming to help, and figuring they'd be busy keeping the zombies in, he decided to try leaving town again. While re-packing his truck, he'd had his first up-close encounter with a zombie. Thankfully, his shotgun had been within reach, but the blast drew in every one of his neighbours. *It had been like ringing the dinner bell.*

After leaving his home, Todd drove through town, amazed by all the chaos. He made it as far as the public library, where he found a group of survivors fighting off a cluster of zombies. Knowing he had a lot to make up for, he decided to stop. With his help, they killed the zombies in the immediate area and finished securing the windows of the library. For his assistance, the survivor group offered him a hot meal and a place to stay. He figured he could stay and pitch in, at least for a few days - he had nothing better to do.

Yesterday, he'd spent the day talking to the residents. He learned that it took between seven and twelve hours for a single bite to kill a person. Someone who died while being ravaged by the undead turned in less than five minutes. Although Todd already knew, each survivor repeated the same thing: the undead needed to be shot in the head, and nothing else would stop them.

This morning, they'd woken to find the power cut off. The melancholy atmosphere in the library quickly turned to fear, and David, the group's leader, calmed them with promises of a generator. Promises, Todd was sure, David couldn't keep.

Squealing tires, followed by a loud crash, interrupted Todd's thoughts. He looked as far up the street as the window allowed, but only saw the ten-or-so wandering zombies turn their attention towards the sound of the crash. Their mouths opened as a chorus of chilling moans filled the air. No longer aimless, they shuffled down the street, seeking living prey. Shouts sounded from the library below, and Todd sprinted through the stacks to the stairwell. Taking the stairs two at a time, Todd arrived on the first floor just in time to watch one of his fellow survivors fling open the emergency door and shout, "Ruuun!"

The library's survivors flooded into the stairwell, curious about the newcomers and eager to see if any of them knew the incoming group. Everyone's hope was that the next group to find the library would be friends or family, people they believed lost in the mayhem of the past three days. Two men, standing nearest to the one holding the door, pulled their guns, aimed out the opening and began to shoot. The loud reports echoed in the small space and the gathered crowd fell silent, collectively holding their breath.

Four more shots rang out; the man holding the door turned to the crowd, "I need everyone to back up," he said, waving everyone back to the library, "Once we're sure they're clean, we'll let them in. You can ask all your questions then." The grumbling crowd slowly returned to the main library as instructed; Todd remained behind, unnoticed. Several more shots fired before a woman, with her arms flung over her head, finally ran into the building.

Once in the safety of the library, she lowered her arms and turned back to the open door. "Dad, Ryan," she motioned frantically, "hurry up."

"Melissa?"

His neighbor turned, obviously surprised to see him there, and said, "Todd, thank god you're okay. I went over to your house earlier today to see if you wanted to come with us, but your truck was gone. We figured you'd gotten out of town before it got bad."

"Who's with you?" Todd asked.

"My dad and Ryan," Melissa responded as she strained to watch her family's progress, "and a girl we found at your house."

"You found someone at my house?" Todd frowned, trying to think of whom she could be referring to; when nothing came to mind, he strained to look out the door. Ryan, Melissa's boyfriend, had his arm slung around Ezra, her father, helping him as he limped towards the safety of the library. Behind them, a woman walked backwards, shooting at any zombies who approached the retreating survivors. *She's a good shot,* he thought, watching another zombie fall to the ground, but he worried the gunfire would draw in every undead within hearing distance. "What about your mom and your brother?" Todd asked Melissa, still trying to see who the woman was; the way she moved seemed familiar.

Melissa's voice broke as she spoke, "We found my brother, eating my mother in the kitchen this morning. Ryan had to take care of them. Afterwards, we packed up and left. We were on our way out of town when one of my dad's friends stumbled in front of us; he swerved, trying to avoid him, even though he was already dead. Dad clipped a wrecked car and we crashed." With her dad and her boyfriend almost to the library door, Melissa shouted, "Hurry up. More are coming down the street."

The woman, finally clear of all immediate threats, turned and dashed across the parking lot towards him; Todd finally recognized her. "Misty!" he called, waving his arm out the door. Raising her arm in greeting, Misty jogged silently as she scanned the area for more undead.

Ryan and Ezra approached the open door; the group of men guarding the exit backed up. The two men stumbled through the door and collapsed into the small area.

"Are any of you bitten?" David, the leader in the library, asked. He gave a pointed look at Ezra's bloody leg, "We'll need to see that."

"He hurt it in the crash." Melissa roughly pulled up her father's pant leg, revealing the long, deep gash in his calf; Ezra grimaced as the blood-soaked jeans, pulled away from the wound. "None of us were bitten."

A gunshot echoed in the stairwell and everyone turned to see Misty, stuck on the lawn as six zombies closed in on her. She aimed her gun at the nearest zombie and pulled the trigger; the gun clicked empty. Her eyes went wide and flicked to Todd; she gave him a small apologetic smile.

She doesn't think she'll make it in. "Do something," he shouted, spinning to look for a firearm. He cursed himself for leaving a small armory in his truck, *and my handgun in my bag.* Being without a gun was no longer an option; now, you never knew when you might need to protect yourself from one of the undead. He cursed his lack of forethought, fingering the knife strapped to his belt. His mind raced, trying to think of options. *If I go out and distract them, maybe she can get in,* he took a step forward, hesitating, *but will I make it back?*

"Here," Ryan nudged his arm. Todd tore his eyes away from the zombies encircling his friend, and glanced down at the offered gun, "use mine."

Todd didn't waste time; "Thank you!" he said, pushing his way past the men at the door. He shot the zombie closest to Misty. Giving David a cold, hard stare, he snapped, "Now was that so hard?"

David snorted. "She has a gun and should've counted her bullets. We'll tell her to run around the building, and when it's clear, she can come in. We can't waste our ammo, when the solution's so easy. Who knows when we'll find more?"

Aiming at the next closest zombie, Todd fired another round. The side of the zombie's head flew off, but it didn't stop the creature; he hadn't hit the brain. He aimed again, taking care to steady his shaking hands. The second shot lodged in the zombie's head and it crumpled to the ground. "She's out of ammo and she'll die if we don't help her."

David shrugged, "She's a big girl. She can take care of herself."

Todd put down a third zombie, giving Misty the opening she needed to run the remainder of the way; he turned on David, "You son-of-a-bitch." Before Todd knew what he was doing, he sucker punched the leader in the mouth.

"Todd!" Misty yelled.

Disgusted with David's attitude, Todd glanced back up to see her dodging around the few remaining zombies in the yard. As she passed the final one, between her and safety, it reached out and tangled the ends of her hair in its clawed fingers. The zombie tripped and pitched forward, yanking her off her feet. She fell back with a scream. The zombie clawed its way forward, pulling the handful of hair towards its gaping mouth. Misty struggled to get free, but only succeeded in entangling it more.

Without a second thought, Todd ran out onto the lawn. With his running momentum, he kicked the zombie in the head. It flopped over to its back, lying dazed but not dead. Misty whimpered as he bent down, drawing his knife. "Hey, you gave me quite a scare there."

She looked up at him with wide, terrified eyes. "Cut it. Cut it off now." With a quick slash of Todd's blade, she was free.

As Todd helped Misty up, the zombie also struggled to its feet. "Let's move," he said, pulling her forward.

"You have a gun," David hollered, "kill the dang thing."

Pushing Misty past him, he whispered, "Get inside."

Todd turned around to face the zombie who'd almost killed his friend. He was surprised to recognize it; it was the town's insurance broker, Cindy. A large woman in life, Cindy had waddled around town, always eager to stick her nose where it didn't belong. *I never did like that woman,* Todd thought as he took aim. In death, she'd obviously lost a few pounds, but not in a good way. Whole chunks, torn from her sagging jowls, left gaping holes in her face and neck. Entrails hung from her round, exposed gut, and clumps of her thinning hair were torn out, exposing the white skull beneath. Her torn and blood-spattered Mumu told Todd that whichever zombies had eaten her, feasted well. Cindy's flabby arms jiggled as she stumbled towards him, moaning for his flesh; he swallowed the rising bile in his throat and pulled the trigger.

Upon returning to the library, Todd wished he'd stayed outside and took his chance with the zombies. "What the hell's going on?" he asked, turning to David and pointing to the two grown men, struggling on the floor. One of the men was Ryan and the other was David's right-hand man.

Blood leaked from the leader's nose, but Todd didn't remember blackening his eye. "That son-of-a-bitch punched me," David said, dabbing a handkerchief beneath his nose.

"So did I," Todd replied, curtly.

David waved him off. "I deserved that, for not helping your friend; in your shoes I probably woulda done the same thing. He," he thrust his finger towards Ryan, "punched me because I told him we didn't have the supplies to properly tend to her father's wound."

"Oh, he has them," Ryan grunted, pushing the other man off, "he just won't let us use them."

"What we have is for those people in there." David thrust his finger towards the library. "Medical supplies aren't so easily accessible anymore and we can't waste what we have trying to tend someone who's just shown up. Those people put their lives on the line to make this place safe, and I won't put them at any more risk than they already are."

"But he needs medical attention," Melissa said, "the wound needs to be cleaned, sewn up and bandaged, or he might die from an infection."

David shook his head. "I'm sorry, but I have a lot of other people relying on me. If it'd been my call, I wouldn't have even opened the door."

Melissa gave Todd a pleading look. "Please Todd."

Todd held up his hands. "I'm just here for a few days, but I'm willing to go search the pharmacies for you; hopefully we can find something to take care of your dad's leg." Todd turned to David. "We'll split what I bring back, after Ezra's been taken care of."

"If you go," David warned, "then everything you bring back will be put into the group stock. If you don't agree to that, then you all may as well leave now."

Todd's fist balled at his side, "Next time you step over the line, I'll break your nose." David cringed, stepping away from Todd. "We're going and you're going to allow Melissa to look after her father, in the library, until we get back. When we return, I'll give you part of whatever we find as payment for keeping them safe. Hell, I'll even tell you where to get more." David spluttered, but Todd spoke over him. "We'll leave after we look after Ezra, and if something happens between now and then, you won't get a thing. Got it?" David's face flushed red in anger, but he nodded. "Good. I'll need two volunteers from your group, just in case we run into trouble."

Gathering supplies...

Finding volunteers wasn't so easy; no one wanted to risk leaving the safety of the library. Finally, a man whose son had severe asthma, along with his brother-in-law, who was a RN, offered to go with Todd, Ryan and Misty to look for medical supplies - provided they would also look for inhalers.

"We'll try Wallgreens first, since it's the closest; then, we'll hit the CVS store." Todd outlined the plan, as everyone walked to the Land Rover. "I'd like to stick to the smaller places first and hope we get lucky. It hit so fast that most people didn't have a chance to gather supplies. Provided we don't run into any major trouble, and if both stores are a bust, then we'll branch out. Head down to Walmart and see what's going on over there."

"Phones and internet were already off when I got back to the house." Misty said, as she jumped into the front. Ryan, and the two men, Parker and Jer, climbed into the back.

"It was dawn by the time I was packed and on my way out of town; the blockades were up by then," Todd said to Misty as he turned the ignition. "I don't know what the army's been doing or if they're even still there. They haven't come into town, but I tried three roads outta town that morning, and the last one warned me not to try it again; that they'd disable my vehicle next time."

"Wait," Ryan interjected, "I was at work when I saw my first one. What do you mean, 'it was dawn by the time you were on your way outta town'?" Todd looked at him in the rear-view mirror. "Did you know this was happening when the plane crashed?" Todd sighed; he hadn't spoken a word about that night to anyone. Just then, a zombie stumbled into Ryan's side of the SUV; he jumped and let out a little squeak.

"We'd better get moving." Todd said, pulling out of the parking lot. Driving slowly, he navigated around debris in the road. "Why was Ezra driving so fast through this mess anyways?"

"We were trying to get down to the highway. Ezra took us past the hospital and the place swarmed with them. I'm sure there are survivors on the top floor; I don't think they'd all be there, if there weren't." Ryan stared out the window. "Ezra tried to get around, but the truck got stuck and those things started surrounding us. He'd just lost his wife and son, so I understand why he panicked. By the time we were free of them, I think that he just wanted to get as far away, as fast as possible." The air thick with tension, they drove in silence for the remainder of the way to Walgreens.

Knowing Parker and Jer hadn't been out of the library since the first day, Todd decided to give a brief rundown of what everyone was supposed to do. "We'll try to keep this as quiet as possible; no guns unless absolutely necessary. We'll go in and clear the place first. Then we'll look for items we may need." On top of having guns, each of them carried a weapon that wasn't quite so loud. Todd had a crowbar, Ryan, his machete; Jer and Parker both carried hammers, and Misty had a tire iron she'd pulled from a car. Everyone nodded and got out.

As Todd ran towards the store's door, he could hear the others following close behind him. He looked into the entryway as he pushed on the automatic door; it slid aside, releasing stale, putrid air.

Misty gagged. "I don't think I can go in there if it smells like that," she said, covering her nose.

Something bumped in the dark interior. "I don't think we should go in there at all." Jer finally spoke.

"We need inhalers for Carter," Parker hissed at his brother-in-law.

"He'll be far worse off if you go and get yourself bitten." Jer hissed back.

"Would you two shut the hell up?" Misty snapped. A magazine rack just inside the interior door fell over with a crash, making them all jump. They watched as a zombie rounded the corner and pressed itself against the glass. Most of its neck was torn away and its arm was chewed down to the bone. "Eeww, gross." She backed up several steps.

Two more zombies joined the first, beating their hands on the glass and moaning loudly. Todd stepped back, trying to figure out what to do next. *The door needs to slide open and we'll have to deal with those three right away. It'll be tight with four of us in the entryway, but if we're careful, we can do it.*

Three gunshots rang out in quick succession and the zombies inside fell. Todd spun around, to see Parker aiming his gun into the store. Already sorry he'd agreed to bring the man along, he barked, "What did you do that for?"

Parker shrugged, "We need to get the door open and can't do that safely with those three there. Now it will be easy." More moans began to emanate throughout the store; Parker visibly paled.

"It wasn't just those three in there." Ryan said, pulling on Todd's arm. "We need to get back to the truck and leave now."

Glancing back over his shoulder, Todd agreed. More than a dozen zombies started to press up against the glass, and beneath their weight, the glass around the three holes began to crack. "Run, now," he shouted, just as the glass shattered. The five of them dashed back for the truck; zombies poured out of the store. Once they were all inside and safe, Todd turned on Parker. "If you do something like that again, I'll shoot you myself." He cranked the ignition and the truck roared to life. They drove down the street, trailing zombies behind them.

Round two...

Much to Todd's relief, the intersection at Tyler Street and 21st Avenue was oddly void of the undead. He wasn't sure exactly why there weren't any zombies shuffling around, but he wasn't about to complain as he pulled into the empty CVS parking lot.

"Ryan and I will be the only ones going in to check out the store." Todd gave a pointed look to Parker. "If we decide it's safe, then the three of you can come in and we'll grab whatever we can carry."

"Why can't I go with you?" Misty crossed her arms over her chest, glaring at Todd. "I'm a better shot than you are, even if I can't crush one of their skulls with a crowbar."

Leaning forward to talk to Misty, Ryan opened his door. "We're just going to make sure we can get into the store; we need someone to wait here with Parker and Jer to keep them out of trouble while we go in." He lowered his voice, as if the two men could no longer hear him. "If we all go in, and he does something stupid..."

"I wouldn't do something to jeopardize this run," Parker snapped, "my son could die if he has an attack we can't manage."

Ryan turned on him, "You already did that, back at Walgreens. Just shut up and sit here like a good little boy until we get back. We won't be long."

Sighing, Todd got out of the truck. "Come on Ryan, times wasting."

Cautiously, they approached the door, watching for movement inside. When everything remained silent and still, they pushed the sliding door and entered the small glass enclosure.

"I still don't see anything moving," Ryan whispered as they slowly slid open the inner door; with it open, they could smell death in the store. "Ugh, maybe I was wrong."

Todd walked into the store, scanning the aisles directly in front of him; nothing moved. To his relief, the shelves, while seemingly ransacked, still held an abundance of merchandise. "I think we've hit the jackpot," he whispered to Ryan, walking down the front of the store to check the other aisles.

Something metal rattled in the far back corner opposite them. "What's that?" Ryan hissed, pausing to glance over his shoulder; it rattled again, louder this time.

"Probably a zombie," Todd said, hefting the crowbar in his hand. "Get your gun out, just in case we run into trouble." He quietly walked back the way he'd come. When he reached the third last aisle, he saw the end of the pharmacy counter at the back of the store. Closed, the metal shutters shook as another rattle echoed through the store.

"Please tell me we aren't going to turn a corner and run into a bunch of zombies," Ryan's voice shook as they walked.

In the second to last aisle, Todd saw more of the pharmacy area and the back of a single zombie. His stomach dropped; it was locked behind the counter. "Damn," he said through gritted teeth. "There's more than one, and they're where we need to go."

Turning the corner of the last aisle, Todd stopped abruptly; Ryan bumped into him and groaned when he saw why. Close to ten zombies pressed together in the small space, between the counter and the wall. "How are we going to deal with that?" Ryan asked, pointing at the enclosed area.

Sensing there was living close by, the zombies began to moan and thrash against the metal barrier. "Let's finish clearing the open parts of the store," Todd said over the cacophony as he walked towards the rear, "and then we'll call the others in while we try to figure this out."

When they'd ensured the rest of the store was clear, Todd jogged to the front to motion for the others to come in. Once everyone was inside, he explained the situation. "So, I want the three of you to grab bags and fill as many as you can, with things we'll need. Rubbing alcohol, gauze, anti-inflammatories; look for first aid kits and vitamins. Go aisle by aisle and take as much as you can carry." He handed each of them a large tote bag. "Use these for food - look for protein bars especially. Stick all the bags you fill by the door and we'll carry them all out at once. We don't want to draw attention from outside. Ryan and I are going to see how we can get the zombies out from behind the counter, without splattering their brains all over the medicine."

No one said anything as they each chose a separate aisle and quickly set about their task; even Parker didn't utter a single complaint.

Todd and Ryan returned to the caged zombies, still thrashing against the shutters. The ones closest to the front forced their arms through the narrow rectangle openings, scraping the dead flesh from their arms. "Oh god," Ryan choked, "I think I'm going to be sick."

It looked to Todd as if, when they pushed their arms through, they'd rolled up chunks of their skin. "Come on," he said, pulling his heaving friend towards the undead. The closer he got, the worse the smell became. "I think our best bet is to move these," he stopped beside a set of long shelves, "over here." He moved to the end of the large shelving unit, dividing the last two aisles. "If we block them off here, I think they'll take the path of least resistance, down the first aisle, and we can pick them off as they come around the corner. That way, we'll have decent light and be close to the door if something goes wrong."

"But how are we going to deal with that?" Ryan asked, nodding to the locked shutters.

"I'll shoot off the lock, raise the shutter and run like hell." Todd elbowed him, "just don't shoot me when I come around the corner." He laughed, but Ryan didn't find the joke amusing.

"Their arms are going to be a problem." Ryan inched closer, careful to stay out of reach. "How are you going to deal with that?"

Todd motioned to Ryan's machete, "You'll chop em off first."

Swallowing hard, he looked from his blade to Todd. "I'll do it."

While Ryan took care of the obstacles in Todd's plan, he went in search of Misty; he found her in the feminine hygiene aisle. "That's gotta suck," he said from behind her; he saw her jump, but she didn't utter a sound.

Turning slowly, she let out a long breath. "Don't sneak up on an armed woman," she warned.

"I'm sorry," Todd gave her a half-grin. "I promise not to do it again." They hadn't had a chance to talk since she'd arrived; or rather, they hadn't spoken since the night of the crash. "I'm sorry about Dennis too," he blurted, growing somber.

Misty looked away, "We'll get through it; we always do. Besides, we need to stick together now, more than ever." Her jaw clenched and she leveled a look at him, "Dennis is gone, who we were before that night, is gone; there's nothing you could have done for him, I understand that now." She shifted her gaze out the front of the store, "If we're both around in five years, then... then maybe we can talk about it. For now, let's just get to tomorrow in one piece."

"We're ready," Ryan called over the loud moans from the back of the store.

"Let's get this done and over with," Todd said, moving down the aisle towards the storefront.

After going over the plan with the others, Todd made his way back to the pharmacy area, psyching himself up for what he was about to do. Kicking aside the dismembered arms in disgust, he aimed his pistol at the lock; before he could think twice about what he was doing, he pulled the trigger. The shot echoed, momentarily drowning out the moans of the zombies. With a push, the gate rattled up; by the time the zombies stumbled from their enclosure, Todd was already halfway up the aisle.

"They're on their way," he said, jogging around the corner and towards his companions, three aisles down.

Once Todd joined them, they raised their firearms, patiently waiting for the first zombie. Not wanting to end up in an uncontrollable situation, they'd all agreed to use the guns. The first one was a woman; her long hair caked with blood. She appeared to be relatively intact, missing only an eye and a portion of her tongue. On her arm, two bite-marks stood out in dark contrast, against her pale, mottled skin. Smeared bits of shrivelled flesh clung to her grey-green cheeks. Dried blood crusted beneath her chin and down her shirt. Todd guessed that during the initial blitz of infection, she'd been caught in the store.

Misty fired a round and the zombie fell to a heap on the floor. Two men came around the corner, only their clothes giving away their gender. Their faces, horribly eaten, no longer looked human; one was missing its forearm.

Ryan laughed, taking aim, "I met him earlier."

Just as Ryan put down his zombie, Jer fired, missing his target; the cosmetics behind the zombie shattered into bits. His voice shook when he spoke, "This is harder than it looks."

Todd fired, hitting another zombie rounding the corner, and turned to Jer. "I think we have this under control, if you want to sit out with Parker."

Jer shook his head, aiming again. "I can do it." His hands shook slightly, but when the rapport echoed through the store, it was followed by the thump of the zombie hitting the floor. "My nephew needs those inhalers," he said through gritted teeth, casting a malicious glare Parker's way; and so, on it went.

When they were through, three children and two teens lay amongst the bodies. Both Ryan and Jer had been unable to shoot them, so the responsibility fell to Todd and Misty. Once done, rather than going to gather the medicine, Misty went out to the truck, saying she needed a minute alone. Parker quickly listed what they should look for, and the men set to work, packing as much medicine as they could carry. During the drive back, everyone remained silent, lost in his or her own thoughts.

When Todd turned back onto the library's street, he knew something was immediately awry. *There are too many of them,* he thought, slowing the truck to a stop.

"Something's wrong," Misty said, leaning up from the back, "there weren't nearly as many, when we left."

"Ronnie?" Parker shrieked, flinging open his door.

"Parker," Jer shouted after him, "come back."

"Who's Ronnie?" Ryan reached down, pulling his gun from his bag.

"My sister," Jer said, climbing out after his brother-in-law.

Todd studied the crowd of zombies, now shuffling towards them. "These guys are fresh." When David, the leader, stumbled from a bush beside him, Todd sucked in a breath. "These are survivors from the library."

Mayhem...

They bounced across the lawn of the library, pulling alongside the building. Before the truck came to a full stop, Ryan was already out and running for the door. "Melissa?" he pounded on the fire exit, "Melissa!" Beating harder, he shouted, "Someone open up."

Todd shoved the truck into park, glancing into the back at Jer as he vacantly stared out the window. "Misty, keep an eye on him and shoot anything that gets too close." Jumping out, he turned back into the truck, "when we get inside, drive around the block a few times. I don't want all of them clustered around our escape door when we're ready to leave. I just need to grab my things, his nephew, and Melissa and her dad." Shots fired within the building and Todd glanced up to see the door swing outward. "I won't be long, he promised as he rummaged through his bag, searching for the walkie-talkies he'd grabbed on the way out of CVS.

"Come on Todd," Ryan shouted, shooting a nearby zombie.

He tossed one of the radios to Misty as she climbed out of the rear, "There are batteries in the bag; I'll buzz you when we're ready."

Ryan fired again, "Let's go."

Todd ran for the door, ducking inside just as the Land Rover bumped over a fallen zombie behind him. Inside the stairwell, he found three guns trained on him and skidded to a halt, slowly raising his hands. "What happened?" he asked, glancing from one man to the next; he didn't remember their names. "Where'd Ryan go?"

The tall man with glasses jerked his head towards the stairs. "He's gone to look for his girl."

Another report echoed through the building. Behind the door to the main library, Todd could hear the moans of the undead. He swallowed thickly and asked, "What's going on in there?"

The round, balding man said, "They're picking off the one's still left in the library."

"Fool kids, playing games. Opened the wrong door and gave those things an opening to get in," said the older man, holding an old eight-gauge shotgun. He shook his head. "By the time we figured out what was going on, it was too late to do much of anything. Everyone not bitten we allowed upstairs, where it's safe, and opened the front doors to get the zombies out. There's still a handful stuck in the stacks," Shotgun paused as another round fired, "and we're taking care of them now. We're going to have a lot of cleaning up to do, but we should be able to stay."

"I'm leaving," Todd said, glancing upstairs as another gun went off. "I just need to know if Jer's nephew made it; we saw his sister outside."

"What about Parker?" Baldy asked, frowning. "Where's he?"

Todd shook his head. "He just let his wife have him."

Tall-man pushed his glasses up his nose, with a look of disgust. "Like he walked into her arms and just let her eat him?"

He nodded. "Carter?" he asked again, about the boy.

Tall-man nodded, "his momma saved him. Held em off long enough for Carter to get to the stairwell. She, however, was bitten in the process. He hasn't said anything since then."

"Jer's in shock too." Todd motioned towards the stairs, "is it okay if I go up? I need to figure out what to do about Carter and Jer."

Shotgun nodded, but reached for Todd's arm. "This may sound callous, but that's a sick little boy up there. If Jer can't look after him, I don't know if anyone will be willing to take responsibility for him."

Taken aback, Todd jerked his arm from Shotgun, "I need to find my friends."

"What about the meds?" Baldy asked Todd's back, "Did you guys find anything out there?" He ignored the question. As the second floor door closed behind him, Todd heard him shout, "We have a lot of injured up there. They could really use some help."

"The nerve of that asshole," Todd growled. He scanned the groups of survivors huddled on the floor, spotting Ryan first; his back was to him.

As Todd approached, he heard Melissa saying in a hushed voice, "I don't know what's wrong with these people. It was bound to happen, eventually. Now they know what to do next time." She paused, "They're treating him like a leper, but he's just a little boy. If his parents are gone, Jer's all he has left."

"I think the stress of today, and seeing his sister like that, got to him," Ryan said. "In his state of mind, he won't be of any use to Carter right now."

"What's going on?" Todd asked and Ryan jumped.

Melissa glanced up at him with a grave look. "Carter was the one who opened the door." A boy of no more than five peeked around her side; she rested a hand on his head. "The kids were playing hide and seek in the staff area; he thought he was checking a room, when it was really the rear entrance. It doesn't matter that his mom died saving him, these people just want him gone. I think that, even if Parker came back, the group would ask them to leave."

Todd glanced around, searching for Ezra. "Where's your dad?"

Melissa bit her lip and her eyes filled with tears; she slowly shook her head. "We couldn't move fast enough and no one would help me. When he fell, they were too close and I couldn't get him back to his feet."

Todd scowled, tossing the radio to Ryan, "Let me grab my stuff and then we're out of here. Radio Misty and tell her to meet us at the door in five."

The survivors said nothing when Melissa led Carter to the stairs. They averted their eyes as Todd made his way through the stacks to his corner. *Thank God I kept my stuff up here,* he thought, collecting his things. A moan drifted up from the lower level, quickly followed by a shotgun blast - the survivors remained silent. When he neared the door, the hushed whispers finally began behind him. "I hope you all rot in hell," he said, flipping them off over his shoulder.

The clang of the door closing behind him, echoed loudly in the stairwell. Tall-man looked up and said, "You didn't answer Pete's question about the meds."

"You guys aren't getting shit." Todd growled, taking the steps two at a time. Just as he reached the bottom, Misty honked from outside. Ryan hurried Carter and Melissa out, while Todd faced-off with Shotgun. "You going to shoot me and try taking what we scavenged today?" Shotgun gave Todd a once over then shook his head.

"Watch out for the dead ones," Baldy laughed as the door closed behind him.

Jer and Ryan sat in the back with Melissa and Carter, who'd curled up on her lap; Misty stayed in the driver's seat. Stopping at Ezra's truck, they gathered up their belongings and began to head north. Before his death, Ezra told his daughter of a little-known hunting road at the edge of town; it was Todd's hope that the military hadn't known about it. They were almost to their turnoff when a canvas military truck loomed over the rise.

Misty slowed down. "Didn't you say they threatened to disable your vehicle if they saw you again?" she asked Todd, pulling up beside the stopped truck.

"It doesn't look like there are any army personnel around right now." Ryan said, scanning the area. "Let me out and I'll see what's in the back." Misty stopped; Ryan got out.

Lifting his foot on the back bumper, he heaved himself up and poked his head through the canvas. After a long moment, Ryan pulled his head out of the back, jumping down and hurrying back to them. He climbed in and slammed the door. "Go," was all he said.

Todd turned around in his seat. "What was in there?" he asked Ryan, who was now ghostly white.

"I found the soldiers," Misty said, speeding up.

Todd turned back around, in time to see zombies in camouflage and helmets, stumbling out of the bush lining the road. "I'm sure as hell glad that we don't have to deal with those guys." He nodded at a nose-less zombie as it struggled up the ditch.

"What was in the truck, Ryan?" Melissa asked softly.

"It looks like they were going to put a bomb in the center of town," he replied in a faraway voice, "they were going to blow us all to kingdom come."

"Then I'm glad they got eaten," Misty said, grinning at Ryan in the rear-view mirror.

"Me too," said Todd, wishing the same fate on those they'd left in the library.

Volume 12: Finding Patient Zero

Two weeks after the first zombie sighting...
Andy stood in a large crowd of reporters in the courtyard of San Diego's City Administration Building. They'd gathered for a press conference, held by Senator Rickford, to assure the press that the situation in Texas was under control. He scanned the throng of reporters, but couldn't find his partner Trina; she'd been filming the press conference from somewhere off to his left. Spotting the senator and his entourage of security, Andy pushed his way through the crowd.

"Senator," Andy shouted, waving his arm. "Senator, I have several questions, regarding the cause of the riots in Texas." *I have many other questions, but that can wait until I have your attention.* "Senator!"

Pausing mid-stride, the senator turned and gave Andy a wary look. "I have nothing more to add. As I said in my statement, the riots continue to plague the state of Texas, and we're working as quickly as possible to clean up the contaminates."

The senator turned to leave, but Andy wasn't done. "Senator, I've received reports from a trusted source in the area that we're not dealing with a simple spill here. That something's infected the population and they're turning on one another." He pushed his recorder into the Senator's face. "I've seen footage of Synergy Pharmaceutical's head honcho; you know he committed suicide. I've also seen video of the experiments his company was working on. Do you have any comments regarding that?" When the Senator motioned for his security to move on, Andy decided to lay it all on the line. "Did you know that, in the company's labs, a dead woman broke free of her restraints and ate a man alive?" *I hope that gets his attention,* he thought, doggedly pursuing the senator.

Rickford stopped walking and snorted, "That's preposterous. I don't know where you found these videos, but they're obvious fabrications; the dead don't rise up - they don't eat the living. You've been watching too many movies." He turned away and continued towards the waiting limo.

Andy pressed on, following after him, "Why is it then, that the US government shut down all communications within the state? Why, if the story's so preposterous, were all flights in and out of Texas cancelled as of yesterday? Who made that decision?"

The senator gave Andy a disgusted look. "I have no further comment," he snapped.

Andy followed behind the senator's entourage, shouting questions he knew would never be answered. "Why has FEMA set up a camp in Oklahoma where the displaced residents of the state are being held, and why has the CDC been called in to investigate? Why did a plane, flying out from Dallas yesterday, crash into the Louisiana bush? Who's responsible for that?" A man wearing a dark suit and sunglasses stopped Andy from approaching the limo, as the senator climbed in. "What happens when the dead start attacking people in San Diego senator? Can we also expect to be cut-off from the rest of the country and abandoned? Left to fend for ourselves, while the politicians run and hide, ignoring the bigger issue?" The car began to move away from the curb; Andy shouted after it, "Will you answer my questions, once the dead come knocking on your door?" Agitated by the encounter, he stood on the curb, staring after the limo until it was lost in traffic.

"Did you really expect a straight answer?" a soft female voice spoke from behind him.

Turning, Andy saw Trina and gave her a small smile, shaking his head. "No, but I'd hoped he'd let something slip." He shoved his recorder into his pocket, jerking his head towards their car. "Let's get back to Paul's; he should be packed and ready to go."

Crossing state lines...

Everything on the drive to Texas seemed perfectly normal; that was, until they reached the small town of Valdo. The traffic on the interstate, just north of the town, slowed to a stop. Andy craned his neck to see what the holdup was all about; all he saw ahead of him was a line of halted cars. "We're so close to Texas, don't tell me we'll have to backtrack and find another route," he sighed, tired from being in the van for the past ten hours.

Trina turned in her seat, "There's army personnel up ahead; I'm not sure why they're stopping traffic though."

"Wasting taxpayer's money," Paul grumbled, "that's what they're doing." The van inched forward.

"Notice how light the traffic's been in the northbound lane?" Trina pointed out.

Andy thought back, remembering no more than a handful of cars in the past several minutes. *She's right.*

"Yeah," Paul nodded, "I've been wondering about that since we got on the I-10."

"If they're stopping people at a checkpoint, what are we going to tell them when they ask why we're headed into Texas? We can't just say that we're headed to where this all started." Andy said, as his heartbeat quickened; he hadn't considered that the army would be stationed just outside the state lines. He'd hoped they could get in and, once finding the checkpoint, find another route.

"We're visiting friends in El Paso." Paul said, pulling forward with the traffic. "Andy, make sure all the equipment's covered and put Trina's camera away. Try to arrange the bags on the floor behind you; that way, if they open the sliding door, hopefully they'll just think its luggage."

Andy did as asked, saying, "If we're just visiting friends in El Paso and we've come all the way from the west coast, wouldn't it raise suspicion if the van appeared too tidy?"

"What if they've been told to flag certain things? If they see my high-tech camcorder sitting out, they may pull us over and do a more thorough search; our story won't hold up under scrutiny and I'd rather not take the chance." Flustered, Trina dug through her bag. "I'll do a quick search on my phone, and find a name and address to give them - just in case we're asked."

"Good thinking," Paul said, reaching over to the glove box. "Here's my press card; can you put it with yours in your purse?"

Andy dug his out of his bag as well. "Here's mine," he said handing it over.

Traffic began to move and the trio stayed quiet until they came to another stop. "Did you get out the map?" Paul asked, glancing at Andy in the rear-view mirror.

"Right here." He waved it in the air.

"Good. Check for another road where we can cross the border east of here; hopefully, we can find another way out of Anthony. Look," Paul said, pointing out the windshield, "there's a blockade closing off the entire highway. It looks like all traffic's either being turned around or routed into town."

"I told you we should have stuck to back roads," Andy grumbled, folding his arms over his chest. "I should have taken a nap."

They sat in silence for the next ten minutes as traffic crawled forward. When they reached the blockade, Paul rolled down his window. "Hello Sir," he nodded to the approaching soldier. "What's going on?"

The tired and worn-out looking soldier, didn't smile as he said, "I'll need your driver's licences."

Trina smiled brightly at the soldier, "May I ask why you need it?" she said, leaning over Paul, to hand him her licence.

He returned Trina's smile, holding up the scanning machine in his other hand. "I just need to scan your ID; and I need to know why you are headed into Texas. You know there's a lot of civil unrest in the state right now, due to the spills, and access to certain areas has been cordoned off. The whole state, east of Fort Stockton, is in total chaos and it isn't safe for a pretty girl like you to be wandering around." Trina blushed as the soldier swiped her ID and handed it back to her; he held out his hand for Paul and Andy's ID's.

"We're going to visit friends in El Paso," Trina said, taking the lead. "They're taking us to visit the state park." She cast a mock-worried look to her two companions, before focusing back on the soldier with wide eyes. "You don't think that we're going to run into trouble, do you? We've been looking forward to this trip all year. Our friends didn't mention anything when we spoke on the phone, two days ago."

The soldier handed Paul back the ID's after scanning them; Andy noticed he didn't bother to look at the screen to review his or Paul's info. The soldier gave Trina a brilliant smile. "Oh, you should be fine, Miss. The park is beautiful and there haven't been any issues reported in El Paso. I suggest booking a tour with the park; it's better with a guide."

"So are we cleared to leave then?" Paul pointed down the interstate, beyond the barricade.

The soldier nodded, scribbling something down on a piece of paper. "You'll have to get off the highway here though. Take Frontage Road until you come to Anthony Drive; follow that road, continuing down Main St until you reach Wildcat Drive." He tore the slip of paper from his clipboard. "Give this to the blockade on the other end of town and they'll let you back on the highway, after they've looked through your vehicle."

"Thank you." Trina said in a singsong voice, giving the soldier one last flirty grin.

Paul took the offered slip of paper, handing it to her. "Here, put this somewhere safe." He rolled up his window and pulled forward. "Andy, is there another road we can take? I want to stay off the highway from now on."

"I think so, but I'll have to check the map of Texas to make sure," he replied, trailing his finger along the map.

"Get out my camera," Trina demanded. Andy looked up as they passed a newly erected sign, directing anyone seeking refuge from Texas, to a FEMA camp five miles west of town. "Andy!" Trina practically shouted, "Can I have my camcorder, please; there's another one coming up."

Thankful he'd only tucked it beneath his seat; Andy dug out the camera and handed it to her. "Now can I please find us another way into Texas?" They rode in silence; Paul driving while Trina filmed everything they passed. After turning onto Anthony Drive, Andy finally spoke. "Okay there's another way over the state line, off of Ohara Road, but first, I think we should pull over for a pit stop. We don't know what we'll find after crossing into Texas."

Out for a run...

The buzz of the alarm pulled Andy from sleep. After hitting snooze, he lay in bed, listening to Paul snore in the bed beside him. *Why did Trina get her own room while I have to share with Paul Bunyan?* "Paul," he croaked, sitting up, "it's time to get up."

After the checkpoint the previous afternoon, Andy took over, and they crossed the state line without hassle. After another three hours of driving, they decided to stop for the night, in the town of Van Horn. The hotel, when they arrived, was mostly vacant. The trio thought it was best that they set out in the early morning, so as not to arouse the local's suspicions.

The phone rang and Paul groaned, rolling over in his bed. Andy let it ring two more times before picking it up - not to make the caller wait, but to annoy Paul awake. "Hello?" he said into the receiver.

"Andy," Trina was breathless, "You have to come see this; I'm down in the lobby." She hung up the phone without saying more.

"Paul," Andy shouted, climbing out of bed.

With a snort, Paul's eyes flew open, "What?" he groaned.

Hastily pulling on his clothes, Andy said, "I'm going to see Trina in the lobby; get dressed and meet us down there. After a quick breakfast, we're leaving."

Andy found Trina in the lobby, flushed with excitement and a twinkle in her eyes. "You have to watch this," she handed him her phone and pressed a button. "It's too bad that's all I had; with the HD cam it would have been a lot better." The phone's display flickered; a road; a treetop; the palm of a hand; flashes of coherent images, but nothing out of the ordinary. "Sorry," Trina ducked her head in embarrassment, "I was on my way back from my run. It took a few seconds for me to check that I was using the right setting on the phone."

The footage stilled, revealing an overpass on the road ahead. A line of Humvee's and canvas-covered trucks rumbled over the bridge; a lone truck sat, idling on the ramp. The camera zoomed in. Two men stood at the hood of the truck, looking at something on its surface. Trina's voice, almost too low to hear said, "I think it's a map." The camera zoomed in further, giving little-more detail. "Stupid piece of crap," she hissed, creeping across the street and up under the bridge.

Now the camera was close enough to see the men's faces and zoom in on the map, although, none of the detail could be made out. One of the soldiers stood talking into his radio; his words muffled. Trina spoke in a low tone, "Just in case my mic isn't picking this up; the guy talking into the radio is saying that if they don't get them in

Fort Stockton, Van Horn's their last option. Apparently, the citizens in this cozy little town are ready for the evacuation order, and everything should go smoothly. Now, he's talking about the charges they've set but he doesn't think it will be sufficient to stop them."

"He goes on to say something about how they should be looking for a backup location for the refugee camp. That if they can't stop it in Fort Stockton, they won't be able to stop it here either. They'll lose El Paso two days later and the refugee camp outside of Anthony after that." Trina giggled, "Oh shit, I think his superior officer just dressed him down. I heard 'none', 'business' and 'task at hand'. It looks like the guy with him is trying not to laugh." She laughed aloud, before slapping her free hand over her mouth. Thankfully, another group of trucks rumbled overhead, drowning her out. Folding the map, the soldiers climbed back into the truck and drove back onto the interstate. The footage ended.

Andy looked at Trina with skepticism, "And you were just out running when you came upon these soldiers?"

She nodded with a look that told Andy she'd discovered at least part of the truth, of what was happening in Texas. "What do you think they're planning in Fort Stockton?"

"Fort Stockton's not our problem." Andy snapped, handing Trina back her phone. "We're here for the truth behind those videos, not for the army's response. If we make it to San Antonio and back out, then I'll consider staying to follow this angle. Until that happens, Paul's running the show. You know his friend went to investigate this same story ten days ago and he hasn't heard from her since. This is unlike any story we've ever covered Trina, but for Paul, it's personal."

"What's personal for me?" Paul said from behind them. They gave each other a guilty look and turned in unison.

"I was out for a run and saw this happen." Trina shoved the phone towards Paul; Andy was relieved when her diversion worked.

After he'd finished watching the footage, Paul glanced up at them both, "I suppose this is why the hotel's empty. With the army so close, I say we grab breakfast to go."

San Antonio...

Eight and a half hours later, the trio reached the city. The closer they got to San Antonio, the more frequently they spotted shambling figures in the vicinity around them. Thankfully, they still hadn't encountered one of the undead up close.

I'm not looking forward to that eventuality; Andy thought as they passed by what was left of a military blockade, on the edge of town. A lone zombie still dressed in uniform, stood guard at his post; his ravaged arms, reaching for them. It moaned loudly, clawing at the air with gnarled fingers. Andy hummed to himself in an attempt to block it out.

"Did you see that?" Trina said from the front seat, slowly panning the camera to remain focused on the soldier. After fiddling with the options for a moment, she turned the view screen so Andy could watch the shot. "This is so surreal;" she muttered, "I feel like I've stumbled into an apocalypse movie."

"I'm having a hard time believing what I'm seeing," Andy said, watching as the camera zoomed in on the corpse. The camera shook, with the motion of the van, but as it drew closer, he saw the flailing figure clearly. The zombie's leg was trapped in a pile of rubble; it was unable to do much more than gnash its teeth and wave its arms as the van passed by. Andy couldn't help but focus on the hollow, somehow hungry look in its milky eyes. The creature looked forlorn and pitiful. For a moment, Andy felt bad for leaving it there like that. *That's stupid,* he scolded himself, looking away from the camera, *if we got close, it wouldn't hesitate to eat one of my friends... or me.* After their drive east, he knew all too well, what the undead were capable of.

That morning, after leaving Van Horn, they headed south on U.S. 90. All the towns they'd driven through were vacant - devoid of life - and cell service became non-existent. Evacuation notices, pasted to light posts and windows, made it clear that the town's residents had been ordered to the refugee camp in New Mexico. It wasn't until the trio was an hour outside of San Antonio, that they saw their first walking dead. As they'd driven through Uvalde, they saw a cluster, gathered around a car. The car sat idling in the street, and to Andy, it seemed as if the undead fought amongst one another, in an attempt to get closer. The sound of the van's engine, as they passed, drew some of the undead's attention. As they moved away from the vehicle, he saw the bloody remains hanging from the car's smashed window. *Someone just trying to survive. Since it's still running, they haven't been there for long,* he'd thought, averting his eyes. *If we'd gotten here sooner, would we have been able to stop that from happening?* Andy knew he shouldn't think that way, but it seemed unavoidable at the time.

Now that they were within the metropolis' limits, the undead population grew more apparent. While the city wasn't a sea of undead, everywhere Andy looked he found at least one, aimlessly wandering the streets.

"I expected there to be a lot more." Paul said, navigating around a pileup.

Trina nodded, "The population of San Antonio before the outbreak was one point three million; it was the seventh largest city in the US."

"Then where did they all go?" Andy asked, a knot of dread, growing in his gut.

"I dunno," Trina shrugged, "but since they're not here, it makes it a lot easier for us."

"It doesn't look like people had much warning." Paul said, slowing to a crawl. To their left loomed a Walmart and a break in the trees lining the road. Paul whistled. "I found some. Trina, get out your camera and shoot that," he said, pointing to the parking lot as he pulled to a stop.

"Are we getting out?" Trina squeaked.

Paul nodded. "Look at all of them; but there's a fence there, so it should be okay if we take a closer look." Trina gave him a skeptical look. "Don't you want to get some up close footage while we know there's a barrier between them and us?" he taunted.

"I don't know Paul," Andy said. He wasn't so sure it was a good idea; it was already past four in the afternoon and they needed to locate Synergy and find a safe place to stay for the night.

"You may not get a better chance," Paul said, knowing he was goading her into it, so he could get a closer look himself.

"I'm in," Trina said, straightening her shoulders. A look of determination filled her features as she pushed open the door and stepped out. "Coming Andy?" she asked, slamming the door before he could reply.

Muttering beneath his breath, Andy slung his camera over his shoulder and turned on the recorder he'd tucked into his breast pocket. "This should be interesting," he grumbled, climbing out after them.

Paul and Trina had already crossed the median and were running across the southbound lane, by the time Andy got out of the van. He jogged towards the Walmart parking lot, where an undead mass writhed in anticipation of the approaching living. The air reeked of death. Paul and Trina stopped several paces from the chin-link fence; Andy could tell by their facial movements that they had to shout to be heard over the cacophony of moans.

"What do you think happened to them?" Trina was shouting, as Andy approached.

"It looks like they tried to fortify this place and use it for shelter." Paul pointed to the entrance on the far side of the parking lot; Trina panned the camera. "They've used cars to block it off, but it looks like they ended up trapping themselves, in the end." Paul turned to Andy with a big grin on his face, "Take a few pictures and tell me this wasn't worth it."

Uncapping his camera, Andy raised the viewfinder to his eye. At first, he took pictures trying to encompass the size of the mass, but he couldn't find the right angle. *There has to be more than three hundred people in there,* he thought, wishing for a moment that they'd push together. Badly eaten, some looked only vaguely human, while others had only a bite-mark or two. One zombie was missing half of its face - his cheekbone and his eye socket, one large gaping hole. Andy zoomed in and snapped a picture. *It looks like someone got a gun in its mouth, but didn't aim for the brain.*

A flash of blue caught his attention and he turned, but couldn't see it in the mass. He went around the bush, to another part of the fence. There, he caught sight of a small blue windbreaker, from behind. Just before it disappeared behind a line of bushes, growing through the fence, Andy thought, *he's just a child,* but even children weren't exempt from the apocalypse. Andy jogged down the fence line, hoping for another break in the greenery, but stopped cold, when a small arm poked through.

There must be a hole in the fence. He began to back up. A boy, no older than four, tumbled out of the bushes. His heart racing, Andy squatted, wanting to get a picture at eye level. The boy's nose was missing, along with his lips. Half his hand was gone and the other still held a toy car. Filled with competing emotions, he snapped several pictures of the sad truth. *He must have been terrified when they were overrun. They believed they were safe in there, but the undead are relentless.*

Movement from behind the boy caught Andy's' attention, and he gasped as another zombie wriggled out of the bush. He cursed, snapping one final picture before getting to his feet. As he ran back towards the others, he watched as they turned, wearing matching expression of confusion. That's when Andy noticed the moans had ceased; all the zombies shuffled along the fence.

"What happened?" Paul asked, his face paling when he glanced over Andy's shoulder.

"We have to go," Andy motioned back to the van. Just then, a truck rounded the corner and came to a stop beside it.

"What are you folks doing out here?" a grizzled old man said, leaning out the passenger side window. "You've gone and let all those buggers out." He nodded back towards the Walmart.

"We're journalists," Paul said as he jogged up to the truck. "We just got into the city."

"We've come to report on the truth, about what's being covered up here." Trina said, motioning to her camera.

"More journalists," the man said to the driver before leaning back out and saying, "We had one of those through here ten days ago, or so." He gave the trio a scrutinizing once-over. "She got herself killed; you three trying to do the same?" Moans erupted behind them and they turned to see the leak through the fence had turned into a flood. "Damn," the old man cursed, "you really did it now."

"Who was the other reporter?" Paul asked, eagerly stepping forward.

Trina ignored his questions and folded her arms over her chest saying, "We're not trying to get ourselves killed. We're just trying to make sure our report encompasses the whole story."

The driver, who Andy now saw was a teenage boy, leaned over and whispered to the man. He nodded and turned back to the reporters. "Well since you just arrived in town, and there isn't really anywhere for you three to stay, why don't you follow us back. We have a safe place for you to sleep for a night or two, while you do your journalist thing." Andy, Trina and Paul shared a wary look. The man laughed, "We've only been under siege for two weeks; we're not barbarians... yet. I promise no harm will come to any of you."

Apocalypse storage...

Andy gaped at the fortified fence, surrounding the storage facility. "They live here?" he asked from behind his camera, as he took several pictures of the outside of the survivor's safe house.

"I guess so," Trina shrugged, not taking her eyes off her screen.

"I still think that was Allegra's car back at the Exxon station," Paul muttered, pulling through the gates. "We need to go over there and check it out." As they pulled up behind the truck, the old man closed the gate behind them.

"It's possibly hers Paul," Trina tore her eyes away from her camera to give Paul a sympathetic look. "But even if it is, she may not have left anything in it. We know she came to San Antonio, and that old man mentioned something about another reporter; maybe they know what happened to her."

"He said she's dead." Paul's voice shook and he jammed the van into park. "If he was talking about Allegra, then we'll never know what she found out." He slammed his fist on the steering wheel, and said, "She was so talented," his voice broke, "she was my friend."

Wanting to change the subject, Andy asked, "Now what?" He looked around the enclosed space, not thinking much of the debris-littered parking lot. The door to the facility swung open and a man with brown hair stood, smiling at the old man. Behind him, a woman held a small boy in her arms.

"Now, we get out," Trina said, opening her door.

They got out and approached the survivors, who stood huddled in the entryway of the building. "I'm Cory and this is Veronica," the man with brown hair said, pointing to the woman standing beside him. He held out his hand and they shook it in turn. "Bill's the old guy who found you," he winked at Bill, "and Zach was the one in the driver's seat."

"Who's this little guy?" Trina smiled and poked at the little boy's belly. He turned shyly, burying his face into the woman's shoulder.

"This is Timmy," Veronica said as she adjusted him on her hip. "We found him in a tree and he hasn't said much since then."

Bill and Cory shared a look before Cory spoke. "My friend here," he motioned to Bill, "radioed in a few minutes ago. You guys are journalists?"

Paul nodded, "I think that my friend may have been here; that's her car back in the gas station."

Cory sighed, "That's a long story; one that shouldn't be told standing out here in the parking lot." He motioned for everyone to follow him inside. "We'll give you a tour and show you where you can sleep; then we'll head up to the roof and exchange stories." He turned to Zach. "Can you please run and tell Amanda to put on some coffee?" The boy dashed down the hall ahead of them.

Andy was amazed as he followed Cory through the building. *There has to be at least fifteen survivors living here,* he thought, catching sight of several teens, lounging in one of the units.

"We've had a steady stream of survivors come in, in the past week," Cory said, leading them to a stairwell. "Mike, Stu, Amanda and her daughter were here when we arrived, but they welcomed us in and we've made a home here for ourselves. Since then, we've taken in every survivor who is willing to abide by the house rules."

"This place seems like it has a bit of everything," Trina said, looking around as they walked onto the second floor where the line of lockers stood open. Andy noticed they'd turned each unit into sleeping quarters.

Cory nodded, coming to a stop in front of the last open door. "We've been very fortunate. There's a lot of crap in some of these units, but we can't complain. We have mattresses, clothes, furniture; pretty much anything you can think of. Well," he said motioning into the room, "this is where the three of you can sleep. I'm sorry there's not much room, but with the increase in our numbers, it's been hard keeping up with the additional need for beds."

"This is fine," Paul smiled, but Andy saw the anxiety behind it.

Andy said, "We appreciate you taking us in for the night."

The door at the end of the hall burst open and Zach came running towards them, carrying something in his hand. "What's wrong?" Concerned, Cory hurried towards the boy.

Zach waved him off. "Nothing," he said, holding up a camera. "I figured if these guys were friends of Allegra's..." Cory gave him a look and the boy snapped his mouth shut.

"So Allegra was here." Paul held out his hand for the camcorder. "May I?"

"How about we go up to the roof and sit down," Cory said, taking the camera from Zach. "I can tell you what's been happening

221

here and you can tell me what's going on out there." When Paul glared at Cory, with his hand still held out for the camcorder, he added, "Amanda's put coffee on for us and I'm sure you all could use a hot meal."

"Paul," Trina hissed, when he stepped forward with his fist balled at his side, "these people were kind enough to take us in. He's not saying you can't have it, he's just asking us to wait until we've had some time to settle in. I'm sure they're as anxious about news from outside the city as we are to find out what's going on inside it."

"And I am hungry," Andy mumbled.

With resignation, Paul said, "Lead the way."

When they got up to the roof, Andy was shocked to find the homey set-up. Not only was the roof lined with fencing, but they also had a seating area, a dining area, a garden and a small plastic jungle gym set up for the kids. "You guys found all of this in the units?"

Cory nodded, motioning them over to the seating area with the fire pit. "Mike, Stu and Amanda were here for a week before we arrived; they set this up. We've added to it as we've cleared out the units. It gives us a place to be able to enjoy the outdoors, without having to worry about drawing in an undead crowd."

They all sat and a short woman carried over four steaming mugs on a tray. "I'm Amanda," she said smiling at each of them, "it's nice to have someone from outside San Antonio here. We've had no news since this all started."

"It's nice to meet you." Andy smiled back, as Amanda handed him a mug.

"First," Cory said, taking his coffee, "we'll get the matter of your friend out of the way." He set the camcorder on the table and sat back heavily, taking a long drink of his coffee.

"So that is Allegra's car." Paul sat forward, ignoring his coffee. "What happened to her? The old guy - um, Bill - said she'd gotten herself killed." Cory proceeded to tell the story, leaving the trio in stunned silence. When he was done, Paul sat back with a look of defeat, "So she's really gone." He picked up the camera, but rather than watching the footage, he tucked it into his bag.

Andy saw the tears in Paul's eyes; he felt bad for his friend, but was also eager to see what Allegra had captured. He hadn't known her well, only professionally, but Paul spoke very highly of her. She'd been a bloodhound when she was on the scent of a story, relentless and determined. She'd won many awards for her hard-hitting articles, but now, none of it mattered. *Her ambitions finally got her killed,* he thought, wondering what would become of his group.

"Bill tells me he found you over by the Walmart on the west side of town." Cory said, after giving the trio a moment to absorb what happened to their colleague. "Zach heard the z's moaning from a block over; they've been quiet since the hordes started moving out."

Andy frowned, "Hordes?"

With a somber look, Cory said, "Five days ago, we noticed the z population in the area decrease; at first we couldn't figure out why, but it didn't take long to find out. Zach and I were out looking for food stores, and we were only three miles southeast of here, when we saw a massive group of them walking up the I35; they were headed towards Austin. We ran into another survivor group later that day, and they told us a similar story of the same thing happening on the eastern side of town."

Andy was glad Trina was filming as Cory spoke; if he weren't talking to someone who'd witnessed it, he wouldn't have believed it. Trina asked, "Does anyone know why they moved out of the city in such large masses?"

"The only thing we can come up with is that they migrated out of the area, looking for fresh meat." Cory gazed towards the fence, looking over the city. "The virus, or whatever it is, swept through the city so fast; one day it was life as usual and the next there were zombies everywhere - not many people survived. I think that, when they ran out of easy prey, they moved outwards in search of more." They sat in quiet contemplation for a time. Eventually, Cory asked, "What's going on outside of San Antonio; outside of the state? We don't even know how far its spread or what other cities were overrun."

Paul, Trina and Andy told Cory what they'd seen, about the checkpoints, the refugee camps and the evacuated towns. They told him about the cancelling of all flights in and out of the state, and the crash that happened a few days earlier, in Louisiana. That both the Houston Chronicle and the Dallas News were no longer taking calls or updating their websites. Although he'd suspected as much, Cory grew outraged when Andy told him that none of the national news networks knew, or at least, were reporting on the situation unfolding in Texas. As far as the general populace knew, the oil spills were under control, and they were cleaning it up as quickly as possible.

Paul finished by saying, "We're here to finish what Allegra started. The American people deserve to know what's happening; that's the only way they'll know to defend themselves when it spreads to their area."

Cory nodded in agreement. "The rate at which this spreads is almost inconceivable. I think the army's trying to slow the spread, but I highly doubt it will be stopped at this point."

Amanda came back carrying bowls of soup, and they fell silent. "It's not much but at least it's hot," she said, cheerily.

Andy wasn't sure how she could be so casual, when her world had been turned upside down, but he smiled gratefully and thanked Amanda for the meal. "I'd figured on eating protein bars tonight, so this is amazing."

"What are your plans going forward?" she asked, conversationally.

"We need to get to Synergy," Trina said, taking the bowl Amanda offered her, "We'll do a full web report when we get back to San Diego. We're hoping to find some hard evidence proving Synergy's culpability, and that they're responsible for the virus. We hope that by outing the pharmaceutical giant, the government will be forced to acknowledge the truth. They're current response, when asked, is that oil spills caused the riots."

Amanda shook her head sadly, "There haven't been any oil spills and there haven't been any riots; just the dead attacking the living."

"Mom!" a girl shouted from the door, "they need you downstairs."

Giving the trio another bright smile, Amanda said, "Well, it was nice to see some people from out there. I hope you find what you're looking for," and she hurried over to her daughter.

"Well," Cory said, getting to his feet, "if you guys want to go to Synergy in the morning, Bill and I will take you. We'll have to leave at dawn, so we're not seen by the gang that's taken over that side of town, so I suggest getting as much sleep as you can."

"Gang?" Andy and Trina asked in unison; Paul stared at the camera, seemingly lost in thought.

Cory blew out a breath, "Yeah, their territory extends from the 110, north to the 135. Your pharmaceutical company is right smack in the middle."

Synergy Pharmaceuticals...

They set out at dawn the following morning, the world around them still, and eerily silent. Trina rode in the truck with Cory and Bill; she wanted to get their first-hand accounts taped before they parted ways, Paul and Andy followed in their van.

"Did you watch Allegra's footage yet?" Andy asked, gazing out over the ruined city as they passed. From the downtown area, black smoke billowed into the sky.

Paul shook his head. "I want to wait until we get out of this accursed town. Once we find proof, and I know we can finish what she started, then I'll watch it."

Who knows if we'll even make it out alive. Andy thought, but kept it to himself. The previous night he'd interviewed a handful of survivors and after they'd shared their horrifying tales, they all told him the same thing - that the undead were unpredictable and taking unnecessary risks was a sure way to end up as zombie bait. "Are you sure it will be safe for us to go into the building?"

With a sigh, Paul said, "I don't know, but we have to try. We have enough to blow this thing wide open, but I want irrefutable proof of Synergy's involvement. If we're lucky, we may find proof of the government's involvement as well. They have to be held accountable."

The radio, given to Andy by Bill before they'd left the storage facility, squawked in his lap. Bill said, "We're coming up on the gang's territory; watch out for trouble."

Andy lifted his radio and asked, "How do you know where it starts?"

Laughing, Bill replied, "We'll make a quick stop at the intersection ahead. Trina's eager to get it on film."

Cory stopped in the middle of the street at the next intersection and Paul pulled up behind him. Trina scrambled out of the truck, pointing her camera upwards; Andy rolled down his window and stuck his head out. Looking up, he saw a row of dismembered heads tethered to a cable above him. Andy guessed there had to be close to forty heads, spanning the width of the street. As if sensing the living, the heads shook on the cable, clacking their teeth together in ghoulish chatter. The cable swayed, setting off a loud crash in one of the buildings lining the streets.

"We've gotta move on." Bill called to Trina, who looked disappointed as she walked back to the truck.

The radio squawked again, and Bill said, "It may be early enough that no one noticed that, but that's the alarm system the gang's set up around their territory."

"It's macabre," Andy said into the radio when Bill fell silent. "Were you at least able to get a good angle Trina?"

"Ten-four," she replied.

Without further incident, they drove the rest of the way in silence, reaching the Synergy Pharmaceuticals building just before the sun crested the horizon. After Paul parked behind a bush to conceal their van from the street, Andy climbed out and stretched, before opening the back to grab his gear.

"We need to go in with as little as possible," Paul said as he climbed from the driver's side. He leaned back in to grab his small handheld camcorder from between the seats. "We don't want to be weighed down if shit hits the fan." Trina said something from behind Paul and he turned, slamming the door closed.

Andy cringed as the bang echoed off the surrounding buildings and Bill hissed, somewhere in the distance, for them to keep it down. Hurriedly, he stuffed everything he'd need into a small backpack as Paul rounded the corner of the van, talking to Trina. "...the smallest camera with a light, Trina." Andy turned in time to see her give him a sheepish grin and a small wave.

"You wouldn't believe some of the stories the guys told me on the way over. Bill's a riot." Trina told him, leaning into the van to gather her things. Andy noticed she ignored Paul's advice, and chose her second largest camera; it had a better light on it anyways.

"Make sure to bring backup batteries and a few extra bottles of water," Paul said, from where he stood.

Clipping a small flashlight to his belt, beside the hunting knife Cory gave him, Andy turned to stare up at the six-story building. "I have a bad feeling about this," he said beneath his breath.

"You and me both," Trina said, stuffing the last few items into her bag.

"We hate to leave you here," Cory said walking towards the trio, "but I can't risk going in there when I have so many other's relying on me." He gave them an apologetic smile.

"It's okay," Andy said, extending his hand, "we understand." Cory shook it. "Thank you for bringing us this far; I'm not sure we would have found it yesterday." He shook Bill's hand, giving the old man a nod of appreciation. "Thanks for finding us," he said, with a half-smile.

"Take this," Bill said, handing Andy a gun, "and here's two extra clips, just in case you need them."

Andy stared at the weapon, uneasy at the thought of carrying a piece; he was far more comfortable behind the lens of a camera. "Trina told us you'd had firearms training, during your time spent in Egypt. Take it," Cory said, with a jerk of his head, "don't use it unless absolutely necessary, though; you'll draw in every undead in the vicinity." He added, "and don't forget what we told you last night."

Looking to Paul, he saw he agreed and Andy scowled at Trina. "Thanks," he said, taking the gun and ammo from Bill. He looked towards the building again, noticing three zombies wandering towards them. "We'd better get going."

"Thanks again," Paul said.

"Good luck," Bill called as the trio turned and walked towards their goal, "and don't forget what we told you; if you find one in there that hasn't been blooded, and one of you gets caught, the other two have to get out of there a.s.a.p. It'll stay with its first kill until it rises." Andy shivered, praying they didn't have to worry about that situation.

Thankful he'd asked Bill for a few pointers, he hesitantly walked towards the closest zombie. His heart raced with fear and anticipation. The night before, Bill let him practice the three best kill zones, for downing a zombie quietly. He'd practiced on the twice-dead corpses, around the storage facility, but hadn't yet killed a moving one himself.

"Be careful Andy," Trina whispered from behind him.

Andy looked at the dead man, and his stomach churned at the thought of touching the dirty creature, but it had to be done. Just before he was within arm's reach, he dodged to his left and with a hard shove, pushed the zombie to the ground. Just as Bill taught him, Andy put his foot on the thing's back to hold it in place. It squirmed beneath his boot as he bent and held the zombie's head down. Blowing out a breath, he buried the hunting knife to the hilt in the base of the zombie's skull. It stopped moving and Andy wiggled it for good measure, before pulling it back out; he wiped off the black gunk coating the blade on the grass.

Paul's voice quavered, "You won't have the luxury of time with the next two."

Andy glared at Paul, "You expect me to kill all three of them myself?"

Paul gaped, "Trina's too small and she's filming anyways. I... I," he trailed off.

Pointing to the machete Paul held, Andy snapped, "Hack off its arms if you don't think you can hit it on the top of the head hard enough." The other two were almost to them and Andy could see another one, coming through the lobby. "It will take me all day if we don't both do it."

Using his anger at Paul to his advantage, Andy rushed the next zombie, driving the knife up, beneath its chin. The zombie fell back but he couldn't pull the blade free and lost his grip. Finding himself weaponless, with a zombie closing in, Andy hissed for Paul to do something, as he stumbled backwards. Forgetting about the zombie behind him, he tripped and fell. The approaching zombie loomed over him. He pulled out the gun and, without a second thought, pulled the trigger. The zombie's head snapped back as the report echoed. *Too loud,* his mind screamed as the zombie fell. Still lying on the ground, Andy sighted the second zombie and shot again.

"Stop," Trina rushed to his side, trying to pry the gun from his hands; her camera lay beside them, forgotten for the moment.

Odd I should focus on that, Andy blinked a few times not sure, what had come over him. *I'm cracking under the pressure; I shouldn't be doing this. I'm just a photojournalist.*

"Andy," Trina said, shaking his shoulder. When he looked into her eyes, he realized how much he'd frightened her. "Come on. Get up." She helped his to his feet. "It looks clear for now. Let's keep moving."

Looking down at the dead-again zombies around him, Andy felt a sudden well of pride. "I killed them."

Trina laughed, "You sure did."

Into the belly of the beast...

The large windows to the lobby were shattered, giving the trio easy access to the building. Once inside Trina flipped on her light and scanned their surroundings. The dead bodies were the first thing Andy noticed - and these ones were truly dead. Scattered throughout the lobby, every corpse he saw, sported a gaping hole in their head.

"I wonder what happened here," Trina said, walking deeper into the foyer.

Andy shrugged before realizing they couldn't see him. "I don't know, but I'm getting the creeps, so can we please find the sublevel labs and get the hell outta here?"

In a monotone voice, Paul responded, "the door to the stairwell is in the lobby somewhere. The blueprints weren't clear; it labeled four doors as possible entrances."

The first one they found was an inconspicuous door with a card reader. "Think this is it?" Trina asked, trying to stay out of Paul's way, but still film what he was doing at the same time.

Still irritated that Paul froze up when confronted with the zombies outside, Andy didn't really care to stand around and watch. He wandered away to snap a few pictures. On the only intact window in the lobby, he found a face-print, smeared with dark around the mouth, and took a picture. *Looks like one of those things pressed up on the glass.* He shuddered, remembering how the knife felt, as it slid into flesh. *It's too bad the gun is so loud.* He wandered back towards his friends. *At least with a gun you don't realize you're shooting something that used to be human.* Paul finally got the door open and Trina hissed for him to hurry back.

Paul started down the stairs, followed by Trina, while Andy brought up the rear. At the bottom of the stairs, they found another locked door; when Paul managed to get it unlocked, an alarm began to sound. "Shit," Paul said, "I really hope there aren't any zombies wandering the halls."

Andy glanced back up the stairs, relieved to see the door had swung closed behind him. "At least we shouldn't get any coming down behind us."

Paul nodded and slowly opened the door, revealing a long, stark hallway before them. Doors lined either side of the hall; Andy pushed past Trina and Paul, to try the knob on the first door. "Locked," he said with a sigh.

229

"Here," Trina dug into her backpack, pulling out a small lock pick gun. She handed it to Paul who shoved it into the lock and pulled the lever. With a pop, the lock opened and Paul slowly opened the door. "Be careful Paul," Trina said, her voice shaking.

Rolling his eyes, Paul turned on his flashlight and entered the room. "It looks like storage," he said, backing out and closing the door behind him.

"We're better off looking for the labs," Andy said, turning back to look down the long hall. "They must have the important doors marked."

They tried several more unmarked doors, before finally finding one that looked like a lab. Turning on his own flashlight, Andy scanned the room. Test tubes and microscopes filled the long tables amongst stacks of papers. "This looks familiar," he said, walking further into the room.

"It looks like the lab from Allegra's video," Paul said, walking over to a table and poking through the contents scattered across its surface.

Andy walked towards a large window; the area beyond was pitch-black, revealing nothing of what lay in the dark. He approached the glass, trying to peer through the darkness, but only ended up startling himself when he saw his reflection move. "Holy hell," he jumped back, and then laughed when he realized how high-strung he felt. Every nerve in his body tingled in warning and it had been that way since they'd come into the building.

"Scare yourself?" Trina asked from the opposite side of the room.

"Yeah," Andy moved closer again, pressing his face against the glass. A shadow in the darkness shifted, and a pale face loomed towards him, out of the dark. Jerking back, he watched as an Asian woman pressed up against the glass. Her chin-length hair was matted with blood and her pale eyes bore straight into Andy, as if she could see him. Her mouth worked, and he imagined he could hear the clacking of her teeth.

"I think that's the doctor from the video," Paul said, startling Andy with his sudden appearance beside him.

"The one who did the filming," Trina whispered from his other side.

Other forms appeared from the darkness; a big orderly in scrubs followed by a small man in a lab coat and a woman whose shoulder hung at an odd angle. They pressed up against the glass, trying to chew their way through it. When that didn't work, the orderly began to bang, open-palmed, making the glass rattle in its frame.

"Trina, get footage of these guys, while Andy and I try to find some of his research," Paul said, pointing to the small man wearing a bloody lab coat.

Andy nodded and set to work, flipping through the stacks of folders nearest him. When they only came up with the lab work, done on Mrs. Farner, the trio left in search of the lab Cliff Holbrook worked in.

They were searching the second sub-level, frustrated on the lack of information they were finding, when they found a door marked, Cliff Holbrook, Head Researcher, Virology. When they went inside the office, however, it was bare.

Trina cursed as she panned her camera around the room. "It looks like someone cleaned up in here."

Andy stepped back out into the hallway, glancing further down the corridor. "Dude, the information on the virus has to be here somewhere," he said. Walking down to an adjoining hall, he called back to Paul and Trina, "Make sure to check those rooms as well."

They'd cleared several more rooms before Trina said excitedly, "Hey! I found something." Andy and Paul left the offices they'd been searching and hurried over to where she stood, looking into one of the rooms. "This is a quarantine unit that was in use until recently. See?"

Andy's heart raced in anticipation as he hurried over. *Our first real lead.* They shone their flashlights around, and when they didn't see any zombies lurking in the dark, they entered. Andy moved to the monitoring equipment but didn't find any printouts from the machines. "Whatever was in here is long gone," he said, ducking to look beneath the bed.

Paul shrieked and Andy jerked his head up, just in time to watch the zombie, who'd been standing behind the open door, bite down into Paul's shoulder. There was a sickening snap of tearing flesh and Paul screamed in pain; Trina echoed his scream with one of her own as she backed up, hitting the door jam.

"Get out Trina," Andy ordered, picking up the camcorder Paul dropped.

Panicked, Trina said, "But Andy, we can't just leave Paul here."

"He's gone Trina. Go!" He ordered again, preparing himself for what he had to do.

"Come with me Andy." Trina begged, "Paul is that thing's first kill. He won't leave it until the body's cold or Paul's risen."

With one last look at his friend, and the zombie crouched over him, Andy realized how stupid and arrogant they'd been. Bill warned them to be careful, but they hadn't been, believing they could get into the building and once inside, they'd be safe.

Trina pulled on his arm and he turned, following her as she ran back the way they'd come. The alarm still sounded, allowing them to find their way back to the stairwell. They raced up the stairs, through the lobby and out to the van, only stopping once they were inside with the doors locked. Both of them panted, trying to catch their breath, as they sat staring towards the building.

Andy was the first to speak, his voice coming out in shaking breaths, "What do we do now?"

Between gasping sobs, Trina said, "We leave. We get the story out."

Starting the van and shoving it into drive, Cory sped out of the parking lot, past a handful of the undead, drawn to the building by the sound of the alarm. "We're taking the long way home," he said, more to fill the silence than to let Trina know what he was doing. "We'll head towards Roswell and then figure out where to go from there."

"Who do you think that was?" Trina asked, between hiccups.

"Considering where we found it, I'm willing to bet that was patient zero," Andy replied. "It's too bad we couldn't get some samples from it. I know a virologist who would've looked at it for us."

Silence filled the vehicle and exhaustion washed over Andy, as he drove out of the city. He'd made it out alive, but the virus had taken both Allegra and Paul. *How many more will have to die, before the government starts warning people?* he thought, as the van bumped over a corpse lying in the road. *We'll get this story out to the public; they will not have died in vain.*

###

Thank you for reading When the Dead Rise Series 1: The Beginning. There are many more stories to be told, so be sure to watch for When the Dead Rise Series 2: The Spread.

If you enjoyed Series 1, please take a moment to leave a review at your favorite retailer.

www.ingramcontent.com/pod-product-compliance
Lightning Source LLC
Chambersburg PA
CBHW070612130626
46556CB00001B/346